P9-BZF-858

The Puzzle Bark Tree

Jimmy's Girl

"Most people think of teenage romance as fleeting, but Stephanie Gertler's *Jimmy's Girl* is a perfect reminder of how strong first love can be.... When Emily (who is married with four children) looks Jimmy up on the Internet, we're excited about their reunion but anxious about the repercussions of unearthing their lost love. *Jimmy's Girl* is definitely a page-turner, but perhaps the best thing about this novel is that as you race toward the end, you're not sure what you want the outcome to be."

—*Redbook* (editor's pick)

"An engaging tale of first love ... polished by Gertler's smooth prose and her good sense of detail and structure. *Jimmy's Girl* is believable, and it is not impossible to see how married people such as these might want to return to their more intense first love.... Gertler manages to raise important issues and describe the process of the decision to act, on both sides, with humanity ... a promising debut."

—*Chicago Tribune*

"*Jimmy's Girl* is a sharp-eyed, impeccably detailed novel about a harried mother/wife/artist who trades reality for a little romance."

—*Marie Clare*

"An intriguing subject [and] enormously likable heroine.... Gertler tells her story alternating Emily's voice with Jimmy's, and it's a tribute to her skill that the man's chapters ring as true as the woman's.... Wry wit and hardheaded sensibility make this debut a keeper."

—*Minneapolis Star Tribune*

"Should the past be left alone? In an assured debut themed to situate its author alongside Waller and Sparks, Gertler answers this question." —*Publishers Weekly*

Also by Stephanie Gertler

Drifting

Stephanie Gertler

NAL
ACCENT

FICTION FOR THE WAY WE LIVE

NAL Accent
Published by New American Library, a division of
Penguin Group (USA) Inc., 375 Hudson Street,
New York, New York 10014, U.S.A.
Penguin Books Ltd, 80 Strand,
London WC2R 0RL, England
Penguin Books Australia Ltd, 250 Camberwell Road,
Camberwell, Victoria 3124, Australia
Penguin Books Canada Ltd, 10 Alcorn Avenue,
Toronto, Ontario, Canada M4V 3B2
Penguin Books (NZ), cnr Airborne and Rosedale Roads,
Albany, Auckland 1310, New Zealand

Penguin Books Ltd, Registered Offices:
80 Strand, London WC2R 0RL, England

Published by NAL Accent, an imprint of New American Library, a division
of Penguin Group (USA) Inc. Previously published in a Dutton edition.

First NAL Accent Mass Market Printing, August 2004
10 9 8 7 6 5 4 3 2 1

Fiction for the Way We Live
REGISTERED TRADEMARK—MARCA REGISTRADA

Printed in the United States of America

PUBLISHER'S NOTE
This is a work of fiction. Names, characters, places, and incidents either
are the product of the author's imagination or are used fictitiously, and
any resemblance to actual persons, living or dead, business establish-
ments, events, or locales is entirely coincidental.

To my children, David, Ellie, and Ben Schiffer,
who have always been and
always will be the loves of my life

Acknowledgments

There are so many to thank for this book. People who inspired and taught me.

First and foremost there is Abby Potash and Sam and JoEllen Guttmann and Kyle who opened their hearts and souls and took me on incredible journeys that touched me deeply and taught me how to truly count blessings. I couldn't have done it without you.

As always, tremendous appreciation to Chip Crosby, Ph.D., for helping me sift through, rethink, and conclude.

Thanks to Ellen Udelson, who listens endlessly to everything. For my heritage and history, I thank my parents, Anna and Menard Gertler, my grandparents, Yelena and Abrasha Paull, and my aunt Laura and uncle Joe Paull. Love to all—here and above.

Gratitude to Doug Buschel, Hilda Kogut, and John Staffieri for guiding me through law enforcement; Marcus Suppo, DVM, and Lester Sills, DVM, for their veterinary expertise; Ronni Berger for always being there to answer questions at Dutton, and Amy Hughes, my new kid on the block; Robert Frederick Wang, MD, and Mark Horowitz, MD for ophthalmic explanations; Bob Gilman, Raquel Flatow and Andy and Juliette Lackow for inspiration; Judy Cochran and Joan Salwen Zaitz for legal advice in matters of child abduction and family law; The National Center for Missing and Exploited Children, Team H.O.P.E. and Pamela and Bob Hoch at The Rachel Foundation for Family Reintegration.

My deep appreciation to my editor, Carole Baron.

Thanks to Margaret Wise Brown who wrote *The Runaway Bunny*, the best book ever written that captured the power of motherhood.

And to my husband, Mark Schiffer—with love and thanks for our children.

Chapter 1

Claire's footsteps echoed as she walked across the planked blue-gray floor of the veranda, her pink cotton robe trailing behind her. Her hair was gathered on top of her head in a mother-of-pearl clasp, stray wisps of pale blond framing her high cheekbones. She set her coffee mug on a glass table, rubbing away a frosted circular remnant of someone's drink with her fingertip; her deep-set eyes faced downward, pools of transparent blue mist.

She sat too stiffly in the cushioned wicker chair, the newspaper folded in her lap, and gazed out the salt-sprayed window. The beach in the distance was strangely stilled by the early autumn morning. The sand appeared dark, littered with pine needles. She listened to the pine needles hitting the flat roof outside their bedroom window the sleepless night before as they tapped the shingles like steel pin drops. A flurry of leaves suddenly twirled like a pinwheel in a vortex

of wind and she turned her head to see a blue-and-
white-striped awning loosen from an upstairs dormer.
The American flag hanging over the front porch
twisted around itself like a Chinese yo-yo. Purple and
pink asters, their blooms nearly finished now, strained
in one final effort toward the September morning sun
that struggled through the clouds.

Stella came and sat beside her, tail wagging low; her
eyes, clouded with marbled blue cataracts, gazed up at
Claire. Claire patted the dog's flank, so lost in thought
that she startled when Eli came into the room.

"Good morning, ladies," he said, placing his steaming mug next to Claire's and scratching Stella behind
the ears. He touched Claire's arm. "Penny for your
thoughts."

Claire smiled at her husband. "Hi," she said, as he
leaned over to kiss her. "You smell like mint."

"New soap," he said. "Is that good?"

She nodded and focused her glance on his hands.
His fingers curled around the mug of coffee as he
brought it to his lips. His hands were mapped with
dark spots but still strong. Large hands that had held
their babies, covered their infants' heads, and en-
veloped her the times she thought she might break in
half if not for their salvation. She remembered watching once while he delivered a foal. How deftly he took
the foal from its mother, holding it as if it were made
of fine blown glass. How he looked when he knelt beside the mare, his breath coming in short precise in-
halations, perspiration glistening on his forehead as
she brushed away an errant lock of hair that had fallen
in his eyes. She thought as she sat across from him
now how odd it was that his dark hair was streaked

with silver and wondered when it turned and why she hadn't seen it happen. He was wearing black jeans and a plaid shirt rolled to his elbows; a frayed white T-shirt peeked out at the notch of his neck.

"There's a rip in your shirt," she said tenderly. "At the collar. I can sew it. I've been neglecting you, haven't I?"

Eli shook his head and fingered the tear. "It's not worth fixing," he said. "I'll toss it later. How's Stella this morning?"

"Not so great," Claire said, stroking the golden retriever's back. "She's having trouble lately up and down the stairs."

"Her depth perception's gone," Eli said, lifting the dog's chin, studying her eyes.

"I think she misses the kids. It's too quiet around here."

"It always feels quiet Monday mornings after the guests have gone," Eli said. "Especially this time of year."

Claire lifted her head and looked into his eyes. She wanted to tell him that it wasn't just the quiet of a Monday morning. It wasn't just the time of year. This was different from every autumn morning they'd known for the last twenty-two years. Didn't he hear the absence of Jonah's blaring stereo and rattling of old pipes as Natalie ran a shower so steamy that vapors seeped under the bathroom door and wafted into the hallway? Normally, Claire would have been dressed by now, clearing the breakfast dishes, shooing Natalie out the door after kissing her slightly damp hair, breathing in her scent of rose water and cherry lip balm.

It was a scorching-hot August day three weeks before when she hugged Natalie outside her freshman dormitory. The moment she knew would come all summer long. She could still taste the precise moment when she folded her daughter into her arms and held her motionless, bittersweet tears moistening Natalie's cheeks.

"Mom!" Natalie said. "You promised you wouldn't cry."

"I'm not," Claire said, forcing a smile.

Natalie turned to her father. "Dad, do something!"

"It's a mother's prerogative," he said, laughing. "She's held up real well until now."

"You're going to be just fine," Claire said, smiling through glistening eyes, her breath held visibly. She stroked her daughter's cheek and tucked the loose strands of hair behind her ear.

"Who are you trying to convince?" Natalie teased.

"Remember to take your vitamins, okay? I bought you the ones with iron. . . ."

"Mom," Natalie protested. "Enough. I'm a big girl."

"Yes, you are," Claire said tenderly. "Sometimes I forget."

Natalie turned to her father. "Help her, okay, Dad? She's all yours now."

"I'll call you tonight," Claire said, hugging her daughter one more time.

Eli placed his arm around Claire's waist and steered her from the steps of the ivy-covered dormitory, his arm staying around her although she turned at least a dozen times to wave as they walked down the path and over the crest of the hill to their truck. Natalie stood until they were gone from sight. It was all Claire could do not to run back and take Natalie home. *Wait!*

the voice inside her cried. *I'm not finished yet. Did I tell you everything you need to know? Teach you everything I've learned over the years? How can I leave you now?*

Eli held Claire's hand in the truck. Blasts of hot air from the air-conditioning vents made her breath feel shorter than it was.

"You okay?" he asked, squeezing her hand. "It's going to be okay."

Claire covered her mouth with her hand and began to cry. "I don't know what's the matter with me."

Eli pulled her to him. "You're a mother," he said, drawing her closer to him, pressing his lips to the side of her head.

"Part of me just isn't quite ready to let her go, that's all."

"She's like a kite. She's so ready to fly," he said gently. "You're just letting out the string."

Natalie called that night to say she was fine. To reassure her mother that she'd found the cafeteria and to tell about her roommate from California who brought a microwave.

"You know, you packed enough Q-tips and Band-Aids for the whole university," Natalie said, laughing. "I could start a cottage industry."

"Well, you never know. . . ."

"I love you, Mom."

I love you, *Mom*. The suffixed phrase came so easily to her children though Claire had never uttered it herself. She thought of the times Natalie raced out the door on a crisp fall morning, sweater tied around her waist, dangling beneath her coat, or Jonah darted back inside to retrieve something he'd forgotten. I love you, Mom! he, too, would cry unabashedly. "I love you, too!" Claire would call as they ran for the bus, her words carrying on the wind for eternity, bouncing back to her like echoes in a cave.

"You're usually dressed by now," Eli said, watching her stare away from him again, wondering what she expected to find beyond his eyes. "No patients today?"

"I have some reports to write for DSS. Another week before sessions begin again."

"That's a late start for you."

"Not really. Schools just opened today," she said.

Eli stood behind her now, resting his hands on her shoulders, the two of them staring at the rocky beach, the red-and-white lighthouse motionless in the distance as though it were painted on the horizon.

"Remember when the kids would ask if they swam as far as they could, where they'd end up?" she asked. "Jonah always said they'd be in Barcelona. Where on earth did he get that from? Barcelona?"

She pictured Jonah and Natalie as they fished from the jetty, matching hooded gray sweatshirts, their skinny stick legs streaked with sunburn, protruding beneath baggy shorts. How was it possible they were on their own now? Wasn't it just yesterday that they wore backpacks bigger than they were and she double-knotted their shoelaces? Jonah. He graduated from college the May before and now was at veterinary school in Ohio, Eli's alma mater. He had left the week before Natalie, the black Chevy Blazer packed to the brim, his muscular, suntanned arm frozen in a wave through the open window. I love you, Mom, trailing behind him as he called from the window and drove away.

Claire reached behind her and pressed her husband's hands with her fingertips. "Summer always ends so fast once Labor Day comes," she said.

There was a distinct chill in the air. A breeze blew through an open jalousie and suddenly made her shiver. The few remaining sailboats were anchored in the small marina, rocking to and fro, their masts tinkling like bells. Jonah was ten and Natalie was six when they bought the Inn at Drifting—"Eight-guest-room gem on Dune Beach" in Drifting, Connecticut, as the brochure described it. "Delightful living room with stone fireplace and adjoining bar area. Elegant dining for fifty." The Inn looked like something out of storybook—an old ramshackle Victorian painted a pale periwinkle blue perched on a bluff overlooking the Atlantic.

"I never get tired of this view," Claire said.

Eli bent down and kissed his wife's cheek. "You used to say that about the Jersey side of the Hudson."

Claire was about to answer when she heard the school bus come to a screeching halt. She pictured the children as they climbed clumsily up the wide steps, the door shutting with a screech, the bus chugging down the street leaving a stream of exhaust in its wake.

"Seven-twenty," she said knowingly as the sound of the wheels became distant.

Eli kissed the top of her head. "What are you thinking lately? Tell me."

She turned to look up at him, her lips parted, her eyebrows raised ever so slightly. "Nothing. You know. Natalie. Jonah."

"No," Eli said, shaking his head. "It's more than that."

"Wait a minute. Who's the psychologist, you or me?"

"I speak as a husband, Dr. Cherney."

"Nothing's going on. It's just that all this is so new to me. You know, with the kids away . . . I'm still learning to separate, that's all," she said, brushing imaginary specks from her robe.

"Baloney."

"You make me so damn mad sometimes, Eli Bishop," she said, looking up at him, her eyes fiery.

"I do, do I? How's that?"

"Because you're like some kind of mind reader or something."

"Comes from spending my days with animals."

"Well, whatever it is, it's annoying," she said with a laugh.

"So, are you going to come clean or not?"

"You have to leave. Go!" she said, giving him a playful shove.

"I have a few minutes," he said, looking at his watch. "Spill."

She stretched her arms over her head and relaxed her body. "It's complicated, Eli," she said, blowing out a puff of breath.

"What is?"

"I tell you what—we'll talk tonight. I promise."

"Are you okay?"

"I'm fine. It's just with the kids gone I have all this time to think all of a sudden."

"So that's good. . . ."

"It's good," she said hesitantly, taking his hand.

"But?"

"But I'm thinking about my mother, Eli," she said, swallowing hard. "How do you leave a baby?" She inhaled deeply. "I'm a little too old for this, aren't I?"

"No, you're not too old for this, Claire," he said.

She put up her hand to pull the hair back from her face. "I've got to get myself going. And you're going to be late."

"I don't care," Eli said. "Talk to me."

"I can't just yet. I have to think things through some more." She looked up at him. "Listen, I'll be fine. Resilient's my middle name. You know me. . . ."

He bent down and kissed her. "Very well," he said. "I know you very well."

Chapter 2

Claire listened as Eli's footsteps crossed the floor of the veranda. As he opened and closed the door to his pickup, to the rattle of the engine turning over, and the shush of the tires fading on the damp pavement as the truck rounded the corner and drove down the winding road. She stood, tightened the tie on her robe, and heard the whisper of her every breath. She cranked the jalousie until the window was sealed and took one last look at the ocean in what now seemed an even stiller morning as a soft rain came down. She picked up her coffee mug along with Eli's, tucked the still unread newspaper under her arm, and walked into the kitchen, placing the mugs in the dishwasher. She let go an audible sigh and looked around her. It all appeared too pristine and unfamiliar. The counters were sponged and clean, no crumbs from breakfast toast. A container of warm orange juice wasn't sitting next to a stick of melting butter, a jar of warm jam. There were no dishes piled in the sink. There was the distinct feeling that no one was home. It was the same feeling she had had when she walked into Jack's apartment the Monday morning after he died. She shut her eyes and remembered the way Eli steadied her hand as she placed the key in Jack's door, how the fresh scent of lemon oil and ammonia assaulted her senses and reminded her of being a girl on those still-cool spring afternoons in Manhattan when they'd finished what Jack called their spring cleansing.

At first she'd been alarmed at the orderliness of Jack's apartment, wondering if he knew the end was near and hadn't wanted to burden her, but then she realized that it was spring. He must have spent Saturday afternoon the week before filing his papers and straightening the lace antimacassars on the backs of the armchairs and polishing the beveled mirrors and old glass doorknobs. She could hear his soft voice, etched with the trace of a Russian accent, telling her that April was the month for renewal. Spring ahead! he shouted as Claire dusted and polished and threw away old magazines and newspapers, stopping only to make sandwiches of liverwurst and spicy mustard on thick slices of black bread.

Jack's friend Vince had called at midnight that Saturday night. The Spring Ahead Saturday when they'd traditionally done the cleansing when she was a child. The night the clocks were to be set forward. If only she could have turned them back.

Vince said they'd been playing bocci at Farabutto as they did every Saturday night, eating linguini with red clam sauce and drinking Chianti, when Jack had the stroke. Vince was sitting in the hospital lobby with his

head in his hands by the time Claire and Eli got there
with three-year-old Jonah in tow. They still lived in
Eli's four-flight walk-up on West Fourth Street back
then. Vince said that if it was any consolation at all,
Jack had been laughing. They were placing bets and
flirting with the hat-check girl and remembering the
first time that Vince took Jack to play bocci. And then,
in the middle of the laughter, Jack collapsed. He hung
on for five days. The first stroke left him with a mild
paralysis in his right arm and a droop at the side of his
mouth that slurred his speech and made him difficult
to understand. But it was mild, the doctors said. Claire
spent those five days at Jack's bedside, interpreting
Jack's halting, stifled words, trying to read the desperation in his eyes. She stayed, unwavering, save an
hour here and there where she went home to Jonah
and Eli came and took her place. It was the second
stroke on the fifth day that felled Jack. The second
stroke came out of the blue as she sat by his bedside.
He gasped, gripped her hand and died. Quietly.
Silently. Almost elegantly. The way Jack did everything. So typical for Jack to make dying appear as effortless as living.

"Dear Jack, Today is a beautiful day," Claire wrote in
the letter she tried to read at his funeral. The first of
many letters she subsequently wrote to him over the
years and slid into the back of her dressing table
drawer. "If I listen carefully I can hear the strains of the
balalaika and the poetry of Pushkin. Today is a beautiful day and I will drink a cup of Postum and pretend
that it is coffee and you are sitting beside me as you
did for every morning of my childhood. But how can
today be a beautiful day, Jack? How is it possible as I

stand here and feel the warm spring sun that any of the days can be beautiful without you? . . ."

Every day of her childhood, Jack had awakened her with the words "Today is a beautiful day." It didn't matter if the day was gray or raining or windy or cold. Jack always said it was beautiful. Each day, he said, was filled with the details of living. You have to watch each detail carefully and appreciate every nuance, every sense that otherwise might pass you by. He would sit on the edge of her bed as he awakened her, reciting a poem in Russian, laughing when he fumbled the words, saying his one regret was that he never taught her his language and was beginning to forget it himself.

The endless parade of cars with their headlights shimmering drove up the parkway to the cemetery. Jack's coffin lay in an open grave shaded by a charcoal tent under a cloudless turquoise sky. Dozens of mourners stood in a horseshoe configuration behind the three rows of not enough folding chairs. Claire and Eli took their places in the front row beside Jack's sister, Helen; Jonah curled up on Claire's lap. She'd handed Jonah to Eli when she rose to read the letter. From the corner of her eye, she saw Aunt Helen twist an embroidered handkerchief, dampened from tears, in her thin, veined porcelain hands. She heard Vince blow his nose like a trumpet and gazed at the sea of saddened faces, many of whom she recognized, but strangers as well whom she later discovered all knew Jack. Customers from the pharmacy Jack owned on the Upper West Side of Manhattan for thirty-five years, waiters from Farabutto, owners from neighboring shops along Broadway. And then, while she was reading, trying to celebrate her father's life rather than mourn him, she heard Jonah's small voice ask, "Where's Pa?" Her shoulders heaved and she bent from the waist, doubling over as if someone had punched her in the stomach. Eli waited to see if she might recover on her own, but then he handed Jonah to Aunt Helen and went to Claire. He braced her against his chest with one arm and took the letter in the other. He barely got through the letter himself, stopping at intervals to swallow his own tears and those he wept for her. He placed his lips against the side of his wife's head when he finished and closed his eyes, a tear escaping down his cheek despite his efforts.

The stroke was the first and last thing that ever stopped Jack Cherney. Aunt Helen told her that even after Ursula left, Jack didn't stop for a moment. He fumbled with diaper pins and learned to tie hair ribbons and fasten sashes on organza dresses. He took Claire to the playground on Sundays and sat at the sandbox with the mothers. Yet Claire always called him Jack. Daddy was too generic. Her friends called their fathers Daddy. Jack was different. The other fathers came home at night and the mothers put dinner on the table. Jack came home at night and taught Claire to cook while he taught himself, scalding his fingers as he fumbled with hot pots and laughing at mistimed meals that landed them at the corner deli. He laundered and ironed and went to PTA meetings and doctor appointments and stood outside fitting rooms at Best & Company while she tried on dresses. Calling him Daddy wouldn't have felt right. He was Jack. He was everything.

Ursula, Sulie as everyone called her, was fifteen years younger than Jack. Dark and exotic, Sulie swore she was left on her parents' doorstep by gypsies. How was it possible, Sulie would ask haughtily, that someone the likes of her could be born to people as simple as Frank and Maria Terenzi? A tailor and a housekeeper? There was no other explanation, Sulie insisted. She must have been left by gypsies.

Sulie was cast as Dunyasha in *The Cherry Orchard* at a tiny theater over on Avenue A when she and Jack met. Jack loved Chekhov but he went back four times to *The Cherry Orchard* because he couldn't take his eyes off nineteen-year-old Ursula Terenzi. The fourth time, he waited for her by the stage door with a bouquet of yellow sweetheart roses and a note asking if she'd have coffee with him. Six months later they were married and ten months later, Claire was born. And two days before Claire's second birthday, early in the morning, Sulie left. She'd called Helen right after Jack left for the pharmacy.

"My agent called last night. I got an audition," Sulie said. "Can you come and mind the baby? I'll only be a couple of hours." The baby. She rarely referred to Claire by name.

Claire was in her playpen and a damp diaper when Helen arrived. Sulie was waiting at the door. A small suitcase was by her side, a new black-and-white herringbone coat from Peck and Peck draped over her arm, a pair of red velvet gloves in her hand. She wore black wool narrow-fitting trousers and a black mock turtleneck sweater adorned with a single strand of Venetian beads. Her thick black hair was twisted in a single braid down her back, a bright red lipstick outlined her full heart-shaped mouth. Helen said Sulie was clearly eager to leave, kissing Claire the way she would have kissed her any other morning when Helen stayed and Sulie went to the grocery or the post office or the hairdresser. A perfunctory kiss that barely grazed the child's feathery blond hair and left the faintest trace of red on the side of her forehead where her lips barely touched Claire's skin.

"Why the valise?' Helen asked, gesturing to the weathered brown leather bag.

"Costume changes," Sulie said without blinking.

When Jack came home that evening, Sulie still had not returned. Helen met Jack at the door.

"You're still here?" Jack asked. "Where's Sulie?"

Helen made a brave attempt to be casual. "Those auditions always take longer than planned," she said with a shrug. "Come, I made pot roast. The way you like it with the cloves."

"What about Max?"

Helen waved her hand. "His brother's in town. Come, have your supper."

But Jack barely touched his meal. He rocked Claire to sleep and tucked her into the crib as Helen cleared the dishes. And after Claire was sleeping, he told Helen that Sulie left them. He knew before he checked the medicine cabinet or noticed that her silver-plated brush and comb were gone from the ceramic cachepot on the bathroom shelf and her cake of Castile soap was missing from its porcelain cradle. He told Helen that he knew when he had awakened that morning. It was a feeling he had in his gut as he watched Sulie braid her hair with great precision, refusing to catch his glance in the mirror. He knew before he'd looked on the shelf of the bedroom closet just after the dinner he'd labored to chew and forced himself to swallow and saw that Sulie's old brown leather suitcase was missing.

"Why didn't you tell me she had a valise with her?" Jack asked accusingly.

"She said it was costume changes."

"And you believed her?"

"Yes. No. Oh, Jack, she is so young." Helen dropped her voice to a whisper and clasped her hands as though in prayer, shaking them toward Jack. "Too young for you."

Jack closed his eyes and pressed his lips together.

"You couldn't have stopped her, Jack," Helen said.

"I know," he said. "I know." He covered his mouth with his hands, held his head back and spoke through his fingers. "Where could she have gone? Where?"

The following day, Sulie's note arrived at the pharmacy. It said she was sorry that she had to leave but her star was calling. She'd boarded a Greyhound bus and headed west. She would phone them at some point. Wife and mother were the only roles she could not play with any realism, the note read. They were simply not part of her repertoire.

Jack read the note at the cluttered wooden table in the back of the pharmacy where he sat and ate lunch. He read it twice, disbelieving at first despite the strong instinct he felt the morning she left, then angry as he crumpled the paper in his hand and placed it in a large glass ashtray. He struck a match on the heel of his shoe and set it afire, watching as it turned from orange to black and disintegrated into ash. He was furious, but with himself. Sulie was barely ready for marriage, let alone ready for a baby. Jack recalled the panic on her

face when she told him she was pregnant and yet Jack
was certain that once she saw the baby, held its tender
pink flesh in her arms, she would soften. She never
did. She never cradled her baby girl. Refused to nurse
her. Reluctantly answered Claire's cries in the middle
of the night. She was, Jack said in later years, like an
animal trapped in a cage. He excused her. It wasn't her
fault, he said. It was youth. And besides, she was far
too spirited for the mundane, ironically the quality
that made him fall in love with her. It was Eli to whom
Jack made this confession. Jack and Eli sat at the
Formica-and-chrome dinette in the kitchen of Jack's
apartment, an icy bottle of vodka between them. Claire
was in the living room nursing Jonah, strains of Judy
Collins drowning out the conversation that wafted in
broken tones, high and low octaves, from the kitchen.

"You understand," Jack said, his eyes imploring as
though he was begging for Sulie's exoneration.
"You've cared for horses. Sulie was like a wild mare.
Some of them simply can't be tamed."

"And Claire? Did Claire cry for her? Ask for her?"
Eli questioned.

"She never asked for her," Jack said, leaning toward
Eli, placing his hand on Eli's forearm, speaking in a
hushed tone. "Once, maybe just once in the beginning. It was as though Claire never noticed she was
gone."

"Claire never mentions her," Eli said. "Once maybe.
Years ago."

"Leave it," Jack said. "It's best this way."

"I'm not sure," Eli said thoughtfully. He was about
to say some more when Jack spoke.

"She will talk when she's ready," Jack said firmly.

"Has Claire asked you questions? Has she spoken with you? Ever?" Eli persisted.

But Jack never answered him. He stroked his chin between his thumb and index finger and poured another vodka.

Sulie's parents were heartbroken and not a year after she all but disappeared, they returned to Rapallo, the small Italian fishing village where they'd grown up and married twenty-five years before. They needed simplicity, they said. Life in America had become too complex. There was too much freedom. It was, they said, what ruined their Ursula. What made her a handful throughout her life: wearing false eyelashes and running around with a wild crowd and forsaking the Church for the theater. They'd come here for her, they said. Now that they lost her, they were going home.

For the first seven years of Claire's life, Sulie called on Claire's birthday or a day later and sent postcards from places with storybook names like Angel, Arkansas and Cakebread, Missouri.

"Look, my darling," Jack would say, waving a postcard in front of Claire. "Your mother is becoming quite the actress. She might even be a movie star one day." And Claire would take the picture, look closely, and wonder what to make of this stranger who had borne her. She would smile and nod her head, hand back the photograph to Jack, and then there would be silence until one of them changed to an easier subject or Jack reached into the pocket of his white pharmacy smock and extracted a candy bar or a small cake of soap carved like a rose. "Ah! I nearly forgot!" he would exclaim. "I have a treat for my sweet!"

In the beginning, Sulie sent a black-and-white picture of herself standing in front of a theater's block-lettered marquee where it said "Introducing Ursula Terenzi" or a head shot with her neck tilted backwards, chin turned up, thick black hair cascading down her shoulders, lips parted provocatively. But then the postcards and the calls just stopped.

It wasn't until her thirteenth birthday that Claire had the courage to take Sulie's pictures from the mantel. She'd planned it all day. She'd thought about it with such determination she was sent to the principal's office for not paying attention in class. Jack was still at the pharmacy when she got home. She walked over to the mantel and with not even a caress or last look of longing, she piled her mother's photographs in her arms like schoolbooks. She toyed with the idea of saving the frames and then decided to toss them, silvered frames and all, watching as they tumbled in what appeared to be slow motion and soundless clamor despite the tumult into the inferno.

"Where are your mother's photographs?" Jack asked when he came home from work that evening carrying a bouquet of yellow tulips and a box of Barton's chocolate truffles for Claire.

"Away," she said softly. "I put them away."

"Where? Where did you put them?" Jack asked, looking around the room. "Claire?"

"The incinerator," Claire said, barely blinking, pronouncing each syllable as though it were a separate word.

"The incinerator? Why? Why would you do that?"

"I don't want her pictures anymore," Claire said, holding back tears she'd held back all day long or perhaps for nearly thirteen years. "I don't want to look at them."

"You didn't have to burn them," Jack said, thinking of the note he'd burned in the ashtray nearly a dozen years before.

"I don't care."

"She's still your mother."

"I'm thirteen now. Things happen to girls when they're thirteen, you know," she said, her head hanging down. "A mother's supposed to be here for certain things. I have no mother. Mothers don't leave their children."

"No, they don't," Jack answered, the words barely escaping his throat.

She lifted her eyes to her father. "We don't even cross her mind, can't you see that? She hasn't sent a letter in years. She never calls anymore. Not even on my birthday."

"And what about . . . what about your womanhood?" Jack asked self-consciously. "Aunt Helen could help you."

"She lives too far away. Besides, I figured it out myself," she said, blushing. "The same way I bought my own bras." She swallowed hard and looked her father in the eyes. "Jack, sometimes I sing myself to sleep at night. I've done that since I'm really little. I sing from *The King and I* and it comforts me." Her eyes overflowed now. Her voice lowered. "There are times that I wonder what it would be like if I had a . . . and I can't fall asleep and the light from the street lamp keeps me awake . . . and I just can't understand how she could've left."

"I hear you singing. I hear you. I think you sing because you are happy," he said, sitting down on the sofa, placing his hands on his knees and shaking his head side to side. "What should we do, Claire?" He looked at her in her black velvet skirt and white satin blouse. "You look very much the teenager now. Thirteen! A young woman. I can't believe it."

"We should go to Farabutto and have our birthday dinner. And we should stop waiting for letters and stop making believe. Stop pretending." And then, drawing herself up as tall as she could, she said, "And maybe you should stop thinking about her."

Jack nodded his head, slapped his hands on his knees and stood up. "You are right, Claire. But you should know that she left *me*, she didn't leave you."

"She left *us*, Jack," Claire said. "*Both* of us. But I am *happy*." She smiled at him. "You're enough for me, Jack." It was the last time they spoke of Sulie but just the other day she wrote a letter to Sulie as well, shoved in the back of the nightstand drawer next to Jack's. A letter asking why.

She missed Jack terribly. Since the day he died eighteen years before there wasn't a night she didn't fall asleep without him in her prayers. In her memories. But lately, she missed Jack even more. She longed to tell him how she felt with both Natalie and Jonah away now. How the house seemed so empty. How the last of her touchstones had incinerated like the pictures so many years before. How whatever uncertainty she'd felt the night her baby girl came into the world had dissolved the minute the nurse placed her in her arms. She'd mothered Jack and then Eli and Jonah but the notion of mothering a daughter was daunting until the moment she held Natalie's slippery flesh naked next to her chest. But more, perhaps, she wanted to ask him about Sulie. She wanted to know how a mother could leave her child. She wanted to know the depth of Sulie's demons.

Perhaps Jack had taught her too well to mind the details. Details distressed her now. She bought milk in quarts. No more bulky gallons. Two apples, two pears, four bananas. There was no large bowl of fruit on the kitchen counter that was eaten overnight. No chips, no salsa, none of what Natalie called the snacky foods. There were two loads of laundry each week instead of each day. Claire's shampoo was where it was supposed to be with the cap on and her hairbrush and comb remained where they belonged. The basketball sat nearly deflated in the corner of the garage. The car wasn't low on gas. Even Stella's cloudy eyes and slow gait marked the passing of time with finality and silent pronouncement that an era was over. All the details that had once distracted her so reliably were gone. Now there was far too much time to ponder what never existed.

She dried the coffee mugs and hung them on the hooks in the cabinet. Fixed the tie on the lace curtain that hung across the kitchen window, lingering as she watched the frothy waves roll up the shore. It felt like yesterday that they'd moved to Drifting. Natalie was conceived the night before they moved, a poignant nine months after Jack died. They had considered moving into Jack's apartment but Claire said it would always feel empty to her. Aunt Helen and Uncle Max had retired to South Carolina when she was ten years old. There was nothing to keep her in the city anymore. Cherney's Pharmacy was sold to the young man who'd been Jack's assistant, and just seeing the old block-lettered sign come down and the new one, STAN-LEY DRUGS AND COSMETICS, go up in a garish hot-pink neon script, tore Claire apart. Eli had never been one for Manhattan anyway. She knew he had stayed for her and for Jack although Eli insisted it wasn't so.

It was pure serendipity that Doc Wilson's ad announcing the sale of his country veterinary practice had been in the journal. They drove up to Drifting one Sunday in late December and not three weeks later were packed and ready to move. They didn't go to Doc Wilson's right away. They drove down Main Street and parked in the empty lot near the beach. The public baths were closed for the winter, their doors battened down with padlocks. The unadorned flagpoles were bare sheaths of metal, their canvas straps slapped by the wind. They pushed Jonah's stroller along the boardwalk and felt the cool salt spray sting their cheeks and wondered aloud if it would be possible to live in a town as tiny as the postcards that lined the shuttered beachfront kiosks. Yet both knew there was no question when Mrs. Wilson opened the door to the small animal hospital on Olivia Street and led them up the bare wooden stairs to the small cozy apartment above. Doc Wilson was dozing in a worn corduroy armchair, his steel-rimmed half glasses perched crookedly on the bridge of his nose, an overweight black Labrador and a mottled dachshund sleeping by his side.

"Martin! Martin! Wake up! That young man who's going to take over the practice is here!" Mrs. Wilson proclaimed as though it was a fait accompli.

Claire knew they were meant to be in Drifting from

the moment Mrs. Wilson took her on what she called the grand tour of the tiny apartment. She peered into every cupboard lined meticulously with gingham-checked paper, every drawer filled with neat rows of worn scratched cutlery and small wire baskets neatly holding oddly paired items—corks, string, safety pins, vegetable peelers, bent paper clips. Mrs. Wilson showed her the four-burner stove with the double oven, telling her proudly about the meals she'd cooked for her three children, how the top oven baked Rome apples far better than the lower oven but the lower one never failed to roast the perfect chicken. And later, when Claire and Eli were back at the board-walk, sitting across from one another at a picnic table, steaming coffee warming their hands while Jonah slept bundled in the stroller, Eli asked, "Can you do this? Can you live in this town?"

She nodded yes. "Can you?"

"It's easy for me. I'm just a small-town boy. You grew up in the city. No shops and department stores and ethnic markets? No Central Park?"

"I can live anywhere as long as I'm with you," she said.

It hadn't been easy to get Jonah to sleep the night before the move. Even Maggie, their old springer spaniel, paced the apartment. Eli said that children and animals have similar instincts. That both Jonah and Maggie had a sense of something changing. They'd tried to explain the notion of moving to Jonah but he remained baffled by the empty cabinets and cardboard boxes filled with his toys and books piled high in the living room. He tossed and turned in his bed as he had for the last several days while they packed, coming out every ten minutes or so, perspiring and weepy, rubbing his red-rimmed eyes. Claire convinced him to drink a cup of warm milk and honey. "It's what Pa gave me when I was little and couldn't sleep. It's like a magic potion, Jonah. You'll see." Claire often mentioned Pa, never wanting Jack to slip from Jonah's young memory.

Claire rocked Jonah while he drank the elixir from the sippy cup, his eyes growing heavy until he could no longer resist. Eli took him from Claire's arms and laid him on his bed, tucking his plaid blanket with the frayed satin trim under his chin. He kissed the boy on his forehead and tiptoed from the room, leaving Maggie curled at the foot of his bed. They waited to see if he would stay sleeping, wrapping the last of the dishes and glasses in newspaper while they listened for his pajama-slippered footsteps.

"Don't wrap those yet," Eli said, taking two wine-glasses about to be rolled in newspaper from Claire's hands. "Let's finish last night's wine."

They made love on a down comforter amid the boxes that night, whispering as Jonah slept. The whispers led to Natalie.

Claire looked at the children's graduation pictures on her dresser next to their baby pictures. Jonah was fair-haired and blue-eyed like Jack and herself but had Eli's strapping build. She smiled to herself. How was it possible that her seven-pound baby boy was suddenly taller than his six-foot-one father? Natalie was petite like Claire and dark-haired like Eli although Natalie had a caramel to her skin and a drama in her dark eyes that were unmistakably Sulie, traits that Claire recalled from the pictures that once sat on the mantel. No question, Sulie was beautiful. Natalie once asked if there were any pictures of her grand-mother.

"Granny's picture is in the living room," Claire answered, puzzled. "On the piano."

"No," Natalie said softly. "*Your* mother."

Claire felt herself bristle. "I have none."

"Mom? Do you remember her at all?" Natalie prodded.

"No," Claire said, shaking her head. "I was way too young when she left."

"Why did she leave?"

"Because *she* was way too young," Claire said quietly.

"Who told you?"

"Aunt Helen mostly. And Jack."

"Was she pretty?"

"Very pretty," Claire said thoughtfully. "Beautiful, really."

"You remember?"

"No. Just from old pictures."

"Where are they? I thought you said you don't have any."

"I don't," she said. "I threw them away a long time ago."

"Do you ever wonder, Mom? I mean, do you ever wonder where she is or want to find her or anything?"

"I did." Claire sighed. "After you were born. Jack was gone and I thought about her pretty intensely for a while. I think it was because you were you, you know, a girl. I wondered how her pregnancy was with me . . . you know, things like that."

"So?"

"So what?"

"So maybe you should try to find her. People do

things like that nowadays. Like kids who are adopted and stuff."

"I know," Claire said. "It's just that I don't know what I'd do with her if I found her. If she said she was sorry I don't know that I could forgive her. And if she wasn't sorry then I think I might feel as if she left me all over again."

A stack of papers long overdue for the Department of Social Services sat on the chair in the corner of the room. She showered and towel-dried her hair, pulled on faded jeans and a worn baby blue Oxford shirt that Eli had discarded, and gathered the papers under her arm. She turned off the lamp, closed the bedroom window and headed downstairs.

The glass door in the small lobby was frosted with fog. The drizzle had become a heavy rain. Claire's office was in what had once been the old barn behind the inn. A short hop down the path, but she surely needed an umbrella even to run the short distance. The frosted glass obscured the man standing outside. She was about to take her umbrella from the brass stand when the front door opened. The man's umbrella appeared first as he pushed open the door. One of the spokes jutted out and water dripped onto the floor as he struggled to close it. He looked at her apologetically. In his late forties, maybe early fifties, he was powerfully built with steel-blue eyes and sandy-colored hair. His khaki trousers were wrinkled and one of his white shirttails hung visibly beneath his tweed jacket, a corner of one lapel turned up.

"Sorry," he said. "The wind turned it inside out."

She pushed a small metal trash can over to him.

"Here. You can put it here," she said. "Can I help you?"

"I'd like to check in," the man said, placing the umbrella in the trash can.

"I don't believe we have any reservations."

"What do you mean?" he asked. "Are there no vacancies?"

"Oh, no. Plenty of vacancies," she said, thinking he had an oddly stilted way of speaking. "It's just that I don't recall taking any reservations for today."

"I never made one," he said, slightly flustered. "I just assumed there would be a room."

"We always have rooms this time of year," she said. "How long will you be staying?"

"A few days. Maybe more. A week, perhaps," he said. "I'm not quite sure."

"A week?" She felt herself become nervous. He was obviously uncomfortable.

"Is that all right?"

"We usually don't have such long stays off-season," she said, looking around, wishing someone else was there. "We're really semiclosed. Are you by yourself?"

"My daughter's with me. She's in the car."

"Your daughter," Claire stated with a nod. She took exception to men who traveled with their "daughters" during the week. May-December romances where the men and their "daughters" took separate rooms and the couple went to great pains to make the "daughter's" room appear slept in. "Well, we have room seven with an ocean view and king-size bed. That's forty-five for the night. And then we have room five with a garden view and queen-size bed and that's forty."

"Is that with breakfast?"

"We don't serve breakfast once the season is over," she said stiffly, wishing she had said they were closed altogether.

"I see," he said. "That's fine, but do you have a room with twins or two doubles? My daughter's used to sleeping in her own bed. She's only seven."

"Seven?" Claire's mouth fell open. "Oh, for goodness sake. When you said you were with your daughter . . . "

The man gave a slow smile and appeared to relax. "Ah, you thought I had a companion, as they say. Nothing that exciting, I'm afraid. Just a dad taking his little girl for a long-promised vacation at the shore. I've been promising her the beach all summer but work got in the way." He reached behind him and tucked in his shirt. "Her school starts next week."

"Our schools started today," Claire said.

"You have children?"

"Two. They're in college now, though."

"Kayla—my daughter—goes to private school," he said. "We don't start until next week."

"Well, we have room eight with twin beds and an ocean view," she said. She pushed the leather-cushioned registration card in front of him. "That's forty. If you would just sign here and give me a credit card . . . "

"I'd rather pay cash, if you don't mind," he said. "One thing I can't stand is getting the bill a month later. Spoils everything. I can pay in advance if you like."

"A two-night deposit will do just fine and then we'll take it from there. As I said, our dining room is closed but there are some cute lunch places in town and a couple up the road in Meadville."

"What about breakfast? I'm afraid Kayla's going to wake up starving. She had cereal early this morning but she mostly played with it."

"There's a coffee shop in town. Gus's," Claire said, handing him the room key. "Here you go. Top of the stairs. Fourth door on the right. Room eight." She glanced at the registration form. Nicholas Pierce, 88 Central Park West, New York City. "Welcome to the Inn at Drifting, Mr. Pierce. I see you're from the Upper West Side. I grew up there and my husband and I used to live in Greenwich Village."

"Ah, urban transplants," he said. "I've thought about getting out many times myself but you get so ensconced, you know? Are you the owner?"

"My husband and myself," she said. "I'm Claire. Claire Cherney."

"Pleased to meet you," the man said, extending his hand. "Nick Pierce."

"I can help you with your bags, if you like. Cora, our housekeeper, will be in around ten. Anything you need or need to know, just ask her. Pillows. Extra blankets. Directions. . . . " She reached for her umbrella. "Just make sure you get everything by noon. Cora leaves early off-season."

"You might want to take a rain jacket as well," he said. "It's really coming down."

Claire took a fleece-lined slicker from the brass coatrack to the side of the desk. She was slipping her arm into the sleeve when he walked over. "If I may," he said, holding the empty sleeve to her arm.

Her breath caught in her throat. Jack always said

that—if I may. He made a ceremony out of helping her on with her coat. *If I may, M'Lady,* he would say. "Thank you," she said, wondering if he heard her heart skip.

"Dreadful weather, isn't it?" Nicholas said. "I certainly hope it clears."

He held the door for her as they walked outside but then he stopped in his tracks. The rear passenger door of his blue Taurus sedan was open. He ran to the car and looked inside. "Kayla!" he called. "Oh, God. Kayla!" He turned to Claire. "She's gone!"

Claire's eyes widened as she looked around her. "I'm sure she awakened and just went to explore. Maybe she walked down to the beach. . . . "

"No, you don't understand—"

"Mr. Pierce, please, I'm sure she's fine," she interrupted him, trying to calm him. "She can't have gone far. Kids can never wait to see the ocean. The beach is just down those steps over—"

"You don't understand," he said, biting each word. The color had drained from his cheeks. His hands were shaking. "Kayla is blind. She's blind."

And so it was, until that September morning, life in Drifting had gone along with a flow as certain as the tides that went in and out every day with the pull of the moon.

Chapter 3

The weariness that had been so apparent on Nicholas Pierce's face turned to desperation. The circles under his eyes took on a darker hue. He began to tremble, turning one way and then the next, crying out his child's name. Claire ran to the backyard. The old tire swing was still. Nicholas ran toward the beach steps and called Kayla's name. He started down the steps when Claire placed her hand on his arm.

"Let me look," she said. "You should wait here. What's the likelihood she made it down the steps? Is she . . . is she that independent?"

"She can be," he said. "I'm not sure." He twisted his hands while his eyes darted this way and that. "Where is she? Where could she have gone?"

Claire took a deep breath. "Not far. She's here. And if she comes back to the car and you're not here, then what?" She didn't want to alarm him but she had to make the suggestion. "I can call the police if you like."

He paled even more. "Not yet."

"Let *me* check the beach then. We're just wasting time. She can't have gone far. Wait here," Claire implored him.

"I need to do something," he said. "I can't just stand here."

"Give me fifteen minutes. We'll find her, Mr. Pierce," Claire said as she ran down the steps. "I promise you."

She knew the feeling he suffered all too well. Jonah was four when he'd gone missing. Gone missing. The term had never been in her lexicon until that moment when he was by her side one instant and the next, he was gone.

They were just coming off a snowstorm. One of those storms where the snow began to fall early on a Sunday morning in January. Small flakes began as lacy sprinkles of confetti and grew to the size of silver dollars that blanketed the countryside. The sky was ivory and the wind blew so fiercely that power lines swung precariously and most of the roads were closed despite the efforts to salt and plow. It wasn't until Tuesday that the sun shone and they heard the welcome sound of ice melting from the trees. There were just so many LEGO towers four-year-old Jonah could build, so many videotapes to watch over and over again. They had used the last of the milk to churn "butter" in a bowl. They baked cupcakes and made blue paste from flour and water and food coloring. Played hide the button and Candyland. Claire was running out of ideas.

Claire bundled up the children against the icy air, popped them into their car seats, and headed to the Big Ace in Meadville. The Big Ace Supermarket was the size of two football fields and sat in the middle of a shopping center that was like a small city. Claire rarely went to the Big Ace. It was overwhelming. Those were the days she longed for the corner grocer in Manhattan where she'd buy what they needed for the evening and breakfast and walk home, plastic bags hanging over the handles of the stroller, Jonah munching a sprinkle-coated cookie while she browsed the shop windows.

Claire was standing on the checkout line, Jonah behind her playing with a plastic Ninja Turtle. She could hear him chattering to himself, banging the plastic figure on the counter, making war whoops so loud she hushed him every few minutes. Two clearly harried mothers, carts overflowing, toddlers in the seats, waited on line ahead of her. The line stretching behind her was endless. Claire had just checked her watch when three-month-old Natalie began to whimper in the Snugli that hung on Claire's chest. She felt her breasts tensing and knew it was past the time to nurse her. Claire took off Natalie's pink knit cap and fished around the diaper bag for her pacifier. She rocked as she stood in place, trying to soothe Natalie when the toddler in the next cart suddenly reached from his seat in the grocery cart and tipped over a bucket of heart-shaped lollipops. His mother was prying them from his clenched fist as he screamed to have them back, trying to distract him with the jingle of her keys and the small flashlight on their chain. She was placing the candies back into the bucket as quickly as the child grabbed for them again and tugged on her hair as she bent over. Claire was trying to help and struggling with Natalie who had started to scream. She rocked her more vigorously, perspiring in her down jacket. It was chaos. She'd tuck the cart someplace, she thought, nurse Natalie and get back on the line. So much for the outing. What was she thinking? Always too ambitious.

"Jonah, come," she said without turning around, fussing with Natalie, trying to get her to suck the pacifier. "We're going to go feed Nat and then we'll get back on the line." She turned to take his hand. "Jonah? Jonah? Come! Where are you?" How long had it been since she'd hushed his chatter? "Are you hiding, Jonah? Jonah?" she called, the pitch of her voice escalating. She could feel the panic ripple through her body and her mouth parch. Her heart pounded in her chest. She turned to the line of people behind her, straining her neck over their blank faces. She visibly trembled. "Has anyone seen my little boy? He was here just a moment ago. . . ."

A woman in a paisley scarf tied beneath her chin curled her lips and shrugged. "I didn't see any kid," she said with what Claire thought was a sinister look.

"What's he wearing?" a man asked. "How old?"

"A red jacket," Claire said, trying to breathe through her nose since her chest felt like it was caving in. "He's four. Blond."

"Yeah, he was here just a moment ago," the man said. "He was playing with some kind of toy. One of them character dolls."

She felt sick to her stomach. Two women murmured that some people just don't watch their children. It's always something, another complained. Either the register tape runs out or someone with coupons holds up the line.

"Please, please, let me through," she said, shoving

people aside. Maybe he was at the gum ball machines, she thought. She ran to the front of the store where the machines lined one wall by the automatic exit door. No Jonah. She ran down the aisles that held sodas and juice and cookies and ice cream, calling his name in a voice that barely resembled her own and came from someplace else. She felt the blood rush from her face and her skin become clammy. He knew not to wander. She'd told him over and over. She called his name again and again, the sound of her voice becoming more shrill, breathless, and distant. She held the back of Natalie's head as she ran, trying to ignore Natalie's cries that were now so incidental. Why wasn't I holding his hand? she thought. What was I thinking? He's only a baby. Sometimes she wondered if she expected too much of him since Natalie was born. Six and a half pounds of Natalie was so feather-light and when Jonah climbed into her lap he felt so big. He wasn't so big, she thought. He was small and helpless and gone. She stopped and began to sob, her knees buckling although she wouldn't allow them to fail because of the baby hanging on her chest and the mission to find her son. It was then that Annie appeared. An angel in a long brown print skirt that hung unevenly over laced-up boots. She had rose-colored cheeks and dark blue eyes that sparkled beneath a teal wool cap pulled down to her brows. Her child, a girl around six with strawberry-blond hair tied in pigtails, held her hand.

"Let me help you," Annie said, grabbing her arm, stopping her from running. "I've been chasing you down the aisles. Boy? Girl? How old?"

"Four. My little boy," Claire sobbed. "He was right next to me on the checkout line and I turned around and he was gone."

"What's his name?"

"Jonah," Claire said, breath exhaling in a stutter. "Oh, God. He knows better."

"They never know better when they're four," Annie said reassuringly. "What's he wearing?"

"A red jacket. He was playing with his Ninja Turtle," Claire said, placing her hand over her mouth. "Oh, God. Where is he?"

"You have to calm down," Annie said firmly. "We'll find him. Maybe he went to play on the horse."

"Horse?" Claire asked, hopeful for a moment, wiping her tears with the back of her hand. "What horse?"

"The shoe store put up one of those mechanical horses a couple of weeks ago. Come, I'll show you," Annie said. She turned to Natalie in the Snugli. "Who's this little one?"

"Natalie," Claire said, sniffling. "He doesn't know about that horse. What if someone took him?"

"No one took him," Annie said. She pointed as they stepped outside the market. "Look over there! Is that your Jonah?"

There was the red jacket. The striped blue-and-red scarf around his neck. He was sitting on the painted wooden horse in front of the shoe shop.

"Jonah!" Claire ran to him, Natalie bouncing on her chest.

"It won't work, Mommy," Jonah said, shaking the horse's neck, pulling on the plastic reins. "It's broke. It won't go."

"You have to put in ten cents, see?" Annie's little girl

said, taking a dime from her pocket and popping it into the slot. "See?"

"Jonah, you can't walk away like that," Claire said, tears rolling down her cheeks, as she kissed him all over his face. "You always have to ask. You know that."

"I did tell," Jonah said. "You said 'uh-huh.' Why are you crying, Mommy? You're makin' me all wet."

"How did you know about this horse?" she asked as he continued to shake the reins, ignoring her distress.

"Daddy took me after we got my hairs cut," Jonah said. "Daddy let me do three rides. Mommy, you're kissing me too much!"

Claire turned to Annie. "I swear, there are times I don't know whether to laugh or cry. I mean, did I answer him? The little boy in front of us was pulling down all the lollipops and can you please tell me why on earth they put candy by the checkout? Besides, it's still over a month to Valentine's Day. It's to torture us, isn't it?" She managed to laugh. "You must think I'm a lunatic."

Annie placed her arm around Claire's shoulders. "Listen, I only have the one and there are times my head spins," she said gently. "I'm Annie Merrill by the way. My husband Sam and I live on Crawford Lane in Drifting. He's the new deputy. We moved here from Southport last month."

"Claire Cherney," Claire said, wiping her cheek with her fingertips. "My husband's the vet. Eli Bishop. You know, I heard that you'd just moved to town and I've been meaning to call and welcome you but I get so busy all the time. It's ten at night by the time I come up for air and that's too late to call. We've lived here for a year and I still don't feel quite settled."

"Believe me, I understand," Annie said, her head bobbing up and down emphatically. "I doubt I'll ever get out of boxes." She handed Claire a small packet of tissues from her purse. "Here. Take the whole thing."

"You know I'm still shaking? Thank you, Annie. Thank you for helping me." She hugged her. They were no longer strangers.

Annie patted her back. "I would have been scared, too. Like I said, I just have Lizzie here and I can't imagine what it must be like having to keep track of two."

"They keep me busy, that's for sure," Claire said, smiling weakly. "Do you want to get some coffee or something?"

"I'd like that," Annie said. "What about your groceries, though? I just started my shop when I spotted you."

Claire waved her hand. "My cart is officially abandoned. I'll pick up something for dinner in town. Listen, there's a place up the road where the kids can have an ice cream and we can sit and have a cup. And I have to nurse this little girl before she realizes that pacifier's dry and I explode. I'll wait for you out front. What are you driving?"

"I have an old Wagoneer. I'll follow you, okay?"

"I have a Rambler wagon," Claire said. "Yellow."

"A Rambler? Those are practically antiques."

"It was my father's," Claire said, a warm smile coming over her as she thought of Jack. "It's a sixty-two."

"You must have been slipping and sliding all the way over here."

"It wasn't bad," Claire said. "My husband put on snow tires." She didn't tell her that sometimes she pretended Jack was driving. How when she was a child she sometimes wondered what it would be like if Sulie were sitting up front next to Jack as she sat in the backseat singing.

Claire stopped at the bottom of the wooden steps that led to the beach. The rain had subsided but the fog remained thick. I'll find her, she thought. Jonah hadn't gotten far that time. Of course Jonah wasn't blind. She picked up the emergency phone encased in the rusted metal cabinet, wondering if it still worked. She dialed 911 and prayed that Sam would be at the station.

"Drifting Police Emergency," the voice answered. "Chief Merrill."

"Sam? Oh, I'm so glad you're there. It's Claire. Chief! I'm not used to that yet."

"What's going on? You came in on the emergency line."

"I know. Listen, a man just checked in with his little girl. He left her in the car and when he came out, she was gone. I'm heading down to the beach now to have a look."

"How old?" Sam asked.

"Seven, I think."

"How long has she been gone?"

"Fifteen, maybe twenty minutes. Not that long. They just checked in."

"What's she wearing? What's she look like?"

"I don't know," Claire said breathlessly. "I didn't see her. But she's blind."

"Blind? Oh, for God's sake. Not bad enough to leave any kid in a car . . ."

"She was sleeping."

"Doesn't matter. Where's the mother?"

"They're traveling alone. She's back home, I guess." Where's the mother? People always asked where her mother was. Jack would say she was out of town and then change the subject. *Well, it's not a lie, is it, Claire?* Jack would say.

"Where're they from?" Sam asked.

"New York. Manhattan."

"I'll radio Kent to keep his eyes peeled. He's directing traffic on Main. They're putting more cable lines in today and it's a mess down there between the crew and the rain. I swear, they won't be done for months. Do you know what these roads will be like come December? I'm on my way," he said. "Is the father with you?"

"No, I told him to wait by the car out front of the inn. I thought in case she found her way back he should wait. . . ."

"Good idea. Name?"

"Pierce. Nicholas Pierce."

"No, the child."

"Kayla."

"I'll be right there."

Claire replaced the receiver and scanned the beach, shielding her eyes with her hand as she squinted through the fog. She could barely make out the jetty to the right. An old cabana had tipped over in front of the McPhersons' dilapidated beach house to the left. Claire ran and turned it over on its side, wondering if the child had taken shelter underneath. Her heart pounded. What if they couldn't find her? What if she'd gone into the ocean? Sam was right. What was that man thinking when he left his child, a blind child no less, alone in the car? What kind of father was he? So what if she was sleeping? She was trying to decide which way to turn when she saw the silhouette of a figure standing at the shore quite a distance to her left. The tipped cabana had blocked the sight of her at first. Claire sprinted toward her, slowing as she approached the child. Kayla was standing ankle-deep in the surf, her head tipped backwards as she caught raindrops on her tongue. The hood of her navy blue parka hung down her back; the front was unzipped. Her sneakers and socks were strewn behind her next to a soiled beige teddy bear, barely escaping the roll of a wave before Claire rescued them.

"Kayla?" Claire asked softly as she approached her, shoes and socks in hand. "Kayla, is that you?"

"How do you know my name?" the child asked, turning in Claire's direction.

"Your daddy told me. He's looking for you. Come out of the water, sweetheart," Claire said, reaching her hand to Kayla.

She didn't take Claire's hand but came obediently. "Who are you?"

"I'm Claire. I own the inn where you'll be staying," Claire said, taking Kayla's arm and pulling her gently, realizing the child hadn't seen her outstretched palm. "Come, I'm going to take you back now. It's okay. Your daddy's waiting."

"The ocean's really big, isn't it? I went to the beach with my grandma when I was little and we made sand castles but she died," Kayla said, taking a deep breath as she turned to Claire. "Can you see anything out there? Like boats? I'm blind, you know."

Claire caught her breath. The child was so

straightforward, so obviously well-adjusted and bright, she thought. "No boats today. But when my son was a little boy, he thought Barcelona was on the other side."

"What's a Barcelona?"

"It's a city in Spain."

"Oh," she said, licking her fingers then lifting her face in Claire's direction. "Salty."

Claire knelt beside the child. "Come, I have your sneakers. You must be freezing."

"A little. I wanted to feel the water. You know, I hollered to Daddy. I said where I was going," Kayla said, running her fingertips lightly over Claire's nose and mouth.

"I'm sure you did but he was inside checking in," Claire said, holding still while Kayla's fingers felt her face like butterflies. "You have to make sure next time that Daddy answers you. That way you know he hears you. Here, hold on to my shoulder and give me one foot at a time so I can dry them." Claire untucked her shirt from her jeans and used the tails as a towel. Kayla's toes had remnants of chipped pink polish on the long toenails. There was a raw blister on the back of her heel. "They're like little icicles. Footsicles."

"Footsicles." Kayla giggled. "That tickles."

"Let's get these socks on first," Claire said, stretching the damp socks over Kayla's feet. "Now for your sneakers."

"I can lace myself," Kayla said. "I know how."

"Go ahead," she said, handing a sneaker to Kayla, thinking how well she'd been taught to be self-sufficient. Too well, considering her adventure. "How did you find your way here?"

Kayla began to hop up and down. "I heard the waves and I followed the sounds."

She was the sweetest child. Short-cropped nearly white blond hair. Arms and legs as thin as toothpicks. A little turned-up nose. She must look like her mother, Claire thought. Nicholas Pierce had more pronounced features: a strong nose, a broad jaw. Kayla was delicate. Waiflike. Almost too tiny for seven.

Claire laughed. "You're all sandy again. Here, give back that sneaker." Claire clapped the sneakers together and shook out the sand. "There you go," she said, handing them to Kayla. She took off her jacket and draped it over Kayla's shoulders. "Put my jacket on so you don't catch cold."

"Won't you be cold?"

"I wasn't standing in the ocean. Let's zip up your parka, too."

"You can't," Kayla said. "The zip is broken."

Kayla forced the once-white sneaker onto her foot and tied the laces meticulously, slowly. "The water was kind of cold," she said, shivering. "I don't think I'd like to swim in it."

"Oh, in the summer it's warm," Claire said, thinking Kayla's sneakers were too small for her. No wonder she had a blister. "You'd love it in the summer."

"Are there boats then?"

"Uh-huh. Lots. Mostly sailboats. All different colors . . . reds, blues, yellows. My favorite has a rainbow sail. There're only a few left in the marina right now. Soon, they'll all be put away for the winter."

"Where do they go?"

"It's called dry dock. They put them inside and stack them up until the thaw."

"What's that?" Kayla asked, turning her face to the sky.

"Seagulls," Claire said, wondering if she should have mentioned the colors of the boats. "They fly over the beach looking for food. Sometimes they swoop down and steal people's french fries."

"You know, when I was little I could see shapes and stuff," Kayla said, heaving the sigh of an old woman. "I sort of remember." She took a pair of tinted glasses from the pocket of her parka and placed them on her face. One of the arms was bent. "I can't see the shapes anymore though and light really bothers me. My mom wants me to go to blind school."

"Blind school?" Claire asked.

"Yeah, where blind kids go," Kayla said, rolling down the cuffs of her pants.

"Oh?"

"You live there," she said. For a moment, she seemed lost in thought.

"Like a boarding school?"

"I don't want to talk about it anymore," Kayla said abruptly. "Where's my bear?"

"Right here," Claire said, handing it to her. She wouldn't press her about the school although she was curious.

"I take him everywhere with me," she said, hugging the bear to her.

"He looks like he's been with you for a long time," Claire said.

Kayla nodded. "Forever."

"Ready now?" Claire asked. She reached her hand to Kayla then realized again that she should speak. "How about we hold hands when we walk back, okay?"

"How come?" Kayla asked.

"It'll just be nice, that's all. You feel warmer when you hold hands."

"What did you say your name was again?"

"Claire."

"Wait! I forgot my cane. I put it down somewhere. . . ."

Claire looked around her. A spot of the red tip jutted out from the sand. "I see it," Claire said. "Do you want it now?"

"Not now," Kayla said, slipping the cane into her jacket pocket. "I'll just keep it in here. Daddy doesn't like me to use the cane."

"Oh, no?"

"No. He says that I should be independent."

"Well, you certainly proved that today, didn't you?"

Sam was writing in a small brown notebook as Nicholas held Sam's large black umbrella over the two of them. Nicholas craned his neck past Sam, looking to the beach. His hand was pulling at the side of his face when Claire and Kayla came up the steps.

"Here we are!" Claire called.

Nicholas ran over to his daughter and lifted her into his arms. "Don't ever do that, Kayla," he said, suddenly stern. "Never leave like that, Kayla. Never."

"I'm sorry," she said, hanging her head down.

Nicholas smoothed her hair and spoke tenderly now. "You scared me half to death." He turned to Claire. "Where was she?"

"Ankle deep," Claire said, wiping raindrops that dripped from her hair onto her forehead. "Quite a way down the beach, though. She's pretty spunky."

Nicholas smiled. "That she is," he said. "She never lets anything get in her way."

"Good thing the swells are calm today. No undertow," Sam said, snapping closed the notebook and slipping it into the breast pocket of his shirt. He bent down to Kayla. "Now you listen to your daddy, young lady, and don't ever run off like that again. Okay?"

"Are you a policeman?" Kayla asked.

Sam nodded and then realized he should speak. "I am."

"Daddy!" Kayla cried excitedly.

Nicholas laughed heartily. "Oh, Kayla. Darling. The policeman was just trying to help me find you. You haven't done anything wrong."

"Want to hear the siren?" Sam asked. "Come here. I'll let you press the switch but don't tell anyone, okay?"

"Daddy?"

"It's okay, my love. It's okay." Nicholas turned to Claire and laughed. "Highly developed sense of right and wrong, my child has."

"I guess you have to work on the 'police are your friends' thing," Claire said with a laugh.

"Well, the chief's taking care of that," Nicholas said, gesturing toward Sam and Kayla.

Kayla took Sam's hand as they walked over to the black-and-white car. Sam placed her hand on the switch and the siren gave out a whoop.

"One more time?" Kayla asked.

"Just once or folks are going to think we're calling the cavalry," Sam said. He turned to Claire. "What are you up to?"

"Well, first I need to change. I'm soaked," Claire said. "Then some paperwork. I'm way behind."

"Heard from Nat?"

"She calls every night. She's made a couple of friends. Loves everything including the food. She misses having her own bathroom. More than she misses me, I think."

Sam laughed. "Don't kid yourself. You're right up there with plumbing. How's the roommate?"

"Sloppy but nice."

"I'm so sorry for all the commotion, officer," Nicholas interrupted.

"Not at all," Sam said. He pointed to the dented fender streaked with white paint. "That's quite a smack you got there, sir."

"The hazards of driving in Manhattan," Nicholas said, shaking his head. "The cabbies are wild men."

"I hope you got him."

"You know how it is, you can never find a police officer when you need one." Nicholas laughed.

Sam's radio crackled in the patrol car. "Merrill," Sam answered. "Kent? We've got her. You can call off the dogs. Yeah, she took a stroll on the beach. Who? Oh no, not again. Okay, I'll meet you over there." He turned to Claire. "Chief Larsen cracked up his car for a change. I swear, I should pull his license but I don't have the heart. I mean, Christ, I was his deputy for years." Sam straightened the holster on his trousers and walked over to Nicholas who held Kayla in his arms. "Well, I gotta run. Have a good stay, sir. Remember what I told you, young lady. Talk to you later, Claire."

Nicholas watched Sam's car drive away. "I've got to get this little girl a hot bath and some dry clothes," Nicholas said. "How did he know to come here?"

"I called him from the beach phone. It's a hotline for the lifeguards."

"Nice fellow. Very laid back."

Claire laughed. "Chief Sam? Oh, he's the best. We're a fairly sleepy town. There're only two other men on the force and they're part-time. They beef up the force off-season but right now, well, you can see there's not too much going on."

"You know him quite well I take it?"

"He and his wife Annie are our closest friends."

Nicholas was hefting a suitcase out of the trunk, Kayla still in his arms. "A sleepy town is just what Kayla and I need these days."

"Why don't you let me take Kayla upstairs?" Claire asked. "She's shivering. Those suitcases are huge. You sure you're not moving here?"

Nick laughed. "I got a bit overzealous with the packing but I wasn't sure whether it would rain or be cold or we'd have a spot of Indian summer. I wanted her to be comfortable." He passed Kayla to Claire and set a heavy briefcase on the ground, the initials NP stenciled in gold.

"I hope that isn't work," Claire said. "This is a resort town, you know. Even off-season."

He smiled. "Not too much work. Just some blueprints I need to look over."

"Blueprints?"

"I'm an architect."

"My father often said that he wanted to be an architect," Claire said. "He was born in Russia and always wanted to go back to St. Petersburg. He wanted to see the Yelagin Palace. He couldn't get a visa, though. He was a pharmacist."

Nicholas nodded sympathetically. "So many dreams we can't fulfill."

"We'll head up, if that's all right with you," Claire said. "Remember, room eight. Fourth room on the right."

"Thank you, Claire. For everything. We've made quite the auspicious entrance, haven't we?"

"These things happen with children, Mr. Pierce. You know, the kids always say they weren't lost because they knew where they were the whole time."

"It's the truth," he said. "Please call me Nick."

"Nick," Claire said, smiling.

Claire walked up the steps, Kayla straddling her hip the way her children had rested so many years before. An old feeling of satisfaction came over her. Memories of carrying Natalie from the beach wrapped head to toe in a towel while Jonah clung to her arm.

"You should put me down," Kayla said suddenly. "I want to learn the way."

"How do we do that?" Claire asked, setting her down gently. "Remember the cane's in your pocket."

"No cane," Kayla cautioned in a whisper. "Daddy doesn't like the cane. Let's hold hands and walk real slow. Just tell me what's here and there and I count the steps." Kayla's free hand felt the way through the door. She smiled up at Claire. "Do you have any girls?"

"One," Claire said. "A big girl. In college."

"Oh, good. Then you know a lot about girls," Kayla said. She looked up at Claire and smiled. "I'm going to count the steps to our room now, okay?"

"Sounds good to me."

"Claire? I'm going to like it here, I think," Kayla said before she began counting.

What kind of mother, Claire thought, could even think to send this child away?

Chapter 4

"I'm running the water," Claire said as Nick carried the suitcases into the room. "Old pipes. They take a few minutes to warm up. I set up the luggage stands for you."

Nick hefted the suitcases onto the canvas-strapped stands and sat on the edge of the bed. "Thanks for everything," he said. He blew out his breath in a whistle. "Quite a morning."

"How about if I get some peanut butter and jelly for Kayla?" Claire asked. "She must be hungry."

"No, just jelly," Kayla said. "Do you have grape?"

"Kayla!" Nick chided.

"No, no, that's okay. I like a girl who knows what she likes. Just grape jelly then. Can I get you something, Nick? Coffee?"

"We've been enough trouble already. We're detaining you. You were on your way out."

"It's no trouble, really. I just have paperwork to do

and I'm a great procrastinator these days. The more distractions the better."

"Coffee would be perfect. You should double our rates," he said with a weak smile.

"You haven't had my coffee yet," Claire said. "You'll demand a refund." She turned to Kayla. "How about a glass of milk?"

"Chocolate milk?" Kayla asked.

"Kayla! What did I say before?" Nick said with a hearty laugh. "She certainly is comfortable here."

"Well, that's just what we want," Claire said. "And yes, we have chocolate milk. I'll be back in a few."

Kayla was sitting in the floral chintz armchair in the corner of the room, her Barbie knapsack beside her. She sat the soiled beige terry-cloth teddy bear beside her.

"This is Drifting, Bear," she said. "Right, Daddy? Drifting, right? Are we in Connecticut?"

"Right," he muttered.

"Right Drifting or right Connecticut?"

"Both."

"Why do they call it Drifting, Daddy? I don't get it."

"I don't really know, Kayla," he said, exasperated. She always asked too many questions, he thought. Endless, endless questions.

"But there must be a reason. Can you think of one?"

"Probably has to do with boats drifting on the ocean or something like that. Maybe someone just liked the name. I mean, why do they call it Boston or Chicago? It's a name. That's all."

"It's a name, that's why," she whispered to the bear. "Later I'll take you to the ocean again, okay? Maybe you'll see that place in Spain."

Nick knelt down in front of her. "Kayla, don't ever run off like you did today. What were you thinking?"

"Nothing," she said. "I thought it would be okay."

"It wasn't okay. Don't you ever do that again, Kayla. Ever," he said sternly.

"Okay, Daddy," she said, her lips quivering. She held the bear to her. "I'm sorry, Daddy," she whispered. "Really sorry."

He reached up and haltingly stroked the side of her face. "I'll lay out your clothes, Kayla," Nick said, popping open the lid of her suitcase.

Everything was a mess. Kayla's shirts were folded inside out, in halves, not thirds the way Phoebe always had them folded in Kayla's drawers at home. Kayla's drawers. He thought about how Phoebe had separate drawers for solids and stripes. Separate drawers for primary colors and pastels. Labeled, no less, with Braille on adhesive plastic strips. Really, what difference did any of it make at all? Kayla couldn't see what she was wearing anyway. Why did she need clothing with patterns and colors to begin with? It was all for Phoebe, he thought. He took a plastic bag from the closet and began to fill it with Kayla's soiled shirts and socks and underwear that he'd shoved in the corners of the suitcase. A yellow T-shirt with a cherry-colored splotch down the center had bled onto a white blouse. He'd meant to rinse it out better. He'd wiped it off after she dripped that Italian ice all over the car. He didn't like when she wore that white blouse anyway. It was one of the things her mother had bought for her. He needed to do a wash but Kayla hated the Laundromat. She hated the roar of the machines, the churning of the dryer, even the sound of change pushing into the slot on the machines and then tumbling down. The last time they'd gone to a Laundromat she covered her ears and screamed so loud that everyone looked at him like he was some kind of monster. White noise, Dr. Dobson the school psychologist explained the day Kayla had come home in tears after the teacher put a fan in the classroom.

"White noise drowns out the sounds she needs to 'see,' " the psychologist said. "Running water. Air conditioning. Fans. Vacuums. They might be disturbing."

Nick turned angrily to Phoebe. "So then what's all that nonsense about her loving the beach?" Nick asked. "Wouldn't you think the sound of the surf would get on her nerves? How's that different from the fan or the washing machine or the air conditioner?"

"Nick, did you ever close your eyes and lie on the sand?" Phoebe asked. "Those are isolated sounds. Specific sounds. Sounds of the waves splashing, the hushed voices, the gulls. Those are the sounds that tell her she's on the beach. She can differentiate those sounds. She loves the beach."

Damn Phoebe. She was so condescending. Talking to him like he was a child or some kind of imbecile who couldn't understand anything. Talking to him in that overly patient tone, enunciating every word while that supercilious shrink nodded her head and squeezed her beady little eyes together. And then Phoebe said how sometimes she shut her eyes and tried to imagine the darkness of Kayla's world and that shrink got all teary-eyed and Phoebe went on and on about how Kayla didn't even see the flashes of light she used to see and how she couldn't tell day from night anymore unless the sun was shining and warmed her skin but the brightness of the sun hurt her eyes. That was when Dr. Dobson leaned over and took Phoebe's hand and he would have sworn she glared at him like it was his fault that Kayla was blind and Phoebe was crying. If he'd been smarter, he might have taken Phoebe's hand himself and comforted her, but then again maybe he was smart not to have done that because she probably would have just wrenched it away anyway.

He tried it once or twice, closing his eyes to see what Kayla's world was like. All he saw was blackness and when he opened his eyes the light bothered them and it took him a while to focus again until the cylinders of faded colors disappeared. Kayla just didn't make any sense to him sometimes. If her world was dark and colorless and had no images, then why did she ask for a pink shirt just the other day when they were at that mall? What difference did it possibly make to her if she wore pink or blue or black? She couldn't see, for the love of God. Or plaid. She wanted a plaid skirt. The lady on the car radio said plaid's what all the girls are wearing now, Kayla said as they stood in the middle of Kmart's children's clothing section. What is it, Daddy? What's plaid like? She must have asked him a dozen times.

"Plaid is like stripes that crisscross each other," he tried to explain patiently. "Like a tic-tac-toe."

"What's that? What's a tic-tac-toe?"

"*Xs* and *Os*," he said.

"You have to *show* me," Kayla implored, pulling his arm.

How was he supposed to *show* her? How do you show someone who's blind?

The salesgirl overheard them. She was a short, squat young woman with stringy hair that had brown roots growing in under a hideous dyed violet. He didn't like the way she looked at him when he answered Kayla. He didn't like the way she looked at them from the moment they'd walked into her department. She pretended not to listen at first, popping price tags on blouses she pulled from a brown cardboard box. But he knew she was staring at him. He'd tried to temper the impatience in his voice. He wanted to leave. They'd been at the Kmart way too long anyway.

"My cousin's little boy is blind," the salesgirl said, looking up from her task. "You have to show her by making her a pattern that she can *touch*."

The girl insisted upon taking them to the toy department where she opened a can of pick-up sticks. She laid them on the floor, stick over stick, vertically, horizontally, taking Kayla's hand, helping her feel the "plaid" she made.

"Usually the plaid is only three colors," the girl explained. "Most common is red and say, blue or green, and then some white."

"It's nice?" Kayla asked.

"It's real nice," the girl said. "Red is crisp like a cool day in fall. Real nice with a white blouse peeking out under say, a navy blue sweater or something like that." She turned to Nick. "I can help you, if you like, sir."

Nick shifted his stance and forced a smile. "Well, that would be so kind of you," he said. "We could use a woman's touch."

"What's your name?" the girl asked.

"Kayla," she answered so softly that the girl asked her again, but Kayla pretended not to hear the second time.

Red. Navy. Plaid. It was all futile. Ridiculous. He watched now as Kayla walked the perimeter of the room, taking the same precise small step each time. Feeling her way along the walls, counting her steps under her breath, touching the molded wainscoting, running her hand down the cool brass handles on the bureau drawers, finding the oval dressing mirror that stood in the corner of the room, although for Kayla there was no reflection. Phoebe had a mirror in Kayla's room at home. Stupid thing, he thought.

What's the point? he'd demanded the day Phoebe hung the mirror on the closet door. You waste my money.

It's for her friends, Phoebe said.

"I think this is the nicest place we've ever gone," Kayla said, stopping and turning in her father's direction. "It smells like flowers. How come?"

"There's a bowl of potpourri on the dresser top."

He watched as she made her way to the center of the dresser, running her fingers along the dresser top until she found the cranberry glass bowl filled with cinnamon sticks and petals, dipping her fingers inside.

"What is this stuff?" she asked, gathering the dried petals in her palm and sniffing them. "Some of it smells like muffins." A smile came over her face. "Is the water warm now, Daddy? I want to take my bath before Claire gets back. I'm cold."

Nick closed the tub drain and ran the water until it filled halfway while Kayla sat in the middle of one of the twin-size beds.

"Ready," he called to her.

She swung her legs over the side of the bed and felt

for the nightstand, used the wainscoting as a guide to the bathroom. "I want to wear the soft corduroys," she said.

"They're not washed yet," Nick said, watching her walk toward him. "I just bought you new jeans."

"We need to wash them. They're still rough. And the tag bothers me. You'll have to cut it out, okay? Maybe Claire has some scissors we could borrow."

"How can we wash them if you won't go to the Laundromat?"

"Maybe Claire has a washing machine. Or maybe I could stay with her while you go. That would be okay, right?" She waited for an answer. "Right? Or maybe Claire will do our laundry. She seems nice."

"You should get in the tub," he said. "Claire's going to bring you your sandwich any minute."

She tripped slightly over the bath rug. "I'll have to get used to that one," she said, blushing. "Did you put everything where I need it?"

"Oh, no. I . . ."

"Towel by the tub on the floor," she said softly. "Soap and shampoo on the ledge. You can hang the washcloth over the spout. Just show me where it is."

"There's a hair dryer on the wall in there," he called to her when her bath was finished.

"You'll have to show me, please," she called to him. "I've got the towel on."

"Over here," he said, walking into the bathroom, guiding her by the arm to the hair dryer.

"I miss my long hair," she said. "That lady cut it way too short. The other day someone thought I was a boy. Remember that waiter? He called me son."

"I told you, it dries faster if it's shorter," he said. He

didn't want to discuss her haircut. Not again. They'd been through this too many times already.

"Did you put out my white blouse?"

He pictured the cherry stain on the front. "You'll have to wear something else."

"It has pearl buttons, though."

"I put out your new jeans and a T-shirt."

"What color T-shirt?"

"Pink," he lied. The shirt was dark green.

"Maybe I can find something," she said, moving her hands along the bed to the stand holding her suitcase, running her hands through the shirts. "This suitcase is a disaster, Daddy. It's all lumpy."

A disaster, he thought. One of her mother's expressions. This room is a *disaster*, Nicholas, Phoebe would say. You can't leave things lying around. She could fall over these things. Pick up your shoes, Nicholas.

"Look, Kayla, just leave it alone. You wear what I put out for you." He tried to soften his tone. "Where do you want to go today? We can go someplace later on and have a nice lunch."

"Okay. I didn't like my dinner much last night though. I don't like mashed potatoes and the chicken was stringy. What did you say it was called? A greasy what?"

"Spoon."

"That's it. Spoon. Why do they call it spoon?"

"For God's sake, Kayla. I don't know." He could feel his temper rising. Too many questions.

"I don't like those places. They smell bad."

He walked to the window and opened the shade. "It looks like the sun is trying to come through," Nick said, trying to change the subject.

"The sun bothers my eyes a lot more lately. What time is it anyway?" she asked.

"Nearly eleven," he said, looking at his watch.

"Do you think there's a place where I can get some new glasses? I need the lenses to be darker and the arm is loose," Kayla said. "And we have to get my drops. Remember?"

"What?"

"My eye drops."

"Right."

"My eyes are starting to feel scratchy," she said softly. "And you promised we could find some Braille books, too."

"It's not that easy, Kayla. I keep telling you. . . ."

"I know," she whispered. "I know. But I like reading. Unless you want to read to me, Daddy. Maybe you could do that, do you think?"

He didn't answer her. She heard him opening and then closing the briefcase. She heard the clicking sound of the combination lock. He was probably going to work on his papers again. She didn't mean to upset him. He was doing the best he could. But she was losing her touch. Literally. Her touch for the letters. She needed to practice. She pitied her father sometimes. He tried so hard. Spending so much time with her when he had so much work to do. But sometimes it was like he really didn't understand that she couldn't see. Sometimes she felt like he thought if he pretended enough things would change. But she wouldn't see ever again, not that she saw much before. Sometimes she thought that she remembered certain things. Shapes of things and flashes of color and shapes, but they were beginning to fade from her memory now.

Mommy had told her the truth. Mommy sat her down and said it wasn't going to get any better. It was the day after they went to that doctor who smelled like onions and spearmint and did all those tests. After the tests, Mommy told her that the light might begin to bother her more and the darkness would be less filled with flashes of color and those zigzags she saw especially if she squeezed her eyes together real tight. She could tell by Mommy's voice that she was sad because her words sounded funny like a squeaky door, but then Mommy's voice got all excited and she said they were going to the zoo. Then they both got happy again. Mommy knew the zoo lady because one time she'd painted a wall at the birdhouse that Mommy said looked like there were even more trees and flowers behind the birdcages and when they got there the zoo lady said, "Phoebe! It's so good to see you and this must be Kayla! I've heard so many wonderful things about you!" And the zoo lady let them into the elephant's cage and Kayla hugged his leg and felt his trunk and smelled him and Mommy said that she was lucky because most kids only got to *see* the elephants but she got to *feel* one up close. Mommy said that's because she was so special. She remembered how they laughed when the elephant let go a big sneeze through his trunk and they both held their noses and said P-U and Mommy said when they got home they'd take bubble baths and put on perfume and maybe bring a bottle of perfume and some of that doctor's spearmint gum for the elephant because he needed it really bad. It wasn't but a few weeks after that when Mommy and Grandma took her to Aunt Caroline's beach house and Daddy wasn't around so much for a while. But then something changed and Mommy wanted to send her away, but Daddy promised he wouldn't let her go. And then Mommy didn't even want to see her anymore. That's when she was with Daddy all the time. Maybe it was because Grandma died, she thought. Maybe that's why Mommy wanted to send her away to that blind school. Maybe Mommy was just too sad. But Daddy said he was going to take care of her and no one was going to send her away anywhere. Never. Not ever.

Sometimes she wanted to tell Daddy that the only thing her eyes still did really well was cry but he was trying so hard to take good care of her that she didn't want him to know she cried sometimes. That would make him feel bad. She made sure he never heard her so she mostly cried at night with her face muffled in the pillow. Maybe tomorrow she'd tell him that her sneakers were too tight, though. They'd been feeling tight for a while now and she needed a Band-Aid for the blister and the toenail broke on her pinky toe because it pulled when it got caught in her socks. In the meantime, she stuffed a piece of tissue inside her shoe. Her stomach growled. She put on the clothes her father handed her and laced her too-tight sneakers. They'd just have to do for now. But her eyes sometimes hurt worse than her blister. Lately it felt like pins were sticking in them sometimes.

Claire's voice came through the closed door. "Room service," she called brightly.

Nick opened the door and took the tray from Claire's hands. "This is too kind," he said.

"Oh, it's nothing, really," Claire said. She crouched down so that she was level with Kayla. "Did you use the bubble bath?"

Kayla shook her head no.

"Oh, next time you have to use it. It smells great. It's oatmeal and almond."

Kayla nodded, shoving a piece of the jelly sandwich in her mouth. "I like that you cut off the crust," she said. "My . . ."

Claire waited for her to finish the sentence but she didn't.

"I'm going to shower and then we'll head into town," Nick said. "Do some exploring, right, Kayla? Maybe some shopping, too. Someone I know could use some new shoes."

"Lucky girl," Claire said, standing. Claire turned to Nick. "I should have made her more than one sandwich. That's one hungry child."

"She's always had a tremendous appetite," Nick said lovingly. "On Sunday nights, we always go somewhere Italian. The spicier the better. Puttanesca. Fra Diavolo. Hot peppers on pizza. It's a sensory thing, you know."

"I understand," Claire said. "When I was a girl, we went to a place called Farabutto on West Sixty-second Street. I wonder if it's still there."

"Oh, for goodness sake," Nick said. "Now here's an example of the small world. It's one of our favorite spots. To think you went there with your parents!"

"My father," Claire said pointedly. "My father took me. He raised me. Alone."

He nodded. "Ah," he said, shaking his head sympathetically. "Then you know. I do the best I can. But it's not easy. Not easy."

Chapter 5

ᴇɪ was convinced he'd ventured to New York City twenty-five years before because he was destined to meet Claire. For certain, he'd never longed for skyscrapers and cement. He'd grown up in the small Pennsylvania town of Piedmont where he swam fearlessly in snake-filled crystal creeks, climbed jagged rock tables, and skated ponds in winter never giving a thought to whether they were frozen through, yet New York City was formidable. The only sight he'd ever longed for beyond the rolling hills of farm country was the sea.

When he was twelve years old, the A & P displaced the small grocery his parents owned on Main Street. The store, Eli's Meats and Produce, was named by his great-grandfather Eli who'd started it in the mid-1800s when they still delivered ice in blocks and ran horse-drawn carts carrying milk in glass bottles. Eli worked weekends and after school at the grocery, carrying bags to people's cars and delivering their bundles in the basket of his bicycle. His soul tore apart as he watched supplies on the store's knotted pine shelves dwindle as the townsfolk carried brown bags emblazoned with the red A & P emblem into their homes on Saturday mornings. A few loyal customers, guilt-ridden no doubt, still came in to buy a quart of glass-bottled milk or a pound of butter or a small bag of penny candy from the old-fashioned glass jars, but eventually and inevitably, the shelves in his family's store were bare with no call to replenish stock. One day his father hammered the FOR SALE sign on the shop's door.

A few years later, the rest of Main Street—Etta's Dress Shop where the local girls bought their prom gowns, Perry's Stationer that sold the best magic tricks ever, Newton's Drugs where an egg cream was still only thirty-five cents, and even the tobacco shop that had begun to sell incense and rolling papers in a last ditch effort to keep up with the times—fell to the highway developers. The last holdout was the barbershop whose red, white, and blue spiral pole was sold at auction and erected by the owners of the penny arcade in what grew to be a mega shopping center. What had been hundreds of acres of farmland off the interstate was now filled with outlet stores and fast food chains.

The oldest of four brothers, Eli felt a rage well up inside him as he watched the construction crews pave over what had been pasture and his family's grocery was replaced with a check-cashing agency, the only business that remained in town after everything else was gone. Main Street became the hallmark of an impoverished ghost town. Rusted metal gates and wooden boards chalked in vile graffiti covered the once-vibrant storefronts.

Eli was riding his bike through town one morning when he heard the gentle whine of newborn pups from under a pile of rubble. He saw the thin-as-a rail junkyard dog across the street rooting around a pile of sandwich wrappers and empty soft-drink cups. Scraps and garbage that someone had obviously dumped from a passing car. He rode his bicycle back home over stones that had once been smooth paved street, took a wicker laundry basket from his mother, lined it with old towels, and gathered the mother and pups and took them home. Three of the pups died despite his efforts, but he found homes for the four others, saved his allowance and, although he felt it was betrayal of sorts, got a job after school as a bag boy at the A&P where he earned enough money to have the bitch spayed. That was the day he knew what he wanted to do with the rest of his life. Perhaps it was the helplessness and silence of the people in town as they watched their history give way to what the local politicians called progress that made him feel a need to help those who by nature were mute.

At twenty-four, he graduated from veterinary school in Ohio and interned for a country vet who sent him around to area farms where he doctored horses and cows, giving shots and placing balms and salves on abrasions and torn ligaments, and putting animals down who couldn't survive without distress. He'd been reading a journal article penned by vets from the Animal Emergency Clinic in Manhattan when he felt a hankering to witness big city veterinary medicine and the various emergency procedures that bordered on heroism. Urban veterinary medicine involved a great deal of trauma but it was something he wanted to learn. He called Dr. Millard Strongin who was delighted to have Eli "come on board" as he called it. They welcomed a country vet who'd worked with large animals, but he cautioned Eli that he would have to supplement his income. The salary was no more than a stipend. It would be primarily an exchange of knowledge and expertise. They were a clinic, Dr. Strongin reminded him. Much of the work they did was pro bono, relying on charitable contributions.

Eli packed a knapsack and a worn green duffel filled mostly with textbooks and took the train from Piedmont to Pittsburgh and then to Penn Station where the stench of sweat and urine and diesel was worse than anything that had ever met his olfactory sense. He rented a room in what was billed on the outside awning as a residential hotel near the Port Authority. The room, vented by a barred window that wouldn't close, consisted of a bed too short for his frame, a dresser with one of the drawers stuck at an angle, a nightstand with a dim lamp, a tattered area rug and cockroaches that managed to survive despite the pungent insecticide sprayed wantonly every day by the man who washed the floor with a filthy rag mop dipped in filthy water. Five days later, he found an apartment on West Fourth Street. The landlady, Eileen Latimer, had advertised in the *Village Voice* for a janitor and because he was polite, handy, and strong, she let him live there for as long as he paid the monthly electric bill even though his janitorial services weren't fulltime. Mrs. Latimer also had several exotic birds, a cat with feline leukemia, a dog with three legs, and a fortune-teller who occupied a studio on the building's ground floor who had predicted Eli's arrival when she told Mrs. Latimer that a handsome stranger would come into her life. Although Mrs. Latimer was seventy and hoped the stranger would be more her vintage and better heeled, she felt that Eli was meant to be.

Eli tried, but he was never one for the bar scene or the Greenwich Village clubs. He preferred Johnny Mathis and Al Martino to the Rolling Stones. He was too exhausted by the time he finished his duties at the animal hospital and constant boiler repairs in the apartment building to spend his evenings out. He roamed the museums and explored grand hotels like the Plaza and the Waldorf-Astoria on the occasional Sunday, pretending to read the newspaper while he sat in a comfortable chair in a hotel lobby. He watched the silver-haired men in their silky blue suits and the blue-haired women in boiled wool jackets brunch in restaurants where the check came to more than his electric bill. He went to the Statue of Liberty and the Empire State Building and Lincoln Center, sitting where he felt his nose might bleed at the Metropolitan Opera, awed by the set and moved by the music and the story. He walked through Times Square where he was blinded by neon and simultaneously repelled and fascinated by prostitutes and drug dealers and wondered what it was that might be waiting for him in this city he alternately feared and challenged as it drew him in. The brutality of some of the urban veterinary cases broke his heart. A dog burned by warring neighbors, rat poison placed strategically in a dog run in Central Park. Country medicine had been far gentler. To make matters worse, it was becoming more and more difficult to make ends meet. And just as he was preparing to call the practice he left back in Ohio and retrieve his old job, he met Claire.

He was certain he'd been in love before until he met Claire. There was Sallie, the girl he'd dated since eighth grade who eventually married his friend Toby after it became clear to her at seventeen that Eli's dreams did not include her. There was Lisa, the older woman he'd met when he was at vet school, who had a twelve-year-old son from a failed marriage. She was thirty-four and he was twenty-two, yet he never felt the years between them. He lived with her at one point in the summer when her son went to stay with his father. They traveled to Tuscany and stayed at her friend Allegra's villa where she cooked for him and comforted him and loved him with a physical intensity he thought he'd never feel again. And although he tried to convince both Lisa and himself that the relationship could work indefinitely, she wisely dispelled any notions he had for long-term romance. The last relationship he'd had was rather superficial: Nina was a sculptress who lived in a neighboring apartment building in Greenwich Village. She was passionate yet aloof and not at all interested in commitment or exclusivity. She made no demands on the little time he had. He was twenty-seven at the time, pouring himself into Strongin's clinic, trying to decide if this detour to Manhattan was taking him anywhere and grateful for an ersatz relationship when he met twenty-one-year-old Claire Cherney. And strangely enough, he fell in love the moment he saw her with the thought that in some universal way he had always loved her and was simply waiting to find her.

It was a Saturday afternoon in July. The heat in the city was so thick that day it was nearly visible in the air. The pavement burned through the soles of Eli's shoes as he walked up Broadway. He was meeting friends for lunch (a married couple he'd met when their dog came into the clinic after being hit and run by a taxi on the FDR) when he stopped into Cherney's Pharmacy. He was early for his date and peered in the window that advertised FOUNTAIN in simple stenciled letters across the window. The small soda fountain with the gold-speckled Formica countertop and lime-green vinyl stools reminded him of Newton's Drugs in Piedmont where he and his friends ordered egg creams, their bicycles leaning against the storefront outside. Claire was at the register when he walked in the door.

"Thanks, Mrs. Falloon," she said, handing the woman a small white paper bag. "This should do the trick. Feel better, now." She turned to Eli as he sat down at the counter. "What can I do for you?" she asked, coming from behind the register. Her blond hair was swept in a high ponytail that fell halfway down her back. She wore the pharmacy uniform of white pants and white jacket with a pale blue blouse, her name embroidered in pink thread on the jacket's lapel. "How's the weather out there?"

"Hot," he said.

She looked up at the ceiling fan. "I'm afraid that thing's just moving hot air around. Our air conditioner's on the blink for a change," she said. "What can I get you? Cold drink?"

"An egg cream, please. Chocolate."

She groaned. "Mitzi usually makes those and she's out today. I don't know how. How about a Coke?"

"I know," he said.

"Know what?"

"How to make an egg cream."

She pushed up the sleeves of her jacket. "Call out the recipe," she said, smiling. "Let's see if it's as good as Mitzi's. Make it enough for two."

He called out the ingredients and, as she poured the thick drink from the stainless steel canister into two small smoked-plastic glasses, he watched as though he didn't want to miss the slightest movement she made. She raised her glass and toasted him before they took the first sip.

"Not bad," she said. "You could give Mitzi a run for her money." The phone rang. "Excuse me. I'm by myself."

His eyes followed her.

"Cherney's," she said. "Oh, Jack. It's you. No, it's fine. Mrs. Falloon picked up her prescription and Dr. Greene called one in for the Silvers' little boy. He has strep throat again, poor thing. When will you be back? It's lonely here." She smiled and listened to the caller. "Love you, too, Jack," she said.

Eli's heart sank. There was someone else.

"So where were we?" she asked, coming back around the counter. "Oh yes, I was about to ask if you were a professional egg-cream maker." She ran her index finger across her upper lip. "You have a little right there."

He felt his face redden. "I'm a veterinarian," he said, blotting his mouth with a napkin.

"Really? Well, I'll be darned. I've got my dog, Maggie, in the back. I was going to run her over to the vet later today. She's been like a lump all morning. Won't eat or drink."

"How old is she?"

"Somewhere around six or seven, we think. We got her at the pound so I'm not really sure. Listen to this, some people moved out of an apartment and they left her behind chained to the radiator. Can you imagine? Apparently the place they moved to didn't allow pets so they just left her."

"I'll never understand. . . . Can I see her?" Eli asked.

Maggie lay on the floor in the back of the store. When Eli approached her, she wagged her tail the slightest bit, yawned, and rolled over. He felt her belly and looked in her eyes.

"Do you have a thermometer?" he asked. "I'd like to take her temperature."

He took the spaniel's temperature and stroked her head as she squirmed a bit. "Normal," he said. "How long have you had her?"

"Three weeks."

"Well, first of all, she's still acclimating. But think for a moment. Anything unusual happen today? Anything different?"

"Nothing," she said thoughtfully. "Only that Jack's been away all morning. He left early to take a relicensing exam. He usually feeds and walks her first thing, but other than that . . ."

"That's it!" Eli said.

"What's it?"

"She misses Jack."

"You're not serious."

"Oh, yes. Animals are very sensitive—especially animals who have been traumatized the way she has. My guess is that when Jack walks through that door she'll be her old self again."

"And if she's not?"

"Well, if I'm wrong, then you should get her to a better vet," he said with a grin. He reached for his wallet. "I owe you for the egg cream."

"Don't be silly," she said. "On the house."

"Now that's not necessary. And what if my diagnosis is wrong?"

"You still get the egg cream for trying."

"Thanks. Look, here's my card. Why don't you let me know how she does?"

She turned the card over in her hand. "I will, Dr. Bishop," she said. "By the way, I'm Claire."

Claire called Eli's office on Monday morning. She said that as soon as Jack walked in the door, Maggie ran over and greeted him. That after a few minutes, she drank from her water bowl and ate the food that Jack put down for her.

"How did you know that was all it was?" she asked.

"Instinct," he said.

He thought about Claire for the next week until the following Sunday when he knew he had to see her again. Part of him felt like a masher. She was involved, for God's sake, he thought. Maybe even married. He heard her say "love you, Jack," but something told him he had to see her just one more time before he went back to Ohio. She was behind the register when he came in. She wore the same white uniform, this time with a sea-green blouse.

"Dr. Bishop!" she said. "It's so good to see you." She called to the back. "Jack! Dr. Bishop is here! Maggie's new veterinarian. It's official!" She smiled at Eli. "You're a miracle worker."

Eli blushed. "Oh, not at all."

Jack came out in his Nehru-style pharmacy coat. "So, you're the young man who can talk to the animals. I'm Claire's father, Jack Cherney."

Her father. *Love you, too, Jack,* and Jack was her father. Eli's body relaxed when Jack shook his hand. He knew at that moment he would not be going back to Ohio. He suddenly knew why the city had beckoned him and why he'd spent the last six months searching.

"You call your father Jack?" Eli asked when Jack slipped into the back, purposely and too obviously, leaving them alone. "What do you call your mother?"

"Nothing. She left when I was a baby."

"I'm sorry."

"Don't be," Claire said. "I'm not."

He reached down to pet Maggie. "Sweet girl," he said.

"You don't speak like a New Yorker," she said.

"Neither do you."

"Because my father's Russian, maybe. Where are you from?"

"Pennsylvania."

"What brought you here? School?"

He looked at her eyes. *You,* he wanted to say. *You brought me here.* "Not exactly. I wanted to study urban veterinary medicine. I'm working at the Animal Emergency Clinic."

She nodded. "Do you want something to drink?" She smiled. "Egg cream? I can make them now."

"Sounds good."

She made two egg creams and came around the customer side of the counter and sat down on a stool beside him. "So, listen, do animal mothers ever leave their young?"

"Sometimes."

"Why?"

"Well, it's rare," he said cautiously. "It's an aberration. Sometimes when they're too young, they just can't handle it."

"Have you ever seen it happen?"

"Once or twice."

"And?"

"And what?"

"What happens to the babies?"

"Humans take over if the animals aren't abandoned in the wild. Bottle-feed them. Care for them."

"And in the wild?"

"More often than not they perish."

"My mother was very young," she said softly. How odd, she thought to herself. I barely know this man and yet . . . "But the thing is, I'm only twenty-one and if I had a baby tomorrow, I would never leave that baby. Never. Not in a million years." She looked at him. "I'm sorry. This is unlike me. I don't usually get melancholy about this."

"I don't mind," he said, unable to keep eyes off her. There was a moment of uncomfortable silence and then, "Do you think we could have dinner one night?" Eli asked.

"I'd like that," she answered. "Very much." And she smiled the most beautiful smile he had ever seen.

They were married on the fourteenth of December, eighteen months from the day they met that steaming July. Jack loaned them the Rambler and they headed to the Massachusetts coast for their honeymoon, wending their way up beach roads from Sagamore to Sandwich and out to Provincetown where they stayed three nights at a small motel called Rosie's on the Water, a driftwood structure perched on the rocky beach, so close to the Atlantic Ocean that Eli said he felt as though he was on a ship when he looked out the picture window.

"I could live in a town like this," Eli said as they sat on the deck, a full moon lighting the midnight sky. Looking back, he often marveled at the prescience of that night. "I'd like to have a place just like this one day."

"Me, too," Claire said. "But I could never leave Jack."

"He could come with us," Eli said.

"Jack won't leave the city until the day he dies," Claire said with a sigh.

"Then it's settled. We'll stay in Manhattan forever," Eli said, tightening his arm around her. "I'll learn to love the Palisades."

The day they packed Jonah in the Rambler and made the move to Drifting was bittersweet. Eli looked in the rearview mirror and saw his sleeping fair-haired boy, head drooped to one side, the small U-Haul tugging behind them. Claire sat beside Eli, her head resting on his shoulder, his left hand on the wheel, the other holding her to him. They knew they would not be leaving the city behind if not for the fact that Jack was gone. They would have weathered the storms, faced what was a scourge of brutality in Manhattan in the 1970s. Eli would have stayed for Jack despite the dead bolts and chain he placed on their apartment door. They barely spoke as they made the drive to Drifting that day except to remark upon the scenery or how sweet Jonah looked as he slept. There was a sense that they were inextricably bound—as Eli felt they had been long before they even knew the other existed.

* * *

It had taken every ounce of Eli's strength to leave Claire on the veranda that morning. As he drove to work he recalled the time he and Jonah stayed up half the night replacing the transmission on the Rambler. They'd started her engine and she purred and then they covered her with a tarpaulin and left her in the heated garage where she still remained, driven only on the occasional Sunday when the weather was deemed perfect enough. He thought of Natalie on the night of her senior prom. How exotic she looked with her thick black hair shimmering like onyx against the silvery sheen of her gown and yet, as he looked at her, all he could think about was the night she was born, a spindly screaming baby girl. He missed the nights when the four of them sat by the hearth and drank cocoa and ate cinnamon toast until the kids were old enough to realize that Saturday nights held more excitement for them outside. It was true: in some respects the house was almost too quiet now and yet he coveted the time alone with his wife. Sometimes he wondered if he would be enough for her with the children gone. She was so young when he met her. There had been two other men in her life before he came along, men she never cared to speak of despite his insistence that he was grateful they had existed so that one day she wouldn't feel she'd never had opportunity or remained too innocent. She'd laughed at him and dismissed the notion that she would ever feel in the least bit deprived.

"You're so young," he said the night before their wedding as they sat on a bench outside Riverside Park. "There could be a whole world out there. Even graduate school."

"Graduate school? I just finished college, thank you very much. I've been in school since kindergarten nonstop. I think you're just trying to talk me out of marrying you," she said with a pout.

"Oh, Claire, no. I just want you to be certain," he said. "Sow your wild oats—that sort of thing."

"You *are* my wild oat, Eli Bishop," she said firmly, putting her arms around his neck and kissing his lips.

Eli pulled into the driveway of the veterinary clinic and parked in his regular spot. He didn't get out of the truck right away and dash into the hospital as he usually did. *You are my wild oat, Eli Bishop,* he thought with a smile. For certain, she was his.

Until that morning on the veranda, Eli couldn't remember the last time Claire had spoken of her mother. In the weeks before they were married he pressed her for words one lazy afternoon. He asked gently if she wanted to talk about Sulie, but she dismissed the conversation, saying she was so young when Sulie left she never felt what she didn't have. He knew better than to ask Jack about Sulie, assuming the pain and shame of being left with an infant was more than he could bear to recount. The evening spent over a bottle of vodka with Jack was the one time Jack came forth, excusing Sulie and nearly extolling her as a free spirit. Eli wondered if Claire heard them speak that evening, yet she never asked a question. She never said a word. And so Eli buried Sulie according to what he believed were Claire's wishes. But in the corner of his heart he knew that morning that Sulie had been exhumed.

Chapter 6

For forty-five years, Irma Jensen, the last of her gener-
ation, owned and ran the Inn at Drifting and had taken
every one of her seven cats to Doc Wilson and then to
Eli. One particularly bitter December morning (which
happened to be Irma's seventy-fifth birthday) she
came to see Eli alone. Unlike previous generations,
Irma was an only child who had no children. She'd
been married briefly to Amos Rogow, a dapper gentleman who wore spats long after they went out of fashion and slicked his hair back with mayonnaise despite
a sour smell that wafted over him in the hot summer
months. After ten years of marriage, when Irma was
already thirty-seven, Amos ran off with the new
young wife of Drifting's mayor who was pregnant at
the time, presumably with Amos's child. Irma, feeling
barren, ashamed, and forlorn, retrieved her maiden
name to avoid any further association with Amos
Rogow and developed a fondness for purple kaftans,

straw skimmers, and cats. She ran the inn with an eccentricity and old-fashioned flair that drew a loyal clientele, all of whom were "welcome with pets" until the board of health got wind of the situation and notified her that mixing pets and dining facilities was illegal and punishable by hefty fines. The morning that Irma came to see Eli, she convinced him to buy the small eight-room inn. She was tired. Her cousin lived in Maine and she planned to join her. She was tired of living alone. It would be extra income for you—you'll inherit Cora the maid and Ivan makes the best German apple pancakes and the place is small and practically runs itself, she said nearly in one breath. Eli's immediate reaction was to reject the offer, but Irma was insistent. He could offer boarding for pets at the animal hospital and the barn would make a great office for Claire, she went on. Irma had it all figured out. Although practically reclusive at that point in her life, Irma knew everything about everyone in town, including Claire, who had just completed her graduate degree at the University of Rhode Island and needed a place to hang her shingle. At first Eli listened to Irma just to be polite, but the more she spoke, the more sense she made. Besides, the apartment was becoming too small. The price for the inn was right. The barn would serve Claire well. Before he even knew what was happening, he was sold.

Although the inn's main building was in near-perfect condition, needing merely a few coats of paint, new mattresses and new carpeting throughout, the barn was in abject disrepair. The windowpanes were cracked and the dry dirt floor consisted mostly of dust, sand, and broken glass. Cobwebs thick as netting, old chipped clay pots, broken garden tools, and empty mason jars mixed in with dried up cans of paint, rusted gasoline canisters, twisted fencing, and hundreds of moldy empty cans of cat food filled the cavernous space. Eli brought Claire inside with great trepidation.

"Visualize," he said. "Use your imagination."

She raised her eyebrows and moved through slowly, Jonah and Natalie watching and giggling in the doorway of the barn. She kicked aside cat food cans, brushed cobwebs from her path, and screamed when a field mouse ran across her foot.

"What do you think?" Eli asked. "It's something, isn't it?"

"Something, all right," she said, still shuddering from the mouse. She faced Eli with her arms crossed and eyes squinting. "You bought this place, didn't you, Eli Bishop?"

"You know, you'll get lines on your face if you squint like that."

"Never mind that. You bought this place, didn't you?"

"Not exactly."

"Meaning?"

"Meaning I only gave a handshake."

"Uh-huh." She walked over to her husband who stood at the doorway with the children now, hushing them as their laughter reached a pitch.

"I think this place is really cool, Mom," Jonah said. "And there's a great big climbing tree in the yard and it's right on the beach. Nat and I like it, right, Nat?"

Natalie looked less than certain until Jonah poked her in the ribs and she nodded her head up and down at his silent command.

"You like it, do you?" Claire said, kissing the top of Jonah's head. "I think you and your daddy are in cahoots."

"What's cahoots?" Jonah asked, looking at Eli, who was waving his hands back and forth.

"A partnership that's a little shady," Claire said, looking right at Eli. "There might even be bribery involved."

Jonah's face reddened. "Like a basketball hoop?"

"Yes, like a basketball hoop." She walked over to Eli and kissed his cheek. "I must be out of my mind, but I love it."

"You'll see," Eli said excitedly. "You'll see. Claire, it's right on the water. It's what we used to dream about." He turned to the children, who were laughing and jumping up and down. "See? I told you she'd love it."

Eli and Sam worked nights and weekends for nearly two months ripping apart the barn. They cleared out wheelbarrows of debris, hefted new windows and Sheetrock, poured concrete and set wide maple planks over the dirt floor. Jack's old rolltop oak desk, an overstuffed armchair, and a blue velvet couch were pulled from storage, and with odds and ends purchased at local garage sales, Claire had an office.

Claire walked the path from the inn to the barn with Stella at her heels, careful not to slip on the tissue-thin coating of wet leaves. She remembered when Eli had set the path slate by slate to the brightly painted red front door. The barn door stuck a bit as she pushed it open with her hip. She flicked on the switch that lit the ivory-shaded lamps and cranked open the windows on either side of the room. Everything smelled musty and damp. The plants lining the windowsill were yellow and drooping. She truly had been neglecting too many things lately, she thought, Eli among them. And Annie, too. She hadn't called Annie in days. She set the pile of DSS reports on the credenza and collected the pile of unopened mail that was scattered on the floor below the mail slot in the door. She sat down in her desk chair, leaned backwards, twirled around, and pressed the play button on her answering machine, wiping off dust that had accumulated since the last time she'd set foot in the door.

Sylvia Monroe was first on the tape. An unwed mother, Sylvia lived three towns north, in Stanton. Only seventeen, she had had visions of knights on white horses and fairy-tale endings until the boy who claimed he loved her in the back of a Buick one starlit night wanted nothing to do with her once she was pregnant. Sylvia wanted to keep her baby but was terrified that her father would either beat her or toss her into the street. It took six sessions with Sylvia for Claire to win her trust. There was something about Sylvia that touched Claire deeply. She was young and sweet-faced and determined as she wrestled with the fear she held for her father and love for her unborn child. Claire longed to tell Sylvia she would take her in with the baby if her parents wouldn't help her. She wanted to promise never to let anything happen to her. Emotional involvement, Claire chided herself silently in the middle of so many sleepless nights. Rule number one in counseling: Remain objective. Don't become emotionally involved.

It was Claire who made the phone call to Sylvia's parents and explained that Sylvia had been seeing her for some three months. At first, Sylvia paid her a small fee but, after the funds ran out, Claire saw her in exchange for filing and other small clerical tasks that Claire barely needed. Claire recalled that session when Sylvia's parents joined her. How her father's fury frightened even Claire, who kept her hand on the phone, prepared to call Eli or Sam to their rescue. Sylvia's mother merely shook her head and wept, every so often reaching for her husband's arm in an attempt to calm him. An honor student, Sylvia was about to finish her senior year in high school. Her father was shattered.

Claire stared at the dirt under the father's fingernails. He was a hardworking man with a wife and five children. Sylvia, the eldest, was the one who held his dreams.

Claire went to the cigar wrapper factory where Sylvia's father worked. At first he wanted nothing to do with Claire. He was wearing an apron and plastic face mask and she stood in front of him screaming over the machines until finally he took her into a stairwell.

"What do you want?" he asked, tearing the mask from his face and wiping the sweat from his eyes with the dirty apron. "I got nothing to say to you. What she done is immoral."

"Mr. Monroe," Claire said. "She can still have it all if you help her. She can still go to college and get her scholarships. This baby will only ruin her life if you don't help her. She wants to keep her baby, Mr. Monroe. Don't punish her."

"I ain't punishing her. Let God punish her."

"Mr. Monroe," Claire said, guessing, "did you and your wife have to get married? Was Sylvia conceived out of wedlock?"

"That's none of your damned business."

"I'm simply trying to understand."

"I made it right. I married the girl."

"And you had more children and you have a family. Sylvia's carrying your flesh and blood, Mr. Monroe. Just remember that."

Leo Monroe called Claire the next day. "My wife says it's God's will just like Sylvia was."

"And?"

"So, she can stay at home and keep the baby. But I tell you, if I ever get hold of the kid who knocked her up, I'll kill him. I swear it."

"Women carry babies for nine months before the world sees them. We feel them kicking and turning. My babies used to hiccough in my belly. Leave him alone, Mr. Monroe," she said. "Just let your daughter have her baby." When she hung up the phone, she wept uncontrollably. The silver-framed pictures of Sulie tumbling down the incinerator were a fleeting image she tried to push from her mind.

Claire heard the baby cooing on Sylvia's lap when she left her message confirming her appointment. She was managing, she said. "I can't wait to see you, Dr. Cherney. I'm going to bring Leo. He's beautiful." Claire could picture the girl's shy smile over the phone. "Naming him after my father was a good idea. Leo or Leona! Who would have thought of that without you? It's bonded them, you know?"

The next message was from Jake Hanson. Jake had two offenses on his juvenile record. One for a mailbox-bashing spree the year before on Halloween and another on New Year's Eve for drunk and disorderly. Three strikes and you're out, the judge told him. Juvenile detention hall. Jake's father was long gone, if he'd ever been around at all, and his mother, Maureen, only thirty-one years old, had two other children at home from two other men who had been one-night stands. Jake was angry and uncommunicative, another kid who kept Claire awake at night. She knew there was more to Jake than the surly young man who never looked her in the eye when he spoke. The judge was a buddy of Sam Merrill's and if not for that connection, Claire wondered if Jake would have gotten off so easily. Last May, she walked into the billiard parlor where Jake was shooting pool with his friends after the hearing.

"You have to be over eighteen to be here, you know," Claire said, coming up behind him. "What did you do? Use a fake ID? That's against the law, Jake."

"What are you doing here?" he asked.

"We need to talk." She smelled alcohol on his breath. "Drinking is illegal under twenty-one. What are you doing, Jake? Talk to me."

"I don't need to talk," Jake said, aiming the cue. The ball skipped and bounced over the table. "See what you made me do? I got money on that."

"Let's see. We have a fake ID and gambling. And drinking. How about we have a little chat, Jake?"

He placed the pool cue down on the table and followed her outside.

"Get in the car," she said.

"What for?"

"Three minutes of your time, Jake, okay?"

He sat in the front seat and stared at his shoes.

"You want to tell me why you're so hell-bent on self-destruction?"

"You my shrink or my mother? I got a mother."

"Yes, you do. And she does the best she can."

"No, she don't."

"Yes, she does. She's not mean or dishonest, Jake." Claire waited for him to answer. "Jake, you can't be shooting pool and drinking and gambling. It's going to land you in jail, don't you get it? What is it you want, Jake? Tell me. Try."

He stared out the window for the longest time and then turned to face her, tears streaming down his cheeks. "I want to get out of here."

"Just a few minutes and I'll let you go."

"No, I don't mean the car, Dr. Cherney. I mean the town. I want to go away someplace and start all over." He looked at her for the first time. "I was reading in this magazine about these places like towns for boys. I need to go there."

She'd found a school for Jake in Wisconsin. The phone message said it all. "Hey, Doc, it's me. Jake Hanson. I only got a minute and I put in quarters, but I got to tell you, this is the best place. Listen to this—I milked a cow yesterday. And I got this job at the local PD in the mornings before classes where I file sh . . . um, papers and stuff. It's pretty cool. I told the cop who drives me to class it was the first time I ever sat in the front of a cop car. He thought that was pretty funny. Anyway, everything's pretty cool and thanks, Doc. Thanks a lot. I gotta go."

She listened to the rest of the messages on the answering machine. Three from DSS asking for the reports back as soon as possible. A referral from a psychologist in Meadville and one from a psychopharmacologist in New Haven regarding a patient whom Claire hadn't heard from in eight months. Did that patient really think Claire would corroborate her request for a scrip? She barely remembered the woman. She'd come in twice, canceled her third appointment, and that was it. A call from Annie had come in early that morning.

"Where *are* you? You didn't call me all day yesterday. How about steamers and beer on the deck at Lucille's Saturday night? She's closing the outside for the season on Sunday."

The next message was from Natalie. "Hi, Mom, where are you? I tried the inn first. I need my red fleece robe, okay? It's hanging in the back of my closet. I have classes until five-thirty and then a bunch of us are going to Hungry Charlie's. I love you."

Claire listened to Natalie's message twice, let the machine run, and heard Jonah's voice.

"Hey, Mom, where are you?" he asked. "I tried the house but no one answered. I just called to say hi. Spoke to Nat last night and she's doing great so stop worrying because I know you are."

Hi, Mom, where are you? Claire thought. She turned to address the DSS reports when the phone rang.

"Claire Cherney," she answered.

"I'm looking for Mrs. Bishop," the voice said.

It was Eli. "Oh, well, this is her alter ego. Can I help you?"

"I'm hopelessly in love with my wife."

Claire laughed. "And this is a problem for you?"

Eli leaned back in his chair. "Yeah, I'm wondering if she loves me. She hasn't mentioned it lately."

"I love you, Eli," she said softly. "Although I think we need to address some of these insecurity issues."

"Blame my wife."

"Oh, they always blame the wife," she said, laughing.

"Jonah called this morning. He tried you but you didn't pick up."

"I know. Both kids left messages. They sound great and Annie called and wants us all to go to Lucille's on Saturday night."

"Sounds good. What else?"

"DSS is breathing down my neck for those reports. How about you?"

"Sick horse over at the Hayes Farm so I'm going to head out there around two o'clock when Stu Hayes gets in from Boston. Where were you this morning?"

"We had a check-in. A man with his daughter."

"Oh, one of your favorites."

She laughed. "No, actually this daughter is only seven. Sweet little thing. And blind."

Eli shut his eyes and shook his head. He thought of his children. Counting their fingers and toes when they were born. "There but for the grace of God . . ."

"We had a bit of drama when she decided to explore the beach without telling her father. That poor man. Remember when Jonah did that? Took off without telling me?"

"To ride the mechanical horse," Eli said. "Funny time of year for a vacation, isn't it? She's not in school?"

"Private school," she said. "Classes start next week."

"No mother?"

"I'm not sure what the situation is. Some dissension, I think. Kayla, that's the little girl, mentioned that her mother wants her to go to some school but Nick, that's the father, seems to be raising her on his own," she said all in one breath.

"How come you get more information from people in two minutes than I get in two hours?"

"Because you're used to dealing with patients who don't speak to you."

"Yeah, but I can look into their eyes and soul and know what they need."

"Oh, really? Think you can do that with humans?" she teased, leaning back in her chair.

"I don't know. We'll practice later."

"You going to hypnotize me?"

"Only if I have to. So, where're they from?"

"Who?"

"Boy, talk about a short memory. Our guests."

"Sorry, I was trying to be sexy and provocative," she said with a laugh. "Maybe you're the one with the short memory. Anyway, they're from New York. She's so precious. Tiny little thing. I bet she was a preemie."

"That could account for the blindness. ROP."

"What's that?"

"Retinopathy of prematurity. It's just a guess. Sometimes with preemies the retinal vessels haven't completed their growth. The retina detaches. Same thing happens with animals," he said. "So, listen, Dr. Cherney, let's get back to sexy and provocative. How about we meet on the veranda around six and I'll ply you with wine?"

"Hmmm," she said, tapping her pen on the desk. "Better bring those doggie treats you keep in that glass jar just in case, though. I may require temptation."

"You sound like you feel better, Claire," he said tenderly.

"I do. I'm good at picking myself up by the boot-straps, you know?"

"Maybe a little too good," Eli said. "Maybe for once you should just let go."

"And if I fall?" she asked.

"I'll catch you," he answered.

She shuffled the DSS reports and poised her ballpoint pen. There was a clap of thunder. Rain pounded the roof of the barn. Stella came over and nudged her legs.

"Scared?" Claire said aloud, stroking the dog's head. "It's only rain."

It was nearly three o'clock by the time she'd finished the paperwork and headed back to the main house. The reports were grueling. Three of the five cases were evaluations she'd done back in July for custody battles where she'd interviewed the heartbroken children. Another concerned the living conditions of a young mother who had just been released from prison and her five-year-old son. There was a restraining order against the boy's father. The next involved a sixty-year-old battered woman who lived in a shelter and was trying to make her way back into the world. Claire rubbed the back of her neck and stretched her arms overhead, sat back in the chair and looked at the ceiling. Sometimes fate deals such an unfair hand, she thought.

If she hurried, she'd make it to the post office with the reports and Natalie's robe before they closed for the day at four. She placed the reports in a manila envelope, wrote a note to Natalie to accompany the robe, and grabbed a handful of butterscotch candies from the china dish on the coffee table. How many afternoons had Natalie shown up at her office after school, flopped down on the sofa, and popped a butterscotch in her mouth?

Dear Nat,
   Here it is! By the way, the robe can go in the washer on cold (but wash it separately—the color might bleed). Dry it on regular. Remove butterscotch candies from pocket before washing. Pouring here today. I miss you.
                        Love, Mom

I miss you. Love, Mom. The words seemed to jump from the page. She took an envelope from the shelf of the rolltop desk and placed the letter inside. She stood to gather her jacket and call to Stella when she sat down in the chair, her heart beating faster. She reached down and booted up the computer. It seemed as though it took forever to start as she waited, eyes fixed on the screen. She worried that someone might walk in at any moment and discover her secret. She sat stiffly in the chair as she typed in peoplesearch.com. And then hesitantly, stroking what seemed unfamiliar keys, she entered Sulie's names. Ursula Terenzi. Ursula Cherney. Her breath held as the machine flickered and then stopped. *Sorry, no people match the criteria you entered. We recommend other options.*

Claire swallowed hard and shut down. She turned to Stella. "Other options," she said aloud. She wondered what the options would be. She could have re-married. She could have died. But something told her it was more that Ursula simply didn't want to be found.

*   *   *

In all the years she lived in Drifting, Claire never tired of the scent of the sea after a storm. The ground was damp and the sun had retreated through the clouds. Cora had remembered to turn on the porch lights and the inn twinkled in the misty daylight. She was opening the front door as Nick's car pulled up the driveway. He maneuvered the car backwards into the parking space, opened the door for Kayla, reached in for her, helped her to step down and admonished her gently to stand still while he collected some small packages and his briefcase from the backseat.

"Hi," he said as he and Kayla walked hand-in-hand up the steps to the porch. "Good recommendation, Gus's."

"What did you have, Kayla?" Claire asked.

"Blueberry pancakes," Kayla said. "Ice cream for dessert."

"Hmmm, my favorites," Claire said. "What else did you do?"

"We toured the town. That took about twenty minutes," Nick said with a smile. "Kayla liked the candle shop."

"That's my friend Annie's store," Claire said. "You know Sam, the policeman you met this morning? Annie is Sam's wife."

"I like the way her shop smells," Kayla said. "The lady gave me this." She reached into her pocket and pulled out a purple heart-shaped sachet. "Lavender. She said if I put it in my dresser drawers it'll make everything smell."

"Smell *nice*," Nick said, ruffling her hair.

"And she's right," Claire said. "Listen, I have to run into town, but when I get back maybe we can have some tea on the veranda. I'll pick up some pastries. In-season, we always have a tea on the veranda around four o'clock. We can pretend it's June."

Claire felt Nick's eyes on her as she spoke to Kayla. She turned her head and looked up to him. "If it's okay. I should have asked you first."

"It's wonderful," he said, swinging his briefcase over his shoulder. "I haven't seen my daughter this content in a long time."

"Drifting tends to do that for people," Claire said. "You know, your briefcase is safe in the room. We also have a place where we can lock it up in the office if you're concerned."

"I have original blueprints in here for a client in Houston," he said, patting its side.

Claire nodded. "I understand. Well, let me know if you change your mind. I'd hate for you to drag that around all week long." She looked at her watch. "I've got to get my daughter's robe and run to the post office. I should be back in about an hour."

The post office was next door to Annie's Candle Shop. Annie saw her from inside the window and waved. Claire held up her index finger and mouthed, *Be right back.* Annie was sewing the edges together on another sachet heart when Claire came in carrying two paper cups of coffee.

"Peace offering. Hazelnut."

"I was beginning to think I lost my best friend," Annie said, setting down her sewing to hug Claire.

"Between you and my husband, I'm feeling a little pressured," she said with a laugh.

"Why?"

Claire settled herself on a stool near the counter. "He called this morning and wanted to know if I still loved him."

"You're kidding? Wow, Sam never does stuff like that."

"I guess I've been a little remote." Claire sighed. "I tend to retreat when I get the blues, don't I? Every little thing sets me off lately. I mean, the school bus rolled by this morning and all I could think of was when the kids were little and I'd put them on the bus with their lunch boxes."

"And now they live in other cities," Annie said wistfully.

"You're a big help," Claire said, shaking her head and smiling. "Good thing you're not a therapist."

"I'm empathizing," Annie said.

"I need someone to talk sense into me, not empathize."

"How's Nat?"

"She's great," Claire said, taking the lid off her coffee. "So, I hear you met my guests this morning."

"Who's that?"

"Nick and Kayla. You gave her a lavender sachet. . . ."

"Oh, the little blind girl. I tell you, that child pulled at all my heartstrings. You should have seen her. She was running through here like a moth to light—smelling the candles and the sachets and the lamp oils. She loved that lavender. What a sweetie."

"She's adorable. She took a walk on the beach this morning without telling her father. They'd just checked in and he went to the car to get her and she was gone. I thought that poor man was going to die right then and there."

"How could he leave her in the car?" Annie said with a tsk.

"I guess he figured she'd keep sleeping."

Annie sniffed. "What's the story with them, do you think?"

"What do you mean?"

"Think he's divorced? Widowed? Where's the mother?"

"Not widowed. But I'm not sure what the story is," Claire said, taking a sip. "Annie, do you think you'd ask the same thing of her mother? You know, if they were traveling alone together?"

Annie hesitated for a moment. "I think mothers do that mother-daughter stuff more often, you know? Or you just figure the father's working and can't break away or something. No, probably not."

"It's really not fair, you know?"

Annie bit down on her lip. "You're thinking of you and your dad, right? I'm sorry, Claire."

"And my mother."

"Your mother?" Annie placed her hand on Claire's arm. "I can't remember the last time you mentioned your mother. "

"Maybe I never did. I see that little girl with her father and it brings me back. All the questions people asked. You know, trying to find out the story. The funny thing is, I don't think I ever knew the whole story. Maybe there is no story."

"How old were you when your mother . . ."

"Left?" Claire said ruefully. "Not quite two."

"I didn't realize you were so young."

"A baby." She twisted her hair around her finger.

"She had two years with me and left. It's one thing giving a child away at birth."

"Did you ever ask why? Ask your father, I mean?"

Claire shook her head. "Not really. I didn't have the heart and his heart was broken. My aunt Helen told me stories here and there."

"Did you miss her?"

"I didn't miss *her*. Sometimes I missed the idea of her. And when I look at Kayla . . . she said something on the beach this morning about how her mother wants to send her away to a boarding school. Can you imagine?"

"Well, you never know exactly what the reasons are behind things," Annie said, putting a final stitch in the sachet and breaking off the thread with her teeth. "But I tell you one thing, when they first walked in I would have sworn she was a boy. Such a pretty face but with that short hair and those dark clothes. . . . I couldn't help but think if she wasn't blind she'd be screaming for something pink and a hair ribbon. Sort of made me think there wasn't a woman's hand in anything."

"I know, but you have to realize that short hair is probably easier to manage for both of them," Claire said. "I assure you that the short hair is easier on *him*. Even Jack never quite mastered the art of the ponytail— and the braid—forget it." Claire looked at her watch. "I've got to get going. We're having tea on the veranda."

"Now, that's romantic. Eli's coming home early?"

"No, no. Nick and Kayla."

"You're getting involved, Claire," Annie said, wagging her finger.

"They're not my patients. I'm allowed to be involved," she said, smiling. "Besides, I'm just being hospitable."

"Right. That's why your cases keep you up at night and you've been known to make house calls." Annie groaned. "Because you don't get involved. For God's sake, Claire, you nearly had that unwed mother and her baby in residence."

"Never mind." Claire stood and stretched. "I'm going to Molly's. Want anything?"

Annie made a face. "Sure. Get me something sticky and gooey so that I can just apply it directly to my thighs."

Claire laughed and hugged her. "Don't be ridiculous. You're beautiful. We'll all go to Lucille's Saturday night and stuff our faces. I'll call you later."

Annie tugged Claire's arm before she could walk away. "I'm worried about you."

"Don't be silly. I'm fine. Why should you worry?"

"Because your nest is empty and you're ruminating," Annie said with a pout.

"Ruminating? Oh, for goodness sake, Annie. You're one to talk. You were a basket case when Lizzie went off to school."

"Maybe, but you never mentioned your mother before. Well, maybe once but that was ages ago."

Claire's eyes filled with tears. "It's probably good for the soul. Ironic though, isn't it? My kids are at college. I have a husband who loves me. And the best girlfriend in the world." She dropped her voice. "And here I am forty-four years too late feeling like an abandoned child. It's like all of a sudden I feel as though someone cut off my arm. Little late, don't you think?"

"I don't think you ever really thought it through before, did you?" Annie asked gently. "I mean, in all the years we've known each other, it's barely come up."

"Repression is definitely underrated," Claire said sarcastically. She laughed. "Listen, I'm sure some of this is also because I miss Natalie. I told her the other night that I sometimes go into her room and slam her door just for old time's sake."

Annie laughed and put her arms around Claire. "I know," she said softly. "They don't tell you this stuff when they're born. It's like they're on loan or something." She shook her head. "They don't tell you not to blink."

The sun broke through as Claire was driving home from town. It was the first time in ages that she noticed the colors on the trees. Reds and yellows this year. A few of the houses along the street already had scarecrows and pumpkins in the front yards. Almost every one had a brightly colored windsock blowing over the front door. She thought of all the things Kayla wouldn't see in her lifetime. The brilliance of an autumn, lights on a Christmas tree, the way the ocean looked sapphire blue in the middle of July, a snowstorm. She would never see herself in her wedding gown or the way her mouth would look outlined in lipstick. She thought of Jonah—how he stood before the mirror in his tuxedo the day of his prom and straightened his tie, turned his head at a cocky angle, and joked, "Bond. James Bond." How does a parent teach a blind child to "see"? How did one describe things in a way that was tactile and palpable enough to compensate for sight? Where sounds and touch and scent rendered an image . . . and what kind of image would that be? Nick Pierce had his work cut out for him, she thought. Perhaps that's why he didn't want Kayla to use her cane. Perhaps he wanted her to navigate the sighted world without drawing attention to her blindness. How difficult it must be to entrust Kayla to a world where people either step out of her way or take her elbow and lead her. She remembered the deaf child who was her patient. The school had recommended the family sessions since the parents were opposed to him learning sign language and wanted him only to read lips. They didn't want attention drawn to his disability, the mother said. And then the mother wept and confessed she didn't want him to be pitied. Claire thought of the things she never saw or heard. The mother dressing for the evening, standing in a slip before the mirror. A mother's drawer filled with silky stockings or nail polishes. The sound of a mother's voice calling her to dinner. She shuddered and pushed the thoughts away.

Nick and Kayla were sitting on the porch stoop, the teddy bear on Kayla's lap, when Claire returned, the white pastry box tied with candy-cane string in her hand.

"Hi there," Claire called as she walked up the drive so Kayla would know she was there.

"I smell cinnamon," Kayla said, jumping up and pulling her father by the hand. "And something else. What else?"

"Cinnamon cake, chocolate leaf cookies, and a big wedge of Molly's peach pie," Claire said. "You can't leave Drifting without tasting Molly's peach pie. It's amazing."

"I never had peach pie, did I, Daddy?"

"I'm not sure, but I tell you what—I often have pumpkin pie," he said, picking her up and tickling her.

"Well, you're in for a treat," Claire said, a warm feeling coming over her as she watched Nick cuddle his child. "Let's go inside and I'll put on the kettle. Kayla can help me put the desserts on the tray, okay?"

Nick took Kayla's hand as Kayla slipped her other hand into Claire's. Without speaking, Nick and Claire swung Kayla up the porch steps, Kayla's legs kicking as she squealed.

"Again!" Kayla cried. "More! I'm flying!"

Nick lifted Kayla in the air and hugged her to him. "Later," he said, kissing the side of her face. "Plane's landed for now."

Claire turned around to coax Stella up the stairs when she saw Eli. His hand was under the dog's belly, steadying her as she hobbled up the steps.

"She's so arthritic, poor thing."

"You're home early," Claire said.

"Disappointed?" Eli teased.

"Of course not. It's just that I thought you went out to the Hayes Farm."

"I did," Eli said. "It wasn't serious. I've known that horse for eight years now and every year it's the same thing. Colic. I delivered that mare."

"We were just going to have tea," Claire said. "Eli, I want you to meet Nick and Kayla."

Eli kneeled down and spoke to Kayla. "I hear you took a walk on the beach this morning," he said.

"Who told?" she asked, her head dropped down.

Eli laughed. "It's okay. Claire told me."

"I got in trouble. I was supposed to tell first," she said. She raised her head. "I did tell but no one heard me."

"Well, I'm sure you'll tell even louder the next time you want to go someplace. Though I can't say that I blame you. This is my favorite time of year for the beach."

Eli stood and faced Nick. "Good to meet you," he said extending his hand. "How long will you be with us?"

"Not sure, really," Nick said. "A few days probably. I'd love to take the week but we'll see how she does. See how it goes."

"Claire tells me you're from Manhattan. How did you find our inn? We always like to know."

Nick's face reddened. "Darn, I'm so bad with names. Right. The Grants. Steve and Pat Grant. Do you know them?"

"So many folks come through here in the summer, it's hard to keep track."

"Your wife's been very kind," Nick said formally. "I keep apologizing for our intrusions."

"And I keep telling him that we love the company," Claire said. "Kayla? Come, let's get those desserts. I'll watch her, Nick. Don't worry."

Claire heard their voices as she put together the tea tray in what they called the "second kitchen" behind the bar. Conversation came so easily for Eli. She often said he could dance with the devil if he had to. He was talking about the horse he tended that afternoon and how he loved the ruggedness of the beach in fall. Small talk about the veranda, how they'd installed the thermal paned windows a few years ago and now they could sit out there in winter. Nick's voice joined in, more at ease now. He'd always dreamed of putting together one of those coffee table books about old New

England porches, he said. One of the reasons he brought Kayla up to Drifting.

"I wish I lived here," Kayla said, tugging on Claire's sleeve. "Would you let me live here?"

Claire looked at her and tried to read her expression. Her brow was slightly furrowed. She has some big troubles for such a little thing, Claire thought.

"You're going to live here for the next few days," Claire said, stroking the back of Kayla's head. "The best part of vacation is always going home."

Kayla leaned against Claire's hip. "I wish I could stay here forever."

Chapter 7

Kayla had insisted upon a walk on the beach after desserts and tea. Eli opted to stay behind, offering to clean up the tea and baby-sit the teddy bear. He watched through the kitchen window as the child walked between Nick and his wife, descending the beach steps slowly as they each held one hand. Claire gathered seashells for Kayla, their laughter carrying on the wind as the surf touched their feet. And as he heard their cries, the breeze that carried them through the open window had an air of something inchoate. Nick trailed behind the child and Claire, the weight of the briefcase slung over his shoulder holding him back. Kayla and Claire had removed their shoes but Nick plodded through the sand with his sneakers. Why on earth would someone drag a briefcase along for a walk on the beach? Odd duck, he thought. There was something about Nick Pierce . . . rather it was something *not* about Nick Pierce. He had an air of unreality about him. His speech was stilted and formal. He spoke in clipped sentences that appeared calculated and measured. His body language was uncomfortable. If Nick Pierce were a dog, despite what the owner said, Eli might have muzzled him.

Eli rinsed the teacups and plates, dried his hands on the blue-striped dish towel hanging on the refrigerator door, and called the Hayes Farm. The horse Power was perhaps a shade better and certainly not worse, the stable boy said. She seemed to be comfortable though still not herself. Eli said he'd be out again tomorrow. These things took time more than anything else, he explained.

"Claire got seashells for stringing," Kayla called just as Eli was hanging up the phone. She emptied her pockets. "Look, Eli! See them!"

"I see them," Eli said, making a scoop out of his upturned palms and taking some shells from her hands. "Well, I'd say you have enough here for a necklace, earrings, and a bracelet, I think."

Claire bent down and touched Kayla's earlobe. "You have pierced ears. We'll have to figure something out, won't we?"

"She doesn't care for earrings," Nick said.

"No earrings, Claire," Kayla said seriously, shaking her head from side to side.

"No? You don't like earrings?"

Kayla turned her head in the direction of her father. "They pinch sometimes. 'Specially when I sleep. Can we all have dinner together?"

"How can you even think about dinner already?" Claire asked. "You must have a hollow leg!"

"It's enough, Kayla, really," Nick said gently. "We should let these kind folks have some privacy."

"Someone told me that a little girl here likes Puttanesca sauce," Claire said, lifting Kayla's chin with her index finger. "Or maybe Fra Diavolo tonight. There's a great little Italian restaurant about twenty minutes from here. Ernesto's. It's become our Farabutto."

"Daddy, please! Can we go?" Kayla begged, tugging on his sleeve.

"Really, I hate to intrude. It's not right."

Eli saw the expression cross his wife's face as she silently asked him to speak. Her cheeks were rosy from the wind, her hair strewn about her face, her eyes sparkled. "Join us," Eli said. "Please."

"Can I wear my skirt, Daddy?" Kayla asked. "Please?"

"I tell you what, let's save that skirt for Saturday night when I take my best girl to dinner, okay?"

Kayla nodded. "Okay. How about the pink flowered pants? Can I wear those?"

"That's a thought. It's a bit cool out tonight, though. Now, look, who wants a piggyback ride up the stairs?" Nick boosted her onto his back, the briefcase batting his side. "We'll be right down."

"I hope you leave that briefcase behind," Claire called to Nick as he climbed the stairs. "We're going to get you to take your shoes off and kick back before you leave here."

Nick stopped and turned. He smiled. "I need to loosen up, don't I? I haven't had a vacation in years."

"What's with the briefcase?" Eli asked when Nick and Kayla were out of earshot.

"He's an architect. It's filled with original blueprints," Claire said.

"He took it on the beach?"

She shrugged. "Who knows?"

"A little neurotic, don't you think?"

"Maybe. We're all a little neurotic."

"I guess."

Claire slipped her hand in his and they walked upstairs. "Come, let's get changed for dinner."

"I thought I was going to hypnotize you," he said.

She wound her arm around his waist. "You do," she said.

Eli offered to drive to Ernesto's but Nick explained that Kayla might become disoriented. She was accustomed to the Taurus, Nick explained. Familiar with the interior space, the cadence of the engine, the scent of the upholstery. There's a rhythm to it, he said, that we may not hear or sense ourselves but Kayla does.

"We'll follow you," Nick said.

"Why can't we go with them?" Kayla pleaded. "Why not?"

"We'll meet you there, sweetheart," Claire said, kneeling down to the child, picking up on Nick's discomfort, his loss for words. "I tell you what, I'm going to lend you a tape to play in the car."

"What's it called?" Kayla asked.

"Peter and the Wolf."

"I know that one! I love that one! I always played it at home."

"Oh, I'm so glad. You know, my father used to play it for me all the time, too. I bet you're at the restaurant before Peter even meets the wolf."

"One of our favorites," Nick said coolly. "If only I'd thought to bring it along."

Despite Nick's words, Eli could have sworn he saw

a shadow cross Nick's face. Kayla didn't need to see the look on her father's face. She felt the ice of his stare penetrate her heart.

"Why do you suppose he wanted to take his own car?" Eli asked as they drove to Meadville, checking the rearview every few minutes to make sure Nick was following.

"He explained why," Claire answered. "Kayla's more comfortable that way."

"It didn't seem to bother her."

"He must know better. Besides, some people are funny about other people driving their kids. Who knows why? Look, he was pretty traumatized this morning when he couldn't find her. Maybe he just feels more in control this way."

"How come you mentioned Farabutto?"

"We were talking about the city, restaurants and things, and I asked if he'd been there. He said it's one of their favorites."

"That place is still there? I thought it closed."

"Well, I guess not."

"Same location?"

"Apparently. Look at all the restaurants in Manhattan that have been in business for seventy-five years," Claire said. She playfully poked Eli's arm. "Is this a conversation or an interrogation, by the way? You've been hanging out with Sam way too much. What's with you?"

"Nothing. Sorry," Eli said, feeling foolish. He was silent for a few moments. "You know, we should go back to the city one of these days."

"What for?"

"Old times. We're on our own time now, Claire. We haven't been there in a dozen years."

"Since when do you miss the city?" Claire asked, leaning over and patting his hand.

"I just thought it would be nice to get away."

Claire smiled wistfully. "I remember the last time we were in Manhattan. It was years ago. Nat was three and we bought her those hot-pink snow boots. She wore them into May and they barely fit her anymore. I finally bribed her with the rhinestone moccasins."

"I remember."

"She always looked like a powder puff, didn't she? My sweet baby girl who wears black on black now," she said.

They drove in silence until they made the turn to the restaurant.

"You okay?" Eli asked. "Where are you? Back when they were babies?"

"No, not really," she said. "I was just thinking that sometimes I feel like I'm nowhere these days. I was always doing a million things at once—working, cooking, driving the kids, and now . . . nothing. I used to wish I had a moment to myself and now I have so many moments I don't know what to do with them."

"Be careful what you wish for, right?"

She took a deep breath. "So then I start thinking about things that aren't too pleasant."

"Like Sulie."

"Like Sulie," she said with resignation.

"What do you think about her?"

She turned away from him. "I really don't want to talk about it right now."

"You're sure?" he asked, although he knew better than to push her.

She nodded. "I probably should have forced myself to start work today instead of next Monday."

"Maybe I can take off a day this week," Eli said. "We could take a drive up the coast. Stay overnight at someone else's inn. We've always wanted to do that." He reached over and put his hand on her knee. "What do you say?"

She looked at him. "We can't. Not until Nick and Kayla leave."

Nick opened the door of the car for Kayla. She hopped out and slipped her hand into his. Claire remembered the nights Jack would carry her upstairs into their apartment after a dinner out, her belly full, her head resting on his shoulder. She pictured Sulie's face in the photographs on the mantel. Maybe Eli was right. Be careful what you wish for, she thought.

Nick read the menu to Kayla, ordered a Shirley Temple for her and a club soda for himself. He never drank, he explained when Eli asked if he should get a bottle of wine. His father died of alcoholic cirrhosis of the liver and the power of genetics loomed large. Nick tucked a red-and-white-checked napkin into the collar of Kayla's shirt and cut her spaghetti Puttanesca into smaller strips, asked the waitress for a teaspoon instead of the larger soup spoon that sat on the table, and dampened the end of a clean napkin.

"Give me your leg, Kayla," he said. "You got some sauce on those pants."

"Did I make a mess, Daddy?" she asked, alarmed. "Is it bad?"

"Of course not," Nick said, rubbing away the spot.

"Will it stain?" She was clearly upset. "I didn't mean to drip."

"It's nothing, sweetheart. Nothing."

Claire asked Nick about his work and teased him about the briefcase that sat by his side at dinner.

"It's one of my idiosyncracies and I have at least a hundred more," he said with a broad smile. "I suppose I shouldn't be carrying the originals."

"You must keep copies at the office," Eli said.

"Well, sure, but you know . . . it's like an original Picasso to me. There are plenty of copies but still. . . ."

"What are they for?"

"Blueprints for a home by the water in Galveston. Boathouse and guest house. I tell you, it's been a real pain with zoning restrictions since the house is right on the gulf. The insurance on the place is astronomical," he explained, as he guided Kayla's hand to her Shirley Temple, moving the drink toward her at the same time. "It's one of those jobs I regret taking on. I've been back and forth for months now. This is the first time I've had off."

"I thought you said the house was in Houston," Claire said.

"Did I? No, it's Galveston. I do have a project in Houston as well." He laughed. "You see? Sometimes I can't keep track of them. That's why I keep this with me."

"So, you travel a great deal," Eli said.

"Oh, yes. Constantly."

"Daddy, can we get dessert?" Kayla interrupted.

"After all those pastries?" Nick asked.

"Please?"

"You'll get a tummyache."

"No I won't. You know what, Daddy? This is not a greasy spoon, is it?"

Claire burst out laughing. "Greasy spoon? Where did you hear that?"

Kayla dropped her head, her chin nearly touching her chest. "I don't know," she murmured.

"Well, I'm going to have coffee," Eli said.

"So will I," Nick said. "Kayla, how about Jell-O?"

"I don't like Jell-O," she said, getting teary. "I hate Jell-O. I always tell you that I hate Jell-O."

"Even with whipped cream?"

"*No!* It's slimy! I like chocolate. Chocolate ice cream with fudge and nuts."

"Chocolate with fudge and nuts," Nick said patiently. He turned to Eli and Claire. "I think someone's getting sleepy. It's been a long day."

Nick carried Kayla up the stairs. She was sleeping soundly, her head resting on her father's shoulder.

"She was out like a light the moment we got in the car," Nick whispered.

"Do you need anything?" Claire asked, whispering as well. "Extra blankets? It's going to be cool overnight."

"We're fine. The maid put two extra blankets in the closet this morning," he said. He turned to Eli. "Thanks for dinner. The next one's on me."

"Our pleasure," Eli said. "She's a great little girl."

"That she is," Nick said, stroking her back. "She's the light of my life."

Nick opened the door to their room and laid Kayla on her bed. He took off her sneakers and placed them at the side of the bed, her socks tucked into the heels. The blister on her ankle looked angrier now, he noted, as he covered her with the blanket. Tomorrow he'd have to take her for new shoes. If Claire would go with them that would make things easier. She could help him to get the other things they needed as well. New glasses for one. The eye drop prescription. For sure, Claire knew a local pharmacy where he didn't have to get involved in all the computerized rigmarole.

He unbuttoned his shirt and hung it on the back of the desk chair, placed his trousers folded on the crease over that, the belt still in the loops, placed his wallet and car keys on the desk. He took out a fresh pair of socks and underwear and laid those on the chair as well and placed a pair of Docksider slip-ons to the side. Kayla stirred.

"Daddy? Can't I wear pajamas tonight? Please?"

"Not tonight."

"Why?"

"Just go to sleep, Kayla," he said. "You'll change your clothes in the morning. And, Kayla—don't ever screech like that again the way you did at dinner. How am I supposed to know you don't like Jell-O?"

Kayla didn't answer.

"I can't hear you," he said.

"Because I told you," she whimpered, rubbing her eyes. He should know she didn't like Jell-O. Mommy knew. "My eyes feel funny, Daddy. They're dry."

"You're tired," he said. "Don't ever carry on like that again. It's not a good thing, do you hear me? You don't want to be sent away, do you, Kayla?"

"No, Daddy."

"Then think, Kayla. Think before you speak."

He popped open the briefcase and reached beneath a pile of papers and newspaper clippings. He took out three fifty-dollar bills and placed them in his wallet. He closed the suitcases on their stands, turned on the television, and fell asleep gripping the handle of the briefcase on the bed beside him.

"How about a nightcap?" Eli asked.

"Nice," Claire said. "You were sort of quiet during dinner. How come?"

Eli pushed the hair back from his forehead. "Tired, I guess," Eli said, walking behind the bar of the veranda. "What'll it be, ma'am?"

"Hmmm," she said, sitting on a bar stool. "Grand Marnier."

"Good choice. Me, too," he said.

"Maybe you're coming down with something."

He sat down next to her and clinked her glass with his. "To transitions."

She smiled. "And hypnosis."

"So, what do you think? You're the psychologist."

"About what?"

"About Nick. The two of them, really."

"What do you mean?"

"I mean, what's your take on them?"

"I like them. She's so sweet." She yawned. "I think he's lonely. Why? What do you think?"

"I'm not sure. I told you, there's something off about him."

"You keep saying that," Claire said impatiently. "Explain. Off *how*?"

"I can't put my finger on it. It's like he's trying too hard. I can't explain it."

"Maybe he has to try hard," Claire said. "He's a single father with a blind child."

"There's a mother. You said she mentioned her mother."

"Yes, but she said her mother wanted to send her away to some school."

"How do you know that's true? Kids say things sometimes. . . . They make up all kinds of things."

"That's a pretty intense thing to pretend, don't you think? Make-believe is typically relegated to pleasant things."

"I thought it was strange that nothing was said at dinner about her mother or home or school or anything."

"Those might be sore subjects right now."

"Maybe," he said thoughtfully, taking a sip of his drink. "But don't you think she'd talk about her friends or something?"

"Not necessarily. For all we know she doesn't have too many friends," Claire said. "She's not your typical child, don't forget. She's blind and other kids can be cruel. As for Nick trying too hard . . . seven-year-olds are really still babies. God knows Jack must have tried extra hard with me when I was seven and I wasn't blind. And Nick is limited in what he can do with her. It's not like he can take her roller-skating or toss a ball around."

"I suppose."

"Even with Jack and me . . ."

"He's not Jack," Eli said abruptly.

"I didn't say he was Jack," she said, embarrassed. "I know he's not Jack."

He sighed. "I'm sorry. I shouldn't have said that."

He twirled the drink in his hand, the thick liquid painting the sides of the glass. "You know how sometimes someone just sets the hair on the back of your neck on end? My father always used that expression. See what happens? You get old enough and you become your father."

"Look, I think Nick is a bit stiff and formal, too. I can see where another man might not find him particularly engaging, but I've seen enough in my career to tell you that he's a decent person. Troubled? Yes. But not 'off' as you say."

He looked at his wife's eyes and placed his hands on her shoulders. "Don't get too involved, Claire."

"You sound like Annie," she said. "She said the same thing this afternoon."

"Well, that's two to one. You have that tendency, you know," he said gently. "And Kayla's already attached to you. That's apparent."

"What exactly would you like me to do, Eli? Oh, and by the way, the stray dogs and cats I've taken in over the years until you've found homes for them and the ducklings from Jonah's kindergarten class that were headed for a l'orange . . . I suppose you weren't getting involved."

"That's different."

"Why is it different?"

"Those animals were helpless."

"So are children."

"She has a father."

"Eli, I know what I'm doing."

"Just be careful, Claire. I just don't want to see you get hurt."

"Hurt? Why would I get hurt?"

"It's like I said before. There's just something about that guy. . . . I don't know. I just worry about you. Sometimes you trust everyone a little too much."

They left the brandy snifters on the bar and turned out the frosted glass lamps that dangled from the ceiling. Eli turned the bolt on the lobby door and they walked up the spiral staircase, Eli ahead of Claire, his hand trailing behind holding hers. A dim light glowed through the transom of room eight, the low drone of the television coming through.

Their private quarters were up a flight of steps and around a narrow curving hallway to the right. How many nights had they made this journey? Claire thought. Stopping at Jonah's room to ask if he'd done his homework, telling him to turn off the computer and get some sleep. A boy can't grow on four hours of sleep, Claire would say, and then Eli and Jonah would laugh.

"I'm fifteen, Ma," Jonah would say. "I'm six feet already."

Eli would pull her away gently. "He's fine. I grew without any sleep, Claire. Bishop men are night owls."

Natalie's room. Claire pushed open the door. The pink-and-purple quilt was pulled tight over the bed, the pillows poufed in front of the white two-poster headboard. The nightstand was cluttered with small stacks of scrap papers held under a red heart-shaped paperweight. Claire pictured Natalie lying in bed with Stella at her feet, fashion magazines strewn about her, some pages torn out, the stereo playing low.

"I've got all these hairstyles for prom," Natalie would say, shaking the pages, beckoning her to sit down. "Come see them, Mom."

And Claire would sit on her bed studying the photographs, holding them beside Natalie's face. Studying curls and updos and straight styles. The things that mothers do with daughters . . .

"What do you think she's doing now?" Claire asked, leaning against the door to Natalie's room.

Eli looked at his watch. "Talking with friends. Hoping you won't call her first thing in the morning." He grinned.

"I only did that the first few mornings," she said, giving him a soft shove. "You know what it feels like when I walk into their rooms lately? It's like with Kayla. How she wends her way down the corridor and finds the way with her fingertips. She has all these markers. There's a dent in the wall on the way to the kitchen. A spackle mark a few feet after that and then a dip in the floor and two steps into the kitchen. She explained it to me. That's how she finds her way. . . . It's like that with me. I walk into the kids' rooms and they're empty. My touchstones are gone."

"There'll be new ones. Different ones."

"I know that but I feel so disconnected right now. That's what I was saying before. Like with Kayla, if I smoothed that rough spackle on the wall, she wouldn't find her way, don't you understand? I can't seem to find my way lately. I keep looking back and back and wondering if I should have done anything differently. If I did things the right way—with the kids, you know?"

"Look at them, Claire. How can you doubt yourself? They're exactly where they're supposed to be."

"I did it without a legacy, Eli."

"How do you mean?"

"Without a mother. I mean, most women learn certain things from their mothers, right? The funny thing is, I learned so much stuff from Nat. From the time she was really little. I guess she was learning stuff from the other girls who learned from their mothers."

"What kind of things? My guess would be Nat's learned a lot more from you."

"No, I know that. Silly things. Girlie things. Like with her prom stuff. I never would have thought to get makeup done and look for hairstyles. I went to my prom and what you saw was what you got. I didn't even have a manicure on our wedding day, let alone have my hair done. No one told me about that stuff."

"So Jack is your legacy."

She smiled. "He certainly is. But lately when I think about Sulie I feel like I'm betraying him. He tried so hard. I know that now, even though he made everything seem effortless." Her eyes filled with tears. "I wonder how Jack felt when she left him." She shut the door to Natalie's room. "Maybe this is just the time in our lives when we think back."

"Middle age," Eli said. "I think about when the kids were born. How you looked the first day I met you. You were wearing a blue blouse."

"You're guessing," she said. "You're just trying to cheer me up."

"No, it was blue. Believe me, I remember."

"Come on. . . ."

"Oh, no, I remember. But I tell you what. As beautiful as you looked that day, I look at you now and you look even more beautiful."

"Oh yeah, with the lines and wrinkles and ten extra pounds . . ."

"I don't see any of that."

"Your eyes aren't as good as they used to be."

"They're great up close."

"Wrong. You hold everything at arm's length."

"True," he said, drawing her close to him. "But you look better up close."

"Are you trying to seduce me?" She tilted her head back and looked up at him.

"How am I doing?"

"Not bad," she said.

"I didn't mean to stop you from talking," he said as he leaned in to kiss her. "We can talk some more."

"Uh-huh," she said kissing his neck. "Not right now."

Chapter 8

Kayla sat up in bed, swung her legs over the side, pointed her toes until they touched the floor and placed her fingertips on the nightstand that separated her bed from her father's. She took the three steps she had counted the day before, one foot in front of the other heel to toe, and walked over to her father's bed.

"Daddy," she said, poking him gingerly. "Daddy?"

Nick grunted and turned to look at the clock. "It's six-thirty, Kayla. Why are you up so early? Go back to bed."

"I heard a noise."

"What kind of noise?"

"Like a screeching noise."

"I didn't hear anything," Nick said, his eyes still shut.

"Listen," she insisted.

"It's the pipes. It's an old house. Go back to sleep."

"There's something on my stomach."

Now what? he thought. She overreacted to every lit-

tle thing. Heightened sensation, the doctors said. He
opened his eyes and flicked on the light.

"That hurts," Kayla groaned.

"What hurts?"

"The light hurts." She began to whimper. "And this
thing hurts. It's like a hole."

"Pull up your shirt and let me see your stomach. It's
probably just a bug bite." He looked at her stomach.
"It's from the tie on the sweatpants," he said. "It's
knotted. It's nothing. The skin got pressed in a little,
that's all."

"Is it big?"

"You can hardly see it."

"That's why I like to sleep in pajamas. It was dig-
ging into me all night, that knot. It hurt all night." She
waited for her father to respond and shook him again.
"I'm hungry."

Nick sat on the edge of the bed. "I have to use the
bathroom. I'll be right back."

He leaned into the bathroom mirror and stroked the
stubble on his chin. Six-thirty. What was he going to do
with her the rest of the day? Buy shoes, he remembered. That's an hour maybe. What else? There was
something else. He couldn't remember. He looked out
the small bathroom window. The sun was just beginning to rise over the ocean. How much longer could he
go on like this? The problem was, there was no turning
back. Not now.

Kayla was waiting where he left her when he came
out of the bathroom, her hand rubbing the depression
on her sunken white stomach around her navel.

"Stop rubbing it," Nick said. "You'll make it worse."

"I want it to go away," she said, stopping nonetheless. "Can we go back to the place we ate yesterday? The one where we had the pancakes?"

"It's probably not open yet, Kayla. It's not even sunrise. Besides, we don't want to go to the same place twice, do we?"

"Why not?"

He hesitated a moment. "We like to try new places, that's why."

"Maybe by the time we get dressed other places will be open," she said softly. "I have to pee. Look, I undid the knot. Good, right?" But Nick didn't answer her. His head was splitting. He lay back on the bed with his arm crooked across his eyes. She hopped down from the bed and counted the steps to the bathroom. Six to the end of the bed. Fifteen to the wall. Left turn. Six steps. Turn right into the bathroom. Seven steps to the toilet. Counting. Always count, Mommy said. Counting was a good thing; even when she was little, she could count better than any kid in her class. Some of them could only count to ten. By the time she was four, she could count to sixty, but that used to worry her when she couldn't go further. What if she was counting someplace really far and she had to count more than sixty steps? But Mommy told her she would learn to count higher really fast and in the meantime Mommy said that she should just start again with one. Mommy always had a good answer. And she was right. When she was five she could count to one hundred. Besides, they never went anyplace where the steps were too far. Not when she was with Mommy. She rinsed her eyes with cold water and then wrung out the washcloth, placing the cold on her belly as well.

"It's better now," she said as she came from the bathroom.

"What's better?"

"The thing from the knot. I put cold water on it." She wouldn't mention her eyes again, she thought.

"I'm going to shower, okay? Watch television or something." He handed her the remote control and put her finger on the channel button. "Just push this one until you find something you want to watch."

She hated when he said to watch television. She didn't like television. Things happened too fast and it got confusing. She got lucky, though. That cartoon was on, the one she liked about the elephant that sat on the bird's egg. Mommy read her the story. *Horton Hatches the Egg*. Except this time it made her kind of sad since Mayzie, the mommy bird, left her egg with Horton and took off. Even though in the end Mayzie wanted the baby back after the egg hatched. She wished she hadn't left the tape Claire gave her in the car although it didn't matter much since her tape recorder in the suitcase had dead batteries. It always had dead batteries. Their stereo at home sounded better than the tinny tape player with the headphones. Mommy played *Peter and the Wolf* for her all the time. The horns. She loved the horns. She remembered when she and Mommy would sit on the big sofa in the living room and Mommy would hold her really tight and say, "Look out now, Kayla. Here he comes. The wolf is coming!" And they hugged as though they were really scared and screamed and laughed even though they knew the ending. It was so much fun. She thought about Mommy all the time lately. Well, since she got to the inn anyway. Really since she met Claire. Claire had the same way about her as Mommy did. She spoke really softly like she was almost singing her a lullaby. What was that lullaby Mommy used to sing for her? Something about a mockingbird? Hush little baby . . . But Claire didn't smell the same as Mommy and her hair felt different. Mommy's hair was thicker and Claire said her hair was blond and Mommy's was what Grandma called auburn and it had curls. Poor Grandma. She wished she could call Grandma like she used to but she died. She remembered when Grandpa died. She and Mommy went to the funeral in Denver and then to Grandpa's grave and when Grandma put flowers there, she cried. When she leaned against Claire yesterday during tea she felt nice, but it didn't feel the same as Mommy. Mommy was softer. She fit right under the crook of Mommy's arm better. Mommy held her differently, all curled up and cozy.

Maybe Mommy will come back like the Mayzie bird, she thought. But at least I have Daddy. Daddy promised to always take care of me since everyone else is either dying or trying to send me away.

Claire was in the kitchen when Nick and Kayla came down the stairs.

"Well, you're early risers," she said.

Nick pointed to Kayla with his thumb. "Blame my little rooster here."

"Hungry?" Claire asked Kayla.

The child nodded. "Do you think the restaurant is open? Daddy says it's too early."

"I'm sure by the time we get there . . ." Nick said.

"Don't be silly. I have a pot of coffee on and we can

find something here," Claire said. "Kayla, what's your fancy?"

"My fancy?"

"Your fancy. What do you feel like having? French toast? How's that?"

"Good," Kayla said. "I like that."

"Nick?" Claire asked.

"I really feel we're taking advantage," he said.

"Don't be silly. The newspaper's over there on the counter. It's just local news, I'm afraid, but something to read. Coffee? Toast?"

"Just coffee. That'd be great," Nick said. "Thanks."

"Can I cook with you?" Kayla asked, tugging on Claire's brushed cotton robe. "This feels like velvet. What is it? What color?"

"Pink. My daughter bought it for me last Mother's Day," Claire said and as the words came from her mouth she realized what she had said between colors and Mother's Day and quickly changed the subject. "You beat the eggs and I'll get the vanilla, okay?"

"I need to find a shoe store," Nick said. "Kayla needs new sneakers."

"Claire, can you come with us today?" Kayla asked, patting Stella who was standing at her side now. "Come to buy the shoes?"

"I'm sure you have better things to do," Nick said.

"I would love to," Claire said. "You know how we women love shoes. Stand back now, Kayla, in case the butter splatters."

"It smells like the candle shop," Kayla said.

"That's the vanilla. We can go back to the candle shop, too, you know. I'm sure Annie would love to see you again."

Nick lowered the newspaper. "I'm beginning to feel the vacation," he said.

"Well, it's about time. Now if we can just get you to unleash that thing, we'll be in business," she said, gesturing with her chin to the briefcase by his side.

Claire was cutting Kayla's French toast into strips when Eli came into the kitchen.

"Well, this is sure a crowd here this morning," he said. "Everyone sleep well?"

"Like a baby," Nick said. "I'm afraid I've started your newspaper."

"Eli, coffee?" Claire asked. "Give me a moment and I'll put on another pot. This one's dry already."

"I have to run," Eli said stiffly. "Full schedule this morning. What's up for today, Claire?"

"We're going shoe shopping," Kayla said. "Claire, too."

"Well, that's fun," Eli said. He turned to his wife. "I'll call you later." He stared her square in the face wondering if she could read his mind. Too much, he was thinking. Too intimate now. The three of them spending the day together.

"I'll walk you to the door," Claire said, knowing he wanted her to follow him. She turned to Kayla. "I'll be right back. Don't go near the stove now. The burners are hot. Careful."

"Shoe shopping?" Eli asked as they walked down the porch steps. "Claire, for God's sake . . . don't you think it's a bit much? You're going to spend the day with them?"

"She asked me to go. What on earth is the difference, Eli?"

"You don't know the first thing about him."

"I'm not going off with *him*. Is that what's bothering you? I'm going for Kayla."

Eli opened the door to the truck and took a deep breath. "I don't like it."

"What is *wrong* with you?"

"I told you. There's something about him. . . ."

"Don't you think maybe you're making a judgment about him without even knowing him?"

"And you're not?"

"He's seems to be a wonderful father," she said softly.

"No one's perfect."

"I didn't say he was perfect," she said, trying to remain patient.

"Look, I told you . . . I have this . . . this instinct about him. I can't explain it."

"Well, your instincts are wrong. And they're not based on anything concrete. Give me one example of why you have this . . . this feeling of yours."

"And your instincts are based on what?"

"On years of studying human behavior. And you didn't answer me. Give me a reason, for God's sake."

Eli turned the key in the ignition. "You might want to search some more case histories."

"Eli! Why are you doing this?"

"Look, I checked the computer this morning. They never made one phone call home from their room."

"You checked the computer? Why would you do that?"

"I was curious," he said defensively.

"Curious? That's a bit much, don't you think? Maybe he's using a cell phone." She looked rather horrified. "I can't believe you checked the computer. How suspicious are you? What are you thinking?"

"He doesn't have a cell phone."

"How do you know?"

"Because he wasn't carrying one."

"So what? Maybe he left it in the room. Or his car. I think you're taking this too far."

"He doesn't look you in the eye when he speaks." Eli was sitting in his truck now, his elbow leaning out the open window.

Claire touched his arm. "Oh, Eli, come on. I see a father with his child. A child who's needy in more ways than one and a father who's trying to do the best he can under what appear to be arduous circumstances."

"Is that based on your maternal instinct or a documented textbook case?"

"What is that supposed to mean?"

"It means that I don't think you're seeing things clearly." His heart pounded. *You're my wild oat, Eli Bishop,* he thought.

"And I suppose you are," she said defiantly, but he wasn't listening.

How was it possible that they had made love for hours the night before and now she stood frozen as he pulled out of the driveway, listening as his tires screeched down the road?

Eli knew from the look on Daisy's face that something was terribly wrong.

"Dr. Bishop, Stu Hayes called," she said as she followed Eli into his office and shut the door. "About ten minutes ago. He tried to reach you on the cell. The mare died."

Eli felt the color drain from his cheeks. "What?"

Daisy handed him a pink slip of paper. "Here's his number."

Eli reached down for his cell phone. "Shit. It was shut off. What the hell happened?"

"He didn't say, Dr. Bishop. Just that they found her this morning in her stall."

He pulled Power's medical records from the file behind his desk. She had a history of colic. Yesterday was no different. Or at least he thought it was no different. Power was lying down in her stall when he arrived. He prodded her to rise and she whinnied and nuzzled him as she always did. He *knew* her. Sometimes he went out there to ride her on the weekend when Stu was away. Aside from Stu and his daughter, Eli was the only one who rode Power. He'd given her the medication yesterday, checked her gums, her eyes, listened to her heart. She'd bobbed her head and neck up and down almost appreciatively.

"It's the colic again," Eli said. "This should do the trick."

"She doesn't need anything else, Doc?" the stable boy asked.

"I can look at her and tell you this is the same old thing," Eli said, stroking the mare's neck. "She'll be better by the morning. I'll be out sometime tomorrow."

He picked up the phone to call Stu Hayes but decided to drive out to the farm instead.

"The waiting room is full," Daisy said as he walked out the door. "What do I tell them, Dr. Bishop?"

"I have an emergency, Daisy," he said with uncharacteristic abruptness. "That's what you tell them."

The horse was covered by a rough brown blanket in the stable when Eli drove up. Stu Hayes must have just driven up from Boston. His car keys were still in his hand.

"They found her this morning around six," Stu said as he bent over the mare, not looking up at Eli. "I just got here."

Eli peeled off the brown blanket and knew right away. The horse appeared bloated.

"Entrapment," Eli said, his heart pounding. "This time she must have had a spasmodic colic. The intestines twist around themselves and strangulate. I don't know how . . . I'm sorry, Stu. I don't know what to say."

"Could it have been avoided?"

Eli's face reddened. "I didn't do a rectal. I would have felt the bowels."

"Why didn't you?" Stu asked.

"She's eight years old," Eli said. "I delivered her. She always got this kind of thing. This kind of colic. My gut told me she was okay."

"Jesus Christ, Eli. Jesus Christ," Stu said. "I guess your gut's not as reliable as you think."

Eli watched Stu and the men in the rearview mirror before he pulled away. Watched them place the heavy leather straps around the horse and hoist her onto the mechanical platform of the flatbed truck. *I guess your gut's not as reliable as you think.* Stu's words penetrated him. He felt them along with the image he had of Claire standing in the driveway. He couldn't remember the last time he and Claire had that harsh an exchange. In the early years, perhaps. When the kids were tiny and he and Claire were tired and overworked and Claire was going for her degree at the same time as everything else. He remembered one night in particular, shortly after Natalie was born, when Jonah came down with the flu and Claire and Eli took turns getting up all night long for three days straight. That was a rough stretch. But now, now things should be different. He loved his wife. He loved her with a tenderness and passion that nearly frightened him sometimes. Even the night before when he made love to her, it wasn't like a man making love to a woman he had known for twenty-five years. She fit beneath him as though she were a part of him. When he slipped inside her, he was complete.

Eli didn't go back to the office. He exited the highway and drove the road that twisted along the shore through the neighboring Rhode Island beach towns. He stopped at a small bar in Westerly where he ordered a beer and sat with the locals, men not much older than he who looked twice as old, greenish stubble spackling their faces, rheumy eyes. More than likely, they'd been drinking since the bar opened at ten that morning. The television screen above the bar was barely discernible, filled with snow, the audio barely intelligible. Yet the men focused on a game show, their gazes blank. He thought about Nick Pierce again and wondered if the sigh he felt was audible. He wasn't a superstitious man and yet he felt that from the moment Claire opened the door to the stranger something had changed. There was something about the father and his child. Even something about Kayla that transcended her blindness. Something he couldn't put his finger on. Something was wrong. It was like something was missing.

Chapter 9

Claire stood in the driveway for what seemed an eternity, wondering if Eli might turn around. She would have made a fresh pot of coffee, offered him slices of French toast, explained that the shoe shopping was only for Kayla's sake. She'd called Eli's name as he pulled away, the syllables catching the tip of her tongue, her mouth slightly agape. She wondered if her cry had been unsuccessful or whether he had chosen not to reply. She ran her hand down the side of her face and spread her fingers over her mouth. A vaporous stream of exhaust was the only remnant of his departure.

Stella loped around from the backyard, her scrawny, feeble legs soggy with morning dew. Claire tugged the dog's collar gently, guiding Stella up the steps the way one holds the elbow of an elderly woman as she crosses the street. Claire stood motionless in the middle of the steps leading up to the porch. A breeze forced her only movement as she brushed away a strand of hair that stuck to the corner of her mouth. She was hollow.

Kayla sat obediently at the kitchen table, her shoulders rigid, the fork held awkwardly in her hand as she picked up the morsels of French toast. The room was strangely silent. For a brief moment Claire noticed the absence of laughter or conversation. There was no sound but the turning of the newspaper pages from Nick across the table.

"Sorry it took so long," she said uncomfortably, trying to force a smile.

Nick lowered the paper that shielded his face. "Don't apologize," he said. "You look stressed. Everything all right?"

"Oh, fine," she said. "Kayla? More French toast?"

"I'm full," she said.

"Well, it's about time," Nick said, moving the paper from his face and smiling broadly. "You finally succeeded in satisfying this child."

"I need to shower and dress and then I can take you to the shoe store in Meadville," Claire said. "Most of them open at nine so if we leave here in an hour we'll get there before the crowds."

Claire washed the breakfast dishes while Nick took Kayla into the backyard. Claire watched from the kitchen window as Nick pushed Kayla on the swing, her head thrown back. Higher, she called. Higher. And Nick, expressionless, let the swing climb above the treetops. Claire wondered if Jack, too, had the air of sadness that seemed to envelop Nick as he pushed his daughter on the swing. Jack took her to the playground nearly every Sunday morning barring rain or snow. Sundays were grand because the pharmacy opened at noon. They always stopped at the bakery where Jack bought a black coffee and French cruller for himself and a jelly doughnut and milk for Claire. Old cannons lined the street in front of Riverside Park, right before the pathway and they sat atop one of the black cannons with their picnic. Each time, Jack told her what was on the other side of the Hudson River, told her to imagine what the cityscape was like so long ago before the brick buildings changed the skyline—and even though he told her the same story each time, she never tired of listening. And then they would walk the path to the playground and Claire would hop on a swing and Jack would push her above the treetops, singing a Russian song. No, she thought, there was no sadness about Jack, at least none that he made evident to her. Families came into the park as the morning wore on. Mothers pushing navy blue Silver Cross prams and fathers pulling toddlers on tricycles. The mothers sat on benches rocking carriages to and fro while fathers pushed the toddlers on the swings or stood to catch them at the bottom of the slides. "Mommy, look at me," the children cried and the mothers nodded and smiled and waved and it was the only time the park made her melancholy. It was the same sort of feeling she had when holidays rolled around and her friends shopped for their mothers. They bought sweet-smelling bath salts and costume jewelry, flowering plants and silk scarves, perfumes and lipstick cases. She never wrote "Dear Mom" on a card or answered the telephone to greet her mother on the other end. She never saw her mother's hose hanging from the towel rack in the bathroom or sat on the edge of her mother's bed rummaging with her through a jewelry box. When she went to Piedmont for the first time with Eli, Harriet Bishop came to the door wearing a calico-printed apron and the smell of baked apples filled the house. Harriet embraced her and made one reference to Claire being the first daughter-in-law, the daughter she never had what with those four boys she raised. But Claire felt herself stiffen at Harriet's words.

She dried her hands on the dish towel and hung it on the hook above the sink. She called through the window to Nick and Kayla that she would get dressed now and Nick acknowledged her with a wave, saying what sounded like take your time although his words were muffled by the wind.

She thought about calling Eli several times as she dressed and stopped herself each time. She didn't want to argue on the phone. She wondered if he was steeling himself against calling as well. It wasn't like him not to call. It wasn't like him not to make amends. She brushed out her hair and looked at her face in the mirror. In all fairness, she thought, it was unlike her not to call as well. Especially after the night before.

Nick and Claire took seats on either side of Kayla at the shoe store. Except for a young mother with a toddler who had just begun to walk, the shop was empty. Not the usual after-school crowd that Claire used to battle when she took Jonah and Natalie there for shoes when they were small. It had been years since Claire shopped there. The chairs were new, the faces of the sales help unfamiliar. The upholstered wooden chairs had been replaced with streamlined chrome and plastic. The circus posters—how the clowns had always frightened Jonah—were replaced with advertisements for sneakers portraying athletic kids playing different sports. An older man came over with the metal device that measures size.

"Here we go," he said. "Let's have a look."

Kayla took off her sneakers and stood up. Claire took her ankle and guided it to the measurer.

"Ten," he said. "What did you have in mind, son? Sneakers again?" He picked up Kayla's worn sneaker and searched for the size under the tongue. He whistled. "These have seen better days. I can't even see the size. Oh, here we go. Eight? You must have stretched these out pretty good."

"I'm a girl," Kayla said. "You called me 'son.'"

"Force of habit," the man said, reddening. "Got too many grandsons, I guess." He turned to Claire. "Ma'am, what do you have in mind?"

"Me? Oh, no, ask her father . . ."

"No, you go right ahead," Nick said. "Up to you ladies."

"I want pink sneakers," Kayla said.

Nick laughed heartily. "Pink! Everything always pink. How about red or blue? Shows the dirt less."

"Pink." Kayla pouted.

The salesman disappeared into the back of the store and came out with a few stacks of boxes. "I got pink-and-white and then a pair here with daisies on the side." As he pulled them from the box, Nick stopped him.

"We should have told you that we need ones with Velcro," he said. "Laces won't do. And I think we should go with the darker colors."

"But . . ." Kayla said.

"Kayla," Nick said simply.

Kayla knew that tone in his voice before her father even finished the sentence. "Okay," she said compliantly. "It's okay." He knew what was best for her, she thought. He knew. She rubbed her eyes furiously, wishing they would stop burning.

"How about some socks?" the salesman asked. "You might want something a bit thicker."

And as Kayla pulled off the old socks and put on the new, Nick could have sworn he saw the salesman stare through him.

"Looks like those toenails could use a clipping," Nick said, preempting the man. "We'll have to wrestle you down later, won't we, sweetheart?"

"Nasty blister," the salesman said.

Nick pulled a fifty-dollar bill from his wallet and handed it to the salesman.

"You want me to toss the old ones away for you?"

"No," Nick said calmly. "We'll take them home."

"She can't wear them anymore. They're way too small. No good for her feet . . ."

"Yes, we know. But we sometimes get attached to certain things," Nick said smoothly. "We'll figure it out. Thanks, though."

"Want to look in that shop over there?" Claire asked when they stepped outside, pointing to a children's clothing store on the other side of the parking lot.

"No, let's just get back to Drifting," Nick said. "How about the candle shop again, Kayla?"

She nodded. Her eyes stung and her head was throbbing now. It was the first time since she and Daddy had been away that she wondered what would happen if she called Mommy. She didn't feel well. She always wanted Mommy when she didn't feel well. The salesman thought Claire was her mommy. Part of her wanted to tell him that was just Claire. But she knew if she mentioned Mommy's name, Daddy wouldn't like it. And she hated when Daddy didn't like things. He got angry and said things that scared her sometimes. But when they were buying the shoes, she wished Mommy was there telling her how one day she'd get her ballet slippers and they'd go dancing. If Mommy was there, she'd tell her not to rub her eyes and then she would take the drops from her purse and a Tootsie Roll Pop and tell her that would fix her up good as new.

"That's where Eli works," Claire said, pointing, as they approached the animal hospital on the way into town. She craned her neck as they drove around the bend. "That's funny. I don't see his truck. I guess he went out to the Hayes Farm."

"Where?" Nick asked.

"The Hayes Farm. There was a sick horse out there yesterday." Claire turned around to look at Kayla. Tears were streaming down her cheeks. "What's wrong?" Claire cried. "Kayla?"

"I don't feel well," she said, the sobs audible now. "Daddy, please. Get the drops. Please."

"What drops?" Claire asked, leaning over the backseat and then turning to Nick. "Nick?"

"Tylenol drops." He stopped the car and pulled to the side of the road, turned around and felt her forehead. "A little warm, maybe. What hurts you, sweetheart?"

"My eyes," she groaned.

"Do you want to take her to the doctor? I can call. . . ." Claire said.

"No," he said, gritting his teeth together. He breathed in deeply. "I'd better get her back to the inn. Children like Kayla often feel the pain of illness in the eyes."

Claire climbed into the backseat and held Kayla next to her. "It's going to be okay," she said. "We'll take care of everything. You must have a touch of something coming on. Does your throat hurt?"

"Just my eyes," Kayla said, whimpering.

"Maybe it's something else," Claire said, holding Kayla to her. "I'm concerned. Nick, look, her eyes are swollen. Does she have allergies?"

"It's common when she gets sick. She must be getting a cold and the eyes get dry," Nick said, glancing at the two in the rearview mirror. "Stop rubbing them now, Kayla. You know better than that."

"We'll make you some hot cocoa," Claire said, stroking Kayla's head. "Do you like that, Kayla? With marshmallows?"

Kayla nodded, holding her breath, trying not to cry. The salt of her tears made her eyes sting worse.

"We'll get you all fixed up in no time," Claire said. "I'm glad you came this week. Next week I have to work."

"What do you mean? Work where?" Nick asked. "I thought you just ran the inn."

"I'm a psychologist. Typically, I'd be shut up in the barn with patients this time of year."

"You're a shrink?"

Claire laughed. "Well, we prefer the more professional title."

Nick reddened. "Sorry."

"No, that's okay. I'm used to it."

"I had no idea. . . . I thought you just ran the inn. Where's the barn?"

"Down the hill behind the inn by the lower lot. I should really call it my office but it used to be a barn. It's great because I'm working but I'm still home, you know? And we're seasonal at the inn and summers are slow in the *shrink* business," she said. "Kids are in camp and people seem to forget their problems in summer. My hours are shorter. It works out perfectly." She adjusted her arm and cradled Kayla. "She's sleeping."

"Well, that's the best thing for her. I'd like to talk when we get back," he stammered.

"Well, that would be nice," she said hesitantly.

"No, I mean professionally. In confidence, right? I can pay you."

"You don't have to pay me, Nick. I'm happy to talk to you." Or listen, as the case may be, she thought.

"No, I want to. Then it's strictly professional, right? I mean you have those codes of ethics, right? Privacy, right?"

"Right," she said cautiously. Her heart was pounding. Kayla's breathing was slow and labored. Claire placed her lips on Kayla's forehead. "She doesn't feel particularly warm. Are you sure she's all right?"

"She'll be fine. I know what it is—but I need your help," he said. He was clearly desperate. "Just tell me I can trust you, Claire."

"Trust me? Of course, you can trust me."

"I need your help," he said again, glancing in the rearview mirror. "I'm afraid I have a bit of a problem."

Chapter 10

Kayla moaned softly as Nick lifted her into his arms from the backseat of the car. She placed her arms around his neck and laid her head on his shoulder.

"She should be in bed, don't you think?" Claire said in a whisper.

"Can't we go over to the barn? To your office, I mean?"

"Don't you want to get some Tylenol or something into her first? Do you think a cold compress might help?"

"Nothing's going to make a difference."

"I don't understand, I thought you said . . ."

"I need to talk to you, Claire," he said, stroking Kayla's back.

"We can put her on one of the chaise longues and talk on the veranda," Claire suggested. "I can get a blanket and pillow."

"I'd rather go to your office. It's more private there, isn't it?"

"I suppose," Claire said. "But no one's at the inn.

Cora's gone for the day," she said, wondering at the wisdom of the remark as she spoke.

"Isn't there someplace she can lie down in your office?" Nick asked.

"There's a sofa in the waiting room," Claire said. "Why don't you drive down to the back lot? It's a closer walk to the barn. Just let me run upstairs and grab a pillow and blanket from linens. She'll be more comfortable that way."

Nick carried Kayla up the slate path to the barn. He placed her on the sofa and covered her with the blanket, tucked the pillow under her head. She stirred for a moment.

"Daddy? Where are we now?" she asked, half asleep.

"Claire's office," he said and kissed her cheek. "Claire and I will be in the next room. You rest. Try to sleep, okay? I'm right here if you need me."

"Are you going to get the drops, Daddy?" she murmured thickly.

"Yes, baby," he said tenderly as Claire looked on. "Real soon."

Claire brought Nick into her office and sat behind her desk, gesturing with her hand to the sofa that sat across from her chair. She brought a small pad of paper from the drawer and put on her glasses.

"Don't write anything down," he said.

"I thought you wanted this to be a professional session."

"I do."

"Well, usually I take notes," she explained.

"I'd rather you didn't," he said curtly. "Besides, that's for people who'll come back, right? I won't be one of those."

She slipped the pad back into the drawer and took off her reading glasses. She clasped her hands under her chin, elbows leaning on the desk.

"You don't tape things, do you?" Nick asked, looking around the room.

"No," she said simply.

"Can she hear us in here?"

"You might want to shut the door," Claire said.

He settled back onto the sofa and placed the briefcase on the floor beside him.

"Maybe we should start with the briefcase," Claire said. "You're inseparable."

"I told you, it's blueprints."

"Okay," she said trying to appear convinced.

"You want to see?" he asked, placing the briefcase on his lap, starting to pop the lock.

She waved her hand. "That's really not necessary."

"Look, I really would feel better if I, you know, engaged your services. I'd feel like what I'm telling you is confidential."

"I'll keep your confidence, Nick. You don't need to pay me."

"I'd feel better if I did. How about two hundred for the hour? That's what shrinks get in the city," he said, reaching for his wallet.

"No, Nick, please. I'll send you a bill if it makes you feel better and, besides, that's way too much for Drifting. Look, despite the fee, you have to trust me. If you can't trust me, then there's no point. . . ."

"I trust you."

"Then why don't you begin before Kayla awakens? Why is she asking for drops?"

"Eye drops. But it's a problem."

"Go on," she said, steepling her fingers.

He looked around the room, scratched his head and turned back to Claire. "Her mother and I are getting divorced."

"Does Kayla know?" Claire asked, her heart pounding.

"I'm easing her into it. What Phoebe's said to her is another matter."

"Phoebe, I assume, is Kayla's mother."

"Mother," he sniffed. "She doesn't deserve the title."

"Why is that?"

"She wants to send Kayla away to a boarding school for blind kids."

"Why?"

"Because she wants no part of her," he said angrily.

"What does she give as her reasons?" Claire asked calmly, trying to quell his anger.

"She has no reasons. She wants to get rid of her."

"Then why not just let Kayla stay with you? If you want her and Phoebe wants no part of her, I don't see why . . ."

"It's not that simple. Phoebe never wanted Kayla," he said. "She was only twenty-three when Kayla was born. Phoebe's my second wife. My first wife and I split when the kids went off to college. It was one of those situations where we married young, right out of college. We were only married for three months before we had Sean and then when he wasn't even two, we had William and we muddled through the next nineteen years until we just figured there was no sense anymore. Funny, you know? I was twenty-two when I married Nancy and I'd never been alone until we got divorced. You know, I went from my mother's house to Nancy and there I was forty-two years old and living in a one-bedroom apartment. Christ, I lived there for four years until I met Phoebe and I never even used the stove, you know? Never made myself a meal.

"I met Phoebe in Vermont. I'd gone on this singles weekend. Crazy, but I wasn't too good at meeting people and I thought I'd try it. One of my friends, Neil, went on them all the time and met his second wife that way. You know, it was like my circle of friends was destroyed when Nancy and I split up. At first people ask you to dinner and they call to see how you're doing but then that stops. Odd number at the table. They don't want to listen to your problems. They try to fix you up with a friend of theirs and it doesn't work out and all kinds of stories about your personal life start being bandied around. Anyway, there was Phoebe and she was gorgeous. She's still gorgeous. Looks like a showgirl. She was just out of art school and working as a waitress in the lodge. I'd go there at night and eat by myself and she told me later that she'd switch with the other girls so she made sure to have my table."

"You were smitten," Claire said with a faint smile.

"I was. The first night we were all there in a group and then the group would go to other restaurants and I just kept going back to the lodge where Phoebe worked. One thing led to another and a year later we were married. Her folks weren't real happy with the whole thing. Said I was too old for her. We ended up eloping. Got married at the city hall and she got pregnant on our honeymoon. It wasn't what she wanted. She wanted to abort the pregnancy but I wouldn't hear of it. She was carrying my baby. Our baby. Anyway, when she was seven months pregnant, she went skiing with her girlfriends. I told her not to. I told her it was dangerous. She had promised she wouldn't go and then when I got home from work one night there was a note that said she'd left that afternoon and she'd be fine. She was a good skier and I figured maybe I should just back off and let her go. Give her a little breathing room, you know? The next morning when I got to work, I got the call from the emergency room. They transported her by helicopter, for God's sake. She'd taken a bad spill and was in labor. Kayla was born that night. At first the doctors thought it might not be too bad. I mean, Phoebe was seven months and all but Kayla was so tiny. Too tiny. Probably because Phoebe dieted through most of the pregnancy. I swear, I thought she was trying to kill the baby in utero. And Kayla was born blind. Retinopathy of prematurity. She had surgeries and all kinds of intervention, but nothing worked. And Phoebe flat-out rejected that baby. The doctors wanted her to nurse and she freaked out and said she couldn't. She wouldn't even hold her. So for the next, say, four-and-a-half years I was like mother and father to Kayla. Phoebe and I went into counseling and then, about a year ago, I found out she was having an affair with this guy whose apartment she had done."

"What does she do?"

"Faux painting. More trickery."

"How did you find out about the affair?" Claire asked, choosing to ignore his slight.

"She was pretty obvious. Going out at night. Staying out late. Away on weekends. Phone calls where she'd hang up the minute I walked in the door. I followed her one night to the guy's apartment and just con-

fronted her. And she just stood there and said she
wanted a divorce."

"I don't understand, though. If she has no interest in
Kayla, then why not just relinquish her custody and let
you have your child?"

"Money," Nick said. "That night that I caught her at
the boyfriend's, she called the cops after she got home
and said I struck her. I didn't hit her. I would never hit
her. She came home that night and said she'd made
arrangements to send Kayla to this school in Maine for
blind kids. A boarding school. I told her there was no
way she was sending Kayla away and she took this big
glass vase we had in the living room and she hurled it
at me. It broke all over the floor and then she picked
up one of the shards and came at me and I grabbed her
arm. And I'm not proud to say I smacked her but I had
to get her away from me because it was that or I was
going to get cut."

"I thought you said you didn't hit her."

"Right, well, that was different. It was self-defense.
She would have cut me."

"Go on—where was Kayla?"

"Sleeping. We had a big apartment and Kayla's
room was in the back. It was quiet back there and since
she's so sensitive to noise I soundproofed the room
with this quilted batting we use in industrial plants.
Between the batting and the plaster walls, Kayla never
heard the commotion, thank God. But Phoebe called
the cops that night."

"She pressed charges?"

"Yes. They took me in. It looked bad. I bloodied her lip
when I smacked her and there was broken glass and
blood all over the place and she turned on the tears when

the cops came in. I called my lawyer and the next day the cops escorted me home and waited while I packed my bags. Kayla was at school. Phoebe got a restraining order against me and that was when I knew there was no chance of my ever having custody of Kayla."

"I'm still confused. Where does the money come into this? Wouldn't it have been easier on Phoebe to just let you have Kayla?"

"I'm not wealthy but I'm comfortable. If Phoebe kept Kayla, her chances were better for keeping the apartment and getting child support and alimony. A young wife who rejects her child doesn't stand up financially in court if you know what I mean. Smart girl, Phoebe. All I knew was that I needed to get Kayla out of there."

"How, though, if there was a restraining order? Don't you have supervised visits?"

"The order was lifted. I have a little studio nearby so I can see Kayla pretty much whenever I want at this point. As a matter of fact, I even take her on Phoebe's weekends. I guess Phoebe realized that having me as a baby-sitter would make her life easier. Anyway, Phoebe said she was traveling this week for business and I decided to take Kayla up here for a little rest."

"Kayla never mentions her."

"No, she doesn't," he said thoughtfully. "Kids have instincts, you know. I think she's peaceful here. She's peaceful with me."

"But before you said that Kayla doesn't know you're getting divorced yet you don't live at home anymore. Doesn't she ask?"

Nick's face reddened. "I told her we were taking a time out, that's all. She accepted that."

"I see," Claire said.

There was silence now for a few moments as Nick shifted his weight on the couch.

"Why does she need eye drops?"

"She has a condition."

"So why not call her doctor? I'm sure he'd call a pharmacy up here. It's only eye drops."

"Phoebe will use it against me in court."

"I don't understand."

"No one knows what Phoebe's really like, see? Everyone thinks she's the perfect mother and I'm some kind of monster. The doctor will tell her I left the meds at home and she'll tell her lawyer and they'll say I'm negligent or something."

"Nick, I hardly think . . ."

"Look, I'm afraid I'll lose her," he said, standing up now. "You said you were raised by just your father. I guess maybe I was wrong about you. I thought you'd understand. . . ."

"I do understand, Nick," Claire said quietly. "But why would they believe Phoebe over you? Why do you think you would be perceived as the monster?"

"Well, how did your father get custody of you?"

"I don't really think that's relevant," she said. Be professional, she thought. Don't get personal. Emotional.

"What's the matter? Why can't you answer my questions? I thought we were friends."

"We are friends," she said coolly. "But we're in session now, Nick. There's a protocol here."

"I need you to help me."

"How?"

"Look, she has juvenile glaucoma. When she's without the drops for too long her eyes hurt her."

"How long has it been?"

"A few days."

"But you just got here yesterday. Does she use them daily?"

"Look, forget it, would you?"

"Nick, I'm happy to help you. It's just that I don't know if a doctor will prescribe for her without an office visit."

"They're only eye drops, for Christ's sake. You said so yourself."

"I have to think about this, Nick," she said deliberately. "I think you're overreacting to potential repercussions of leaving the drops behind. I really think you could call Kayla's doctor."

He stood abruptly. "No!" he shouted. "Or maybe you think I should just lose my child and everything I own?" He stepped toward Claire's desk. "Maybe I was wrong about you."

Claire swallowed hard, trying not to show her fear. "You weren't wrong about me, Nick. Sit down. I understand. I just have to think about the best way to go about getting you the drops. That's all."

Kayla appeared in the doorway. Her eyes were red and swollen; her father's jacket was gathered around her shoulders. "I heard yelling," she said in a hoarse voice.

Nick walked over and picked up Kayla in his arms. He looked directly at Claire. "Claire's going to get you the eye drops, Kayla. Everything's going to be all right. I promise. You've got to stop rubbing your eyes, though, honey. You're irritating them."

Claire watched as the child buried her face in her father's neck. She envisioned Phoebe holding a shard of glass. She thought of the postcards Sulie sent her when she was small. How some nights she would find Jack sitting in the living room, a drink in his hand, just staring into the fireplace. And she, such a little girl, would curl up on his lap and without speaking so much was said. What would Jack have done if Sulie had taken her when she left? For sure, he would have gone to the ends of the earth to have her back with him. Claire leaned over to stroke the top of the child's head as she lay limply in her father's arms.

"Do your eyes hurt you, Kayla?" Claire asked.

Kayla nodded. "A lot."

"We're going to get you something to make you feel better. I promise," she said. She looked up at Nick. "Tim Boyd is an internist and a friend. I'll ask him."

As Claire reached up to stroke Kayla's face, Nick pressed his hand over hers. "Thank you," he said.

Claire withdrew her hand from beneath Nick's and flicked out the light in the corridor. He walked ahead of her, the child slumped in his arms. She shut the door to the barn and came behind them on the path.

"You can drive around to the front," she said.

"She's peaceful now," Nick said. "I don't mind carrying her." Besides, he thought, the car was in a perfect spot away from the road.

Chapter 11

Claire made a pot of coffee for Nick and cocoa for Kayla. She brought the remainder of Molly's cookies but Kayla had no appetite, something worrisome by itself. Claire tried coaxing her to sip the cocoa but all Kayla wanted was to sleep. Claire looked at her, nestled and pale under the cool white sheet that tipped her chin. Claire couldn't help but question the depth of the child's pain.

"You never told me the name of the drops," Claire said, not taking her eyes from Kayla.

Nick fumbled in his wallet and pulled out a scrap of paper. "There are three of them. Timoptic. Pred Forte. Atropine," he read, handing her the scrap. "Here, you can take this."

"No, I'll just write it down," she said. "There's pen and paper in the desk over there."

Claire studied him. He was ashen and drawn. His eyes were sunken hollows in his head. For the first time, she noticed that his fingernails were bitten down to the cuticles. He was, unlike even the day before, a man who appeared broken.

"I'll do what I can," she said, slipping the paper into her pocket. "Are you sure you're all right? You look a bit peaked."

Nick's eyes darted furtively around the room. "I'll be fine," he said curtly.

She closed the door quietly and stood outside for a moment. Listening for something and not knowing what. She heard the low drone of the television come on, the popping of what she knew was the lock on Nick's briefcase. She tiptoed away, turned the corner in the hallway, descended the small flight of steps to her quarters. Stella appeared out of nowhere suddenly at her heels, following her to the bedroom. Enough was enough. She couldn't recall a time when she and Eli hadn't spoken all day. She sat on the edge of the bed and dialed Eli's office.

"Daisy? It's me. Is he there?" she asked.

"Here? No, he's not here," Daisy said excitedly. "We haven't heard from him all day. I thought maybe he went home. I tried calling. . . ."

"Why would he come home? Was he sick?"

"Didn't he tell you? The horse died up at the Hayes Farm."

"Died? Oh no. When?"

"Early this morning. Doc went up there, oh, I'd say around eight. Right after he came in. You mean he didn't call you?"

"No," Claire said, trying to keep her voice even. "Did you try his cell?"

"I got the voice mail. I left three messages."

Claire could hear herself breathing into the mouthpiece. "I don't understand."

"I'm sure there's a reasonable explanation. Maybe he went to lunch with Mr. Hayes. He was pretty upset."

"I'm sure," Claire said distractedly. "Look, I'll try his cell. I'll let you know if I reach him."

She hung up and dialed Eli's cell phone. Over and over, pressing the redial button several times, hoping if he was ignoring the ring for whatever reason her persistence would win in the end. She heard the door to their quarters open in the hall.

"Eli? Is that you?" she called.

"It's me."

"Where have you been?" she cried. Her relief turned to anger. "You can't do that, Eli. You can't just not call all day long. For God's sake . . ."

"Don't," he said. "Please don't." He walked past her and sat on the oversize armchair by the window. "Power died, Claire." He lifted his face that had been in his hands. She could see his jaw pumping. "I fucked up, Claire. What the hell is wrong with me?"

She kneeled on the floor beside him. "Tell me what happened."

"She had a history of colic. She didn't seem to have anything different yesterday except this time she was strangulating and I missed it."

"What do you mean, strangulating?"

"The bowel. If I'd done a rectal on her, I would have felt it. I would have operated and resected it. But I didn't do a rectal. I just looked at her and she responded the way she always did and I figured it was the same thing it's always been."

"Eli, everyone makes mistakes. Don't be so hard on yourself. . . ."

"Oh, yeah? Tell me how you'd feel if someone came to see you and then a few days later they jumped off a building? You think maybe you'd feel like you screwed up? Think maybe you'd feel guilty and incompetent? You know what Stu Hayes said? He said, 'I guess your gut's not as reliable as you think.' "

"He's upset, Eli. He's angry," she said. "You've been practicing for thirty years. You're only human."

"Maybe that's what's killing me. I always felt like I had this sixth sense when it came to these animals."

"You do," she said gently.

"I didn't this time."

She reached up and placed her hand on his shoulder. "Let's go someplace," she said. "Come on. Let's order a bottle of wine and talk this through. Come on."

"I'm sorry about this morning. I'm sorry I gave you such a hard time. I don't know what I was thinking." He shook his head. "More lousy instincts. I'm batting a thousand."

"Listen, how about we drive up county and go to that little place by the water? You know, the one in Stanton?"

"Pete's Pier? That place is a dive."

"I'm in the mood for a dive. Let's go someplace where no one knows us, where we won't run into anyone, okay?"

He rose from the chair. "I need to get out of these clothes."

"Where were you anyway? You smell like a brewery."

"Some bar in Westerly. Then I just sat in my truck and felt sorry for myself. I parked by the lighthouse."

"Which lighthouse?" she asked, smiling.

"*Our* lighthouse," he said. "How many times do you think we made love there?"

She laughed. "How many? Only twice."

"That was all? I sat there today and felt like we'd made love there a hundred times."

"We'll have to go back." She leaned in and kissed him. "You should have called me today, you know. Don't ever do that again."

"How did everything go? Kayla get her shoes?"

"She did."

"What's wrong?"

"Why would something be wrong?"

"I can tell by the look on your face. What happened?"

"That gut's still pretty reliable if you ask me, Dr. Bishop."

"Are you okay?" he asked, taking her hands. "Did something happen?"

"Everything's fine. Do you think Tim Boyd would call in a prescription for Kayla? She has juvenile glaucoma and Nick left her eye drops at home. She's very uncomfortable."

"Why doesn't he just ask her doctor to phone it in? The Drugmart's twenty-four hours."

"He doesn't want to."

"How come?" he asked, pulling his shirt over his head.

"It's a long story."

"Where are they now, anyway?"

"In their room," she said. "Kayla's sleeping. Can't you call Tim? Please?"

"How come I don't like this?" he asked, dialing

Tim's phone number. "Hey, Tim. Eli Bishop. Listen, sorry to bother you at home but we have a little problem. No, we're all fine. We have some guests staying with us and the little girl has juvenile glaucoma. She needs . . . " He turned to Claire as she shoved the paper into his hand. "Timoptic. Pred Forte. Atropine. Hmmm, I see. No, I know. I'm not sure. Let me put you on with Claire." He covered the mouthpiece of the phone. "He ran out of all three?"

"Tim? Hi, how are you? How's Jeannie? Oh, good. Listen, this little one, her dad left her meds at home and she's really suffering. . . . Oh, that would be great, Tim. Kayla Pierce. Right. With a K. Then P-I-E-R-C-E. The Drugmart in Meadville would be great. Listen, I really appreciate this. Truly."

She handed the phone back to Eli. "Okay if we make a slight detour? He's going to call in the scrip, but if we could just run it back here. . . . She's in pain, Eli. She needs them."

"All three?" he asked, placing the phone on the cradle.

"They work in conjunction with each other, I guess."

"What's going on, Claire?"

"Honestly, I'm not quite sure. We'll talk at dinner. I promise. Let's just stop at their room and tell Nick we're going, okay?"

She tapped lightly on Nick's door. He opened it just a crack.

"Eli called the doctor. We're going to the drugstore," she whispered. "How is she?"

"Still sleeping," Nick said. He acknowledged Eli. "Hey."

"I'm sorry she's not feeling well," Eli said. "I had Tim Boyd call in the prescriptions."

"We'll run and get them and be back in less than an hour, " Claire said. "Can we bring you anything? Something to eat? Pizza?"

"Pizza would be great. Thanks," Nick said wanly. "Appreciate it." But when he closed the door to the room he felt beads of perspiration form on his forehead. Maybe he'd told her too much, he thought. Why did she have to tell her husband about the eye drops? What else did she tell him? Now too many damn people knew his business. She said she'd keep his confidence. Lousy shrink. He should've just left the day before. He was so tired. So damn tired and bone weary. His heart began pounding and his hands shook. He went over to the briefcase and lifted up the blueprints that lined the top tier. Stacks of small bills lay underneath in rubber bands. He neatened the piles, locked the case, and placed it by the side of the bed.

He looked down at Kayla and pulled away the covers. "Time to go, Kayla," he said.

"No, Daddy, please. No.

"It's time, Kayla." Twenty minutes to Meadville, he thought to himself. Say another twenty between the drugstore and the pizza place. Another twenty home. An hour. He had an hour, but he could do everything in less. As always, their bags were packed.

"Let's go, Kayla," he said, pulling her arm. "Now. Shower and the special shampoo."

He needed to color her hair again. The roots were coming in.

Chapter 12

"He opened the door like it was Prohibition," Eli said as they drove to the Drugmart.

"Oh, come on. Kayla was sleeping. He didn't want to disturb her."

"Are you going to tell me what's going on?"

"It's a long story. I told you, I'll tell you over dinner. Over a glass of wine."

"Not even a clue?"

She inhaled. "He talked to me today. As a patient."

"As a patient? For God's sake, Claire . . ."

"He wanted the confidentiality. He felt that engaging my services would ensure that."

"Where were you?"

"In the office."

"Just the two of you?"

"Kayla was there. She was sleeping on the couch in the waiting room."

"And you didn't find that strange?"

"Find what strange?"

"That he wanted to confide in you."

"A little, I guess. But given the story he told me, no. Not in retrospect. He talked to me like any other patient. You know, people hear you're a psychologist and they want to unload."

"Are you going to tell me what he said?" Eli asked, his eyes straight ahead on the road.

"Yes. Don't I always? Pillow talk, right?"

"So?"

"So, it's a little complicated," she said. "Look, there's a spot over there by Gino's."

"I don't know. The guy just bugs me. I don't like him. I don't trust him. He thinks too much before he speaks."

"Why don't you run into Gino's and get the pizza? I'll meet you back at the truck."

"Problems?" Eli asked as Claire came from the Drugmart nearly fifteen minutes later.

"Not really. Long line, that's all. I'm sorry. As soon as I get this to her we'll head right up to Pete's." She looked at her watch. "It's nearly seven-thirty. We'll eat fashionably late, that's all."

"What's with the chocolate?"

"She likes it."

"But you're not getting involved here," he said, putting his arm around her and holding her to him. "You are hopeless, Claire. Totally hopeless."

"His car isn't here," Eli said as he drove the truck into the inn.

"What?"

"Nick's car. They must have gone out."

"Oh, no, he left it down the hill by the barn."

"See what I mean? I'm missing things. How come I didn't notice his car was gone when I was home before?"

"Because you weren't looking for it before, silly. Eli, *stop*. You can't keep questioning every little thing so much. Look, I'm going to take this upstairs and I'll be right back, okay?" She leaned over the console and kissed him.

"So how come he didn't drive it back up?"

She looked exasperated. "I don't really know. He was carrying her. I guess it just made more sense to walk. Would you stop now? Please?"

She was certain she had left the outside lights on when she left. The inn was dark. She flicked on the overhead porch light and opened the door. The chandelier in the lobby was bright enough to light the entryway. She raced up the steps to the second landing and stopped at room eight. She heard the television through the door. She knocked softly. "Nick? Nick? It's Claire. Are you awake?" She waited and knocked again, louder this time. "Nick? It's me. Open up."

She tried the doorknob, left the small white bag on top of the box of pizza outside the door, went back down the stairs, picked up the lobby phone, and called room eight. No answer. Could they both be sleeping that soundly? What if something happened to Kayla and he had taken her to the hospital? She should have given him her cell phone number, she thought as she walked through the veranda to the kitchen and turned on the lights over the back lot. The Taurus was gone. She ran around to the front of the inn. Eli was listening to the radio, head tilted back, eyes closed. She threw open the door of the truck.

"They're gone," she said, her eyes wide.

"What?"

"Their car is gone."

"Maybe they went to dinner, Claire. Maybe she was feeling better."

"That's impossible. She was too sick. Her eyes were all swollen. I want to check the room."

"What the hell is going on, Claire?"

"I'm not sure," she said, trembling. "I heard the television. Just please get the key. I want to go inside. Please"

"Claire, why . . ."

"Just do it, Eli, please," she said. "Please."

Eli took the key from the locked cabinet behind the front desk and followed behind Claire as she bounded up the steps. Claire's mouth parched as Eli put the key into the door and slowly pushed it open. The room was dark save the light thrown from the television. Eli turned on the overhead light. The suitcase stands were empty. A pile of seashells was scattered on the rug. The closet was open and empty. Claire stood frozen in the middle of the room, staring at the turned-down bed where Kayla had slept.

"I don't understand," she murmured.

Eli walked into the bathroom and flicked on the light. An amber bottle sat on the edge of the tub dripping a purple liquid down the tub's walls.

"Claire?" he called to her, picking up the bottle. "Come here."

"What?"

"What is this stuff?

She took the bottle from her husband's hand. "Hair dye." Her face paled and she clasped her fingers to her mouth. "Oh my God," she said shutting her eyes. "I think I made a terrible mistake."

"Talk to me," Eli said as he poured them each a drink at the veranda bar.

"You must be starving," she said.

"Never mind that. Speak."

"I think he took her."

"Took her where?"

"*Took* her," she said emphatically. "Kidnapped her."

"Kidnapped her? You mean he's not her father?"

"No, no. I'm sure he's her father, but I think he's taken her."

"But he's her father."

"It doesn't matter. Would you ever take Jonah and Natalie from me?"

"Of course not."

She took a deep breath. "Nick and his wife are getting divorced. He's afraid he'll lose custody. He said his wife filed bogus charges against him for battery and he's afraid the court will award Kayla's sole custody to her mother. Phoebe, that's his wife, even had a restraining order against him at one point."

"Restraining order?"

"He hit her. But he said it was self-defense."

"Claire, how could you . . ."

"I can beat myself up alone, thank you," she said. She inhaled deeply. "The hair dye. I think he changed the color of her hair."

"But why run now? Why not at least wait to get her meds?"

"I don't know," she said, taking a sip of her drink. "He said that Phoebe was negligent when it came to Kayla. That she didn't even want her. That she'd enrolled her in a boarding school for blind children up in Maine."

"Look, he must have a lawyer. Why doesn't he just go to the courts? There must have been witnesses— family, friends—who could have attested to his capability as a father. Why take her and run? None of it makes any sense."

"But what if he was telling me the truth and he's on the run because he's truly protecting her? What if he's the rare case?"

"What do you mean the rare case?"

"What if Phoebe is as awful as he says? You said yourself that it was strange that Kayla never mentioned her mother. Maybe she's afraid of her."

"This still doesn't explain why he just leaves here. No note? No explanation? Packs up lock, stock, and barrel and runs when the kid's in pain? You're not thinking clearly."

"I don't know what to think. What to believe."

"Claire, listen to me. He tells you this story. You get her the meds. You come back and he's packed up and he's gone. Why's he running? What's he running from? And why wouldn't he wait for the meds if she's in such pain? This is one desperate man, don't you think?"

"But why? What happened?" she asked, frustrated.

"He wouldn't even open the door to the room when we came to talk to him, Claire."

"If he had been just anyone coming to talk to me today I would have said he appeared paranoid. He wouldn't let me take notes. Wouldn't let me tape record. He was irascible."

"What stopped you from going with your gut?"

"My gut kept going back and forth. On one hand I believed him. On the other, he made me feel uneasy. He was rather volatile but I just attributed his agitation to nerves. I mean, he was dealing with a sick child." She raised her eyes to Eli. "Why did he run? What could have happened?"

"People run when they're scared. Like animals."

She shook her head. "Maybe the fact that you knew about Kayla's condition. Maybe he felt I breached his confidence somehow."

"What difference would it make if I knew? At least not if he was telling the truth. That doesn't make any sense. Why would a parent take a child from the other parent, from their spouse? Never mind the rare case— in the usual case."

"Control," she said assuredly. "Punishment to the spouse."

"And what happens to the child?"

"It's horrible. They're frightened. Disoriented. In some ways it's like brainwashing. They trust the abductor because that's all they have. They have to believe in him."

"Okay, so given all that, what made *you* believe him when he spoke to you today? Why have you believed in this guy from the moment he walked in the door?"

"I had no reason not to. What are you getting at? Just because you didn't like him. Just because you thought he was 'off.' "

"Never mind what I thought. Why were you so drawn to him?"

"What difference does it make now?" she cried angrily. "I don't need you to play shrink with me, Eli. And I wasn't drawn to him. I was drawn to *them*. The *two* of them. To the child."

"Claire," he said patiently. "You told me today that we're all only human. Listen to me. I made an assumption based on the horse's history rather than looking for something else this time. You're doing the same thing."

"No, I'm not."

"You are," he said taking her hands in his. "I told you when he first got here, Claire. I knew what you were thinking. You looked at him and you saw Jack and yourself and the phantom of a mother who wanted to abandon her child. You made a judgment based on your own history."

Claire's eyes became distant and looked away from Eli. "We had pictures of Sulie on the mantel when I was a little girl. For a few years she sent postcards and she called on my birthday sometimes. And I remember feeling guilty because I just wanted her to go away altogether. I remember Jack coming with me when I bought my wedding gown and how all the other girls at the shop were with their mothers." Her eyes brimmed with tears. "He was the sweetest man, Eli." She laughed. "He was so hapless standing there. Every dress I put on he said was the one. But I wondered what it would have been like if I had been there with a woman . . . with my mother." Tears ran down her cheeks now though she hardly noticed. "What kind of monster was my mother? How desperate a human being was she?"

"I don't know, Claire. I wish I had an answer for you."

"I mean, once you have the baby—how do you just

leave her? I could barely leave Nat at school last month. And every time Jonah comes home and goes back, I feel like a part of me disappears for a moment. So, explain to me how she . . ." She wiped her damp cheekbones with the back of her hand. "How do I know that Phoebe isn't the same kind of mother as Sulie? How do I know that Nick isn't that child's only salvation? All I know is that they're gone and Kayla is in pain." She stood and walked to the window overlooking the empty back lot.

"What do you want to do?"

She turned and drew her shoulders straight. "Call Sam," she said in no uncertain terms.

She shut her eyes. "Call Sam before it's too late and they get farther away."

Chapter 13

⌒

Kayla was sleeping fitfully when Nick awakened her in the soft white bed at the inn. She dreamed that she was flying. Soaring to the sky, pursing her lips together as tightly as she could, propelling herself into the heavens, heading for the moon. There were astronauts in white garb who floated with her among the stars and then she landed in the belly of a dinosaur. She knocked on the walls of his belly and cried out, listening to the hushed voices talking on the outside who might help her. But no one heard her. No one could help her escape the belly of the beast. She'd tried to dream about Mommy and Grandma and beaches. She thought about the day that now seemed so long ago when the wind blew her long hair around her face as she and Grandma dug the deep hole in the cool wet sand on that hot overcast day and Grandma taught her to make drip castles and the mud slipped through her fingers like chocolate pudding. And all the while she was sleeping, she felt the pain in her eyes but the dreams made her feel better. She felt her father shaking her shoulder, gently at first, then rougher and when she opened her eyes to the familiar darkness, she felt the swelling around her lids, the sharp stabbing pain that had faded in her dreams but now was all too real. We have to get going, he said in that voice she knew too well was etched with urgency. *Get going.* How many times before had he used that same expression when she was in the middle of a meal or had just settled into a bed in a motel room where there was a pillow for her head and a toilet that didn't smell like men's rooms at those highway stops? She didn't know how long she'd been sleeping. She didn't know whether it was morning or night. She let go a cry of protest as he pulled away her covers. But he placed his fingers over her lips. "It's time, Kayla," he hissed. And she knew that meant it was time to go before someone would find them and take her away. She knew better than to ask why they had to leave. He would only say he had his reasons. Claire had told her about the small school where her own children had gone and about the horses in the stables down the road that smelled like hay and apples. They were going to go there tomorrow. Claire said so. She would miss the inn, where the air smelled like pine and vanilla and salt and she could sit on the veranda and feel the warmth of the sun on her back, but it didn't hurt her eyes. Somehow she thought there would be a miracle and they would stay in Drifting forever.

"I don't want to go," she murmured under her father's fingertips.

"You have to get up, Kayla. We need to wash your hair first," Nick said. "Get you all fixed up."

He was going to use that yucky shampoo again. The one that smelled so strong it made her nose run. It smelled like the stuff they used in the bathrooms at school. Ammonia. That was it. But Daddy told her it would make her hair clean and she wouldn't get the head lice. That's when they first used it. Where were they? Some hot town where people kept talking about a dust bowl and her head was itchy and Daddy said there was a special shampoo to cure the itch. She heard the shaking of the bottle. She counted the steps to the bathroom and sat obediently on the edge of the tub, a towel draped over her shoulders while Daddy poured the mixture onto her head. And she waited while the shampoo set in and did its work. The strong smell burned her eyes that hurt so much anyway but there was no point in saying anything again.

She heard her father packing up as she sat with the shampoo in her hair. The clicking of the latches on their suitcases. The rattling of the coat hangers in the closet. She didn't dare say a word. He said to be quiet. When she was sleeping, she thought she heard Eli's voice and then Claire's and something about going to the drugstore and coming back soon. Maybe they would come back in time with the drops and then her eyes would stop hurting and they could all say good-bye. And for a fleeting moment she let herself wonder what would happen if she asked Claire if they could stay. If Claire would promise to take them in and not ever tell anyone where they were.

When Daddy picked her up to get the shampoo out of her hair and stand her in the shower, his hands were damp and cold. The back of his neck was wet and his hair was damp. He smelled funny like Grandma's

basement or the way Uncle Frank smelled when he
came back from a tennis game. Maybe Daddy had a
fever. Maybe that was it. Maybe Daddy didn't feel well
either. The warm water ran down her back as she
tipped her head backwards. She didn't see the pools of
purple running down the sides of the tub. She didn't
see as her father toweled dry the short strands of now
dark brown hair.

Nick dressed Kayla in blue jeans and a black
pullover sweater and her new red sneakers. He made
her sit still on the bed while he carried the bags down
to the car and placed them in the trunk. He came back
to the room, took her handily in one arm, the briefcase
slung over the other. He drove without headlights
down the narrow winding road that led from the inn
to the highway. She sat still as she could in the backseat of the car, holding her bear tightly to her chest.
She tried not to touch her eyes and tried to force herself to sleep again but the pain was nearly unbearable.
They weren't but a half hour from Drifting when she
began to sob.

"Where are we going?" she asked, trying to muffle
her sobs.

"Just going," Nick said, his eyes fixed on the highway.

"Why? Why did we have to leave? Can't we wait for
Claire?"

"It was time, Kayla. I told you. It was time."

"Please, Daddy," she wailed. "Why can't we just go
back to Drifting? Why? Claire said she'd get my drops.
Maybe she has them now. Why can't we just get them
and then leave? Please, Daddy."

"I've taken care of you all these months, haven't I? Have you been cold or hungry or sick?"

Her sobs quieted and she shook her head. "No," she whimpered. "No."

"Then you keep quiet, Kayla, until I figure out just what we're going to do. You don't want to go away to that school, do you? You don't want Mommy to take my money and for me to go to jail, do you?"

"No, Daddy," she said in a whisper. "No."

A small bell went off on the dashboard. The tank was nearly empty. Nick looked at the clock. Claire had surely gotten back by now. She'd probably knocked on the door and noticed his car was gone by now. She had no business telling Eli anything. Eli didn't like him, that he knew. He was certain they'd had an argument about him that morning. He could tell from the way Eli looked at him when the coffeepot was dry and he was reading Eli's newspaper and the look on Claire's face when she came back after seeing him off. She shouldn't have told Eli their business. He confided in her and she betrayed him, he thought bitterly. He turned on the news radio. Some local traffic report and weather saying a fog was coming in that night with rain showers expected around midnight. He could drive another four hours or so, maybe get another two hundred miles under their belt. Cape Cod. It was desolate there this time of year. A good place to hide. But first he needed to fill the tank.

A small sign on the two-lane highway said there was gas and lodging at the next exit half a mile away. He saw yellow lights and a flickering neon sign from a small motel off the exit ramp and a Shell station across the road from that. He was about to make the turn into the Shell station when he noticed an old burgundy Pontiac Bonneville with a FOR SALE sign in the window parked next to the curb by the gas station. He didn't turn in. He drove about a quarter mile down the road and pulled into the darkened parking lot of a boarded-up Chinese restaurant.

"Wait here," he instructed Kayla. "Duck down in the seat and don't get out of the car."

"Where are you going?" she asked, trying to control her fear.

"I'll be right back," he said, trying to soften the edge in his voice. "I'm going to get us something to drink. There's a little deli here. I'll lock the doors." He opened his briefcase and took out two rubber-banded packets of bills, stuffed them into the pocket of his jacket, and tucked the briefcase under his jacket on the front seat.

She slid down obediently, the bear held tightly. She'd been through this sort of thing many times before. But when he opened the car door and she sniffed the air, she didn't breathe any deli smells.

Nick crossed the narrow two-lane road and walked into the Shell station. A boy, around eighteen, sat inside the small shop watching an old sitcom on an overhead television.

"I'm staying at the motel over there," Nick said affably. "I see you have a car for sale."

"Yes, sir," the boy said, jumping up. "Fifty thousand miles but it runs good. My brother gave it to me but I got my eye on something else."

"What are you asking?"

"Seven hundred," the boy said. "But I'm open to offers."

"How about if I give you eight hundred and you give me the keys?"

"But you gotta transfer title and stuff, sir. I can't do it that way. No way, sir. That's not legal. My brother told me I gotta scrape off the sticker and turn in the plates. I gotta go to Motor Vehicle and—"

"Listen, my kid's back at the motel and it's his birthday," Nick said sympathetically. "Eighteen years old today. About your age, I bet. I sell insurance and he's learning the ropes a bit. Traveling with me this week. We've been looking at used cars all day and I pulled into that motel over here tonight and saw this little gem. I really want to surprise him. How about I give you eight fifty, cash, and promise I'll come in tomorrow first thing in the morning and we take care of all the odds and ends? Just let me drive it over there tonight and give him a surprise before his birthday ends at midnight. What do you say?"

"I can't do that, sir. It ain't legal."

"Oh, come on, son. We can take care of all the legalities in the morning. Now, there's nothing illegal about driving a car across the street now, is there?"

The boy looked around him. "What time can you be here in the morning?"

"What time do you open?"

"Seven."

"Seven sharp. You have my word."

"I ain't even vacuumed it out or nothin'," the boy said. "It's got a full tank, though."

"Well, we hardly need a full tank for the distance I'm going," Nick said with a hearty laugh.

"I keep her nice and gassed up for folks who want test drives, you know? Oil and tires are good, too. But

I was going to wash and vacuum her for the buyer. Detail it, you know? It's a little smoky."

"Well, we can do that first thing in the morning. Come on, what do you say? I'm staying right over there. Come on, buddy, you know where to find me. And say, any good places to eat around here? My kid's starving. By the way, what's your name, son?"

"Muldoon. Tommy Muldoon."

"Nick Preston," Nick said, extending his hand. "Now you have my name and my word."

And with that Nick extracted eight one-hundred-dollar bills and one fifty and counted them out to the boy who handed over the keys. Nick drove the car into the parking lot of Benson's Motel while the boy watched. He pulled into a spot, shut off the engine, got out of the car, and held the keys up with a grin on his face as he waved to the boy. He walked toward the lobby door of the motel and watched while the boy turned and went back inside the small shop at the station. Then he walked back to the Pontiac, started the engine, and with headlights out, drove down the street to the empty parking lot where Kayla slept once again in the backseat. He transferred the luggage to the trunk of the Pontiac and picked up Kayla, who never stirred.

They were forty miles down the interstate, heading west, when Kayla awakened. Slowly at first in familiar darkness her hands felt the cool vinyl of the seat rather than the plush of the Taurus. The stench of stale cigarette smoke and beer filled her senses. She felt around the seat and on the floor of the car for the bear. "Bear!" she sobbed. "Please, Daddy. Where is he? Where's our car? You left him in the car." Her cries became more frantic as her father's voice became distant and his words cold and empty. Going back to get the bear, he said, would be more trouble than either she or the bear were worth.

Chapter 14

Sam and Annie Merrill were having dinner at the station house when the call came through from Eli.

"See? I told you," Sam said, reaching for the phone. "The moment I put that lasagna in my mouth there's a call." He swallowed and cleared his throat. "Drifting Police. Chief Merrill."

"Hey, Sam, it's Eli. You busy?"

"Busy? This time of year? Annie and I were just having supper. What's up?"

"Our guests, you know, Nick Pierce and his daughter. They seemed to have left rather precipitously."

"Skipped out on the bill?"

"No, they paid the bill. Paid cash in advance actually. No, it's a little more complicated than that. I think you might want to come over here, Sam."

"What's going on, Eli?" Sam leaned forward in his chair and pushed his plate to the side.

"We don't know exactly, but let me ask you this. The

day you came over here, that first day when Kayla was missing . . . did you run the guy's plate?"

"No, I didn't," Sam said uneasily. "There was no reason. Kid came back. Things were fine. We're not supposed to run plates unless there's cause. I didn't see cause."

"Did you write it down?"

"Sure, I wrote it down." Sam reached into his desk drawer and pulled out the small brown notebook. He flipped back a few pages. "Got it right here."

"I think you might want to run it."

"Jesus Christ, Eli. You want to tell me why I'm running this plate?"

"Claire has reason to think the guy took the child, Sam."

"What?"

"He spoke to her today and there was some talk about custody battles and such. Anyway, it's a long story and I can tell you later but let me just tell you that the child is sick and we'd gone to get her medication. We came back and they were gone. Packed up. Except we found a bottle of hair dye on the bathroom floor."

Sam felt his blood run cold. "Shit. I'll run the plate. Hang on."

Sam swiveled his chair around to face the computer.

"What's going on?" Annie asked, coming up behind him. "What happened?"

"Hang on just a second," Sam said, reading the numbers aloud from his notebook as he punched them into the computer. "I'll be damned."

"What is it?"

"The car was rented to a Nicholas Preston out of a place called PDQ Leasing in Long Island, New York.

There's a warning here that the car was reported stolen on March twenty-first. He's had it for six months."

"Preston? This guy's name is Pierce."

"Well, I tell you what. They got the guy as Preston and I think we've got a problem here. Starting with larceny," Sam said. "I'll be right there. Hey, Eli, you and Claire don't touch anything else in that room, okay?"

"Do you want to tell me what's going on?" Annie asked as Sam stood and strapped on his rig, slipping his Glock semiautomatic pistol into the holster. "Sam! What on earth are you doing?"

"You know the guy with the little blind girl who's staying at the inn? Well, it looks like he may just be a kidnapper."

Annie froze. "A kidnapper? No. . . . "

Sam opened the dented, gunmetal gray, locked steel cabinet. He fumbled with the keys for the padlock. When was the last time he pulled out the evidence kit, the gloves, the plastic bags, the paper satchels? At least seven years. It was long before his promotion when those high school kids drove up from Boston and one of them overdosed at that trailer park on Route 9.

"What is all that stuff?" Annie asked. "Sam, what are you doing? Maybe you ought to call Kent."

"Kent's minding the bridge where the cable guys are working," Sam said.

"What about Nelson?"

"Away with the family this week. It's okay, Annie."

"I'm going with you," she said, covering the remains of the lasagna with tinfoil.

"You going to protect me?" he asked with a twinkle in his eye.

Annie sniffed. "I told Claire that little girl looked like a boy."

Sam led the way up to room eight with Eli, Annie, Claire, and Stella trailing behind him. "You've all got to wait outside the room," Sam said gravely. "This is a crime scene." Sam pulled on clear rubber gloves, inserted the key into the door, turned the knob, barely touching it and opening the door slowly with his foot. He looked around the wall with his flashlight and threw the overhead switch. He opened the closet and shone a flashlight into the corners and onto the shelves. He opened each bureau drawer, kneeled down and looked under the beds and behind the curtains. He walked into the bathroom and saw the bottle of dye sitting on the edge of the sink. He extracted an old Polaroid camera from a canvas bag that hung at his side and photographed the bottle and the bathroom.

"Hey, Eli," he called as he walked to the door, holding the bottle gingerly by the grooved top. "Is this it? Where did you say it was?"

"That's it. It was on the side of the tub," Eli said. "You can see where more or less because the dye dripped down the tub walls."

"Damn, I wish you hadn't picked it up," Sam said, dropping the bottle into a small plastic bag which he secured with red tape. A plastic bag was wedged between the toilet and the tub. He picked it up with a gloved hand and tipped the bag over as he read the labels on the bottles inside.

"What the hell . . ." he said. "We got Timoptic from a pharmacy in San Anselmo, California, dated January 2002. Atropine from Cherry's Drugs in Queens from

March 2002. A Pred Forte from a Lyle's Drug in Santa Fe from May 2002. More Pred Forte and Atropine from a Clark Chemist in Dallas dated July 2002. We got them made out to a Kayla Powell, Kayla Preston, and Kayla Peterson." He turned to Eli. "What is this stuff?"

"Eye drops. I don't know too much about them. Some are steroids," Eli said, his jaw set. "Why do you suppose he dumped it out now?"

"I don't think he dumped it. I think he dropped it."

"How's that?" Eli asked.

"He's been saving these empties. It's a trail otherwise," Sam said.

Claire was shaking. Annie moved next to her and slipped her arm through the crook of Claire's elbow. "What does that mean?" Claire asked although she knew the answer.

"Looks like they've been all across the country since at least January," Sam said. "What are these for? What sort of condition?"

"She has juvenile glaucoma," Claire said haltingly. "Those are the same prescriptions we picked up for her this evening. Tim Boyd called them in for us." She shook her head. "She needs them desperately. She was in such pain all day long."

Sam took out the small brush and powder from the evidence kit. He dusted the mirror and the doorknobs. He took the pillowcases from both beds and dropped them into a large brown paper bag which he sealed again with the red tape. Picked up each seashell by the edge and placed them in another taped bag.

"What now?" Eli asked.

"Now we go back to the station and run the NCIC," Sam said.

"What's that?" Claire asked.

"National Crime Information Center," Sam said.

"And then?" Claire asked.

"And then we see what it has to say about our friend Nicholas whatever-the-hell-his-real-name-is," Sam said somberly. "And hope he's kind enough to make another mistake so we can get him."

Claire leaned her head on Eli's shoulder as they followed behind Sam back to headquarters. They drove in silence, Eli gripping her hand tightly on top of his thigh.

Sam hung his jacket on the hook behind the door and sat down behind the computer. It seemed as though it took forever for the machine to boot. He punched in numbers and letters and then names. Nicholas Pierce. Preston. Petersen. Powell. "No hit," Sam said.

"What do you mean no hit?" Eli asked.

"Nothing's coming up. None of these are his real name," Sam said. "He's obviously got phony ID. Phony license. I'm stumped. Son of a bitch. I should probably call the FBI." He looked at the wall clock. "Nine o'clock. I'm not going to get a soul in there until morning."

"What will the FBI do?" Claire asked.

Sam raised his eyebrows. "I don't really know but maybe they have something on him if he's an abductor. Interstate flight or something like that. To tell you the truth, I never dealt with anything like this before."

"Is that a regular computer?" Claire asked, pointing across the room.

"Yup," Sam answered absentmindedly.

"Can I use it?" Claire asked.

"Yeah, but this NCIC here is the one that runs warrants. If this one isn't helping you can be sure that one's not going to get you a thing."

"There's a Web site for missing kids I want to try," Claire said calmly.

Eli stood behind his wife, his hands resting on her shoulders while Annie and Sam stood on either side of him.

"How do you know about this?" Annie asked.

"DSS," Claire said. "We all check on occasion just to be sure we haven't seen a kid who may not be with the custodial parent. Ironic, huh?"

"Did that ever happen? I mean did you ever find a kid who was missing?"

"Not yet," Claire said, booting up the computer.

She punched in missingkids.com and came up with the Web site for the National Center for Missing and Exploited Children.

"See, you can punch in certain vital statistics and then hopefully get a match with one of the posters. You know those ADVO cards you get in the mail? You know where one side of it says you get a discount on carpet cleaner and the other side is a picture of a missing child? Well, this is the place they come from," Claire explained, clicking on the link. "I just wish we knew her real name. Damn, Sam, this thing is slow."

She filled in the empty fields: first name, age, height, weight, color of hair, eye color. Under type of abduction, she chose family and added endangered missing.

"Why endangered missing?" Annie asked.

"Because she's blind," Claire said softly as she pushed enter and waited for the next phase. "Oh my God."

Two photographs appeared before her on the screen.

There was Nicholas whose last name was Parsons next to a photograph of daughter Kayla. The photograph of Nicholas was a fair likeness. Kayla, although recognizable, looked entirely different: Long auburn hair, tucked behind her ears dotted with small diamond stud earrings, flowed past her shoulders. Her face was full. Her cheeks rosy. She wore a pink blouse with puffed sleeves. Claire read aloud.

Kayla may be in the company of her noncustodial father. She is visually impaired and may be in need of medical attention. Kayla was last seen in San Anselmo, California. She has waist-length auburn hair, however it is believed the hair color has since been changed. A warrant for unlawful flight to avoid prosecution has been issued for the abductor.

The city of report was San Anselmo. The child had been missing since February 26, 2002.

"Now what?" Claire asked, turning to Sam.

"Now I call the FBI. But first I'm putting out an APB for the area. Connecticut, Massachusetts, and Rhode Island."

"And then?" Claire asked.

"Then we pray for something just short of a miracle," Sam said. "And like I said before, we hope Mr. Parsons makes another mistake."

Chapter 15

⌒

Nicholas believed the highway led directly to hell. He turned on the radio and rolled down his window hoping the rush of cool night air would drown out Kayla's low muffled sobs from the back of the Pontiac. His breathing became increasingly rapid; he perspired profusely and ached with nausea although part of him felt he wasn't there. Detached from the space around him. He'd had the same feeling the day he left Santa Fe. The hot sun pulsated through the windshield as he drove down the empty stretch of New Mexico highway that led nowhere. Santa Fe. That widow, Merle Weaver. A plain name for an even plainer woman. She took them into her home and for seventy-two hours he felt a sense of peace. And then just like in Drifting, the chaos set in again.

Merle had seen them at the flea market and taken a shine to Kayla as she felt the woven shawls Merle had displayed in her booth. She passed the time talking to

Nick as he sipped a black coffee and broke off pieces of a stale danish while Kayla listened to a puppet show. He didn't quite know how it happened that he told her his wife had been killed by a hit-and-run driver on a suburban road in Charlotte. She'd been walking the dog, he said with tears in his eyes, when an SUV barreled through what up to then had been the quietest of neighborhoods and taken his beloved that night along with the chocolate Lab, the guide dog they were training for Kayla. He was homeschooling Kayla, he explained, picking up where his wife, Penelope, had left off. Being on the road was not a problem—especially for a man like himself who made a living as a writer. The more new scenery, the more new ideas, he explained as her eyes sparkled, and besides he could no longer stay in Charlotte. It was simply a graveyard for him. The story gathered moss as he unraveled the tale and watched the widow's eyes become wider and then fill with tears. As a matter of fact, he nearly believed the story himself.

Merle was around sixty. She had no children, although she talked his ear off about all her nieces and nephews and he smiled like he was so interested but he just wanted her to stop talking and his jaw ached. Her husband, a long distance trucker, had died just six months before. She wove shawls and sold them at the flea market on weekends but otherwise she was alone in her big house in the desert tending her flowers. Her husband built a hothouse for their thirty-fifth anniversary where she forced orchids and tea roses that otherwise would have been scorched by the southwestern sun. One thing led to another and they left the flea market together, he following her in the Taurus, and for the next two, perhaps three days, life was idyllic. She'd even been kind enough to have her doctor friend call in the prescription for Kayla's drops since he explained that her opthalmologist was on vacation and the covering doctor simply wasn't returning his calls. Everything was fine until he made the mistake of saying his wife had been killed on a winding road in Marietta where they lived when at first he'd said Charlotte. He corrected himself within moments and blamed the error on mental confusion due to grief coupled with the wine they'd had at dinner. That was the night he swore he'd stop drinking. She didn't treat him as kindly as she had the day before. He heard her speaking on the phone shortly after his gaffe and when she emerged he was certain he saw a look in her eye that was no longer trusting. She asked why his car had New York plates and when he said it had belonged to his uncle he knew she didn't believe him. In the middle of that night while she was sleeping, he took the suitcases he had been wise enough not to unpack, loaded the car, and headed for the highway.

It was Eli who drove him from Drifting. Claire was simpler, an even easier target than the widow. It was pure serendipity that Claire had been raised by her father and saw nothing but herself as she looked at him with his child. Of course, he didn't know that at first. At first it was just the perfect stop, a country inn with an empty lot perched on a bluff in that tiny town. But Nick knew the moment Eli shook his hand that he would be less trusting. Men know these things, he thought to himself. Men sniff around each other like dogs. Had she just left things alone and kept her mouth shut they might have stayed there a few more days, and he would be in that warm bed now in that room scented with salt air and the sweet smell of lavender.

He was just beginning to feel the effects of the night air on his face when he was jolted by another scream. Not just the slow and steady sob that he had learned to ignore but a shattering soprano that caused him to swerve the car violently. He crossed the double yellow line, turning the wheel just in time as a car headed in the opposite direction leaned on the horn and careened away, both managing to avoid each other on the dark highway lit only by a thumbnail moon.

"My eyes," Kayla wailed. "You have to help me. Daddy, please. Please."

He reached behind him in temper, swatting at her but unable to reach. "Quiet! Quiet *now*! Quit rubbing them!"

"Please," she sobbed. "Help me. Please."

Flashing red lights reflected on the dashboard; the unmistakable slow steady beep of what would be a siren had it come full force. But it came closer. His heart pounded and his hands slipped on the worn slick steering wheel as he pulled onto the shoulder. The Bonneville would never outrun a police car. He had no choice.

"It's the police, Kayla," he said through his teeth. "Are you happy now? You know what can happen. Be quiet now, Kayla."

She wiped her face with the arm of her shirt and feigned sleep, biting down so hard on the inside of her lip that she tasted blood.

The police officer approached the car and shone a flashlight into the backseat.

"You crossed the double yellow, sir," he said. "License and registration."

"I'm sorry, officer," Nick said as he reached for his wallet then into the glove box praying the kid left the registration inside.

"Your son slept through the swerve, I see," he said. "Were you falling asleep at the wheel, sir?"

"No, not at all, officer. My son has a touch of the flu and a fever. He cried out in his sleep and it startled me."

"Texas driver's license? Rhode Island plates?"

"We're from Dallas, officer. We're heading to my mother's up in Providence. This is my nephew's jalopy. Tommy Muldoon."

"Where were you this evening?"

"At my aunt's house down in Hubbard," Nick said, breathing a sigh. "I don't know if you have kids, officer, but I'm not used to this. The wife is back in Dallas tending to our two older ones. Teenage girls, you know. Can't leave them alone if you know what I mean."

"I got five kids," the officer said, handing back the license and registration. "Look, consider this a warning, sir. Take it slow. I hope your son feels better. Have a good night now."

"Good night, officer. And thanks. You're a gentleman," Nick said formally.

Nick waited while the officer stood a bit onto the road and waved him on before getting into his car. Nick breathed a sigh of relief as he shifted into drive, adjusted his mirror in a show of good faith and gratitude, and thought perhaps this was a sign that things were finally going his way. He even remembered

Tommy's name. Maybe he wasn't losing it after all. He would drive for another two hours, he thought, at which point he would hopefully be at the tip of Cape Cod before midnight.

Tommy Muldoon arrived at the gas station on Wednesday morning at six-thirty with an Egg McMuffin and supersize Coca-Cola. The parking lot at Benson's Motel across the street was dark and seemingly empty except for Floyd Benson's rusted old beige Volvo, which had been parked in the same spot for months since Floyd came down with an attack of what everyone in town called Benson's gout. The Bonneville was probably in the back where the guest rooms lined the rear lot, Tommy thought. He waited at the service station until eight o'clock when his brother, Brian, came in to fill up.

"Hey, where's the Pontiac?" Brian asked, looking around. "You sell it?"

"Someone took it for a test ride," Tommy lied. "Listen, Bri, can you just hang here for a moment? I gotta run across the street."

"What for? I'm going to be late to work."

"I swear it'll only be ten minutes," Tommy said as he flew across the narrow road.

He ran into the back lot first where cars were parked perpendicular to the stained lime-green guest room doors. There was an SUV, an old white Buick, and a beat-up minivan with dry cleaning hung across a rod in the back. No Bonneville. He'd never been inside the dingy motel before. There was a brown folding table in the corner with an old coffeemaker and a stack of Styrofoam cups next to a worn-out sofa and a rack that held some yellowed newspapers and magazines, the pages curled at the edges. Floyd was behind the desk, his glasses perched on his nose, the sleeves of a brown corduroy shirt rolled up above his rough red elbows.

"Hey, Mr. Benson," Tommy said, out of breath. "I'm looking for this guy who's staying here with his son. A man, say, around fifty with a kid around my age."

He shook his head. "Nope" was all he said, not looking up.

"What? No, I met the guy last night. He's staying here."

"No one's here like that," he said, looking at him now, and clearly irritated.

"You sure? Can you see if maybe someone checked in last night or something?"

"Now look here, Tommy Muldoon, I left last night at seven and no one's been in this morning. If someone'd come in last night, I would know. Door's locked. They'd have to ring the bell."

"Thanks," he said, running back across the street.

"Jesus, Tommy, I'm going to be late. What's going on?"

"Listen, Bri. Don't kill me. This guy come in last night and gave me eight-fifty cash for the Bonneville. He said he'd come back this morning so we could do title transfer and all that shit and he didn't show. He said he was staying at Benson's and the car was for his son's birthday. He wanted to bring it across the street to surprise him. Well, he's not there."

"So maybe he's at breakfast or something."

"No, the guy must have lied. Mr. Benson says there's no one there with his son."

"So you're telling me that you just gave some guy the car?"

"I told you, he said the car was for his son. He said

he just wanted to show it to him. And he paid me, Bri. Look here." Tommy pulled the cash from his wallet.

"Jesus."

"I'm scared, Bri. What if the guy is gonna use the car to rob a bank or something?"

"You got to call the police, Tommy," Brian said, shaking his head. "Now. I got to get to work. You call if you need me. And let me know what happens."

"Don't tell Ma," Tommy said.

"I won't tell Ma, but get a grip, Tommy. Grow up a little, would you?"

Tommy went into the small shop and sat for a moment in the torn brown leather swivel chair behind the cash register. He grabbed a fresh bag of nacho chips from the hooks on the wall and took a root beer from the cooler. He pulled out his wallet and counted the money the man had given him the night before, looked across the street at the motel, and hoped maybe the Bonneville had come back. Tommy's father had been put away fifteen years ago for armed robbery. His mother worked as a bus driver and lunch aide at the elementary school, eking out a living to take care of her sons. He pictured his mother's face before him and shoved the money back into the wallet. Brian was working and did two years at the community college. Tommy was another story entirely. He never quite got over the day his father went to prison. He was only three and yet he remembered it like yesterday. The day they came to the house and took him away in handcuffs. He thought about those visits where he saw his father through the plate-glass window at the prison and how those metal bars slammed down behind him when he and Brian and

Mom went to visit. He picked up the phone and dialed the police.

"Sergeant Blanco," the voice answered.

"Sarge? It's me, Tommy, over at the Shell."

"Hey, Tommy. How's it going over there, buddy? What's up?"

"This guy come in last night to look at the Bonneville. He gave me eight-fifty cash and just took off."

"I'm not following you. Slow down, Tommy."

"This guy, he said he was staying at Benson's and he'd come back this morning to do title transfer and stuff. Well, the guy never showed. And I checked with Floyd Benson and the guy never even registered there."

"So you're saying he just took the car?"

"Well, he paid me and all but there's no paperwork, you know what I mean? I mean you can't do that, right? He said he'd come back so we could do it legal and all."

"Right. I'll send an officer over, Tommy."

"Am I in trouble?"

"Not you, Tommy," Sergeant Blanco said sympathetically. He'd watched Brian and Tommy grow up. He knew how hard life had been for their mother. They were good boys, although Brian seemed to bear fewer scars from his father's absence. "You're not in trouble, Tommy. You didn't do anything wrong."

Chapter 16

John Blanco sent out Joe Erickson, one of the younger cops, to see Tommy Muldoon at the gas station. Joe was only twenty-five, not much older than Tommy, and someone who he felt wouldn't be too imposing or make Tommy feel like he'd screwed up as much as he had. Besides, Joe had gotten himself in plenty of hot water as a kid and Blanco knew that.

"Why don't you tell me what happened?" Erickson asked. "Right from the beginning."

Tommy told him about Nick and pulled out the cash from his wallet. "You want this for, like, evidence or something?"

Erickson placed his hand on Tommy's arm. "Put that away for safekeeping. Why don't you give me a description of the guy?"

"White guy about five foot ten, I guess. Little taller than me," Tommy said. "Sort of salt-and-pepper hair. Fifty maybe. Give or take."

"What was he wearing?"

"I don't remember."

"Jacket? Hat?"

"I'm not sure. Maybe. No, no hat. A dark jacket maybe."

"He was alone?"

"Yeah."

"You said he drove it back over to Benson's?"

"Yeah. He said he wanted to buy the car for his kid because it was his birthday."

"And he walked into the station here? He didn't drive in?"

"No, he walked in and I thought it was weird at first but then he said he was staying across the street and all. I mean, the motel's right over there."

Erickson's radio crackled in his car. "Hang on a sec," he said. He walked over to the car and picked up the radio, listened for a moment, and came back to Tommy. "Okay, so we'll keep our eyes open. At this point, there's not much we can do."

"Am I in trouble?"

"You didn't do anything illegal, Tommy. He's the one with the stolen vehicle. You're okay. We'll keep you posted, okay? Try to relax."

"What about the money?"

"Hang on to that right now. Like I said, don't spend it. Just let it sit. Listen, maybe the guy will still show up. Maybe he had an emergency or something. Did he say why he was in town?"

"He sold insurance or something like that. Like a traveling salesman, I guess."

Erickson got back in his patrol car and finished writing in his notebook. The radio crackled again with an

APB for a dark blue Taurus with New York plates be-
longing to an alleged child abductor. Crazy, he
thought, listening halfheartedly, turning down the vol-
ume as he wrote up Tommy's report. He was driving
down the road back to headquarters when he figured
he'd check out the parking lot where that boarded-up
Chinese restaurant was becoming more and more of
an eyesore. The place was nothing but problems. Kids
used it as a meeting place and a lover's lane of sorts.
Two nights ago there had been trouble in the lot when
a group of kids from Hubbard High were caught
drinking. He drove around the back of the lot just to
make sure there wasn't garbage dumped there that
would bring an onslaught of rats like they'd had last
July. There was nothing but a blue Taurus parked in
the rear of the lot. He got out of his car and shaded his
hands over his eyes as he looked in the windows. He
heart began thumping.

"This is Erickson. I'm over at Ming's Wok on Highway 12," he said into the radio. "You want to run that
APB by me again?"

He stared at the license as Blanco read each number
and letter from the plate in front of him.

"I got that blue Taurus here at Ming's Wok," he said.
"Unoccupied."

"Sending backup," Blanco said. "Good deal, Erickson. Ten four."

"Ten four," Erickson said.

Within thirty minutes there were two state troopers
and four local police at Ming's lot on Highway 12. The
Taurus was dusted for prints, the teddy bear on the
floor of the backseat dropped unceremoniously into an
evidence bag. Tommy Muldoon saw the lights and

heard the sirens as he sat at the Shell station. He remembered when there had been all those rats back in
July, but this was an awful lot of activity for a bunch of
varmints, he thought. Someone should just rip that
place down. No one had been into the Shell for hours,
typical for a Thursday morning. Well, one couple who
needed directions and checked their tire pressure and
some guy who used the squeegee without even filling
up. This time of year most of the traffic was on weekends when people drove through town on their way to
the Cape or tooled around New England to see the fo-
liage. He shut the door of the shop, flipped the sign
around from OPEN to CLOSED and walked down the
road to Ming's. Sergeant Blanco had just pulled in.

"Hey, Sarge," Tommy said. "What's happening?"

"We're looking for someone. This guy," Blanco said,
showing him a computer printout with National Center for Missing and Exploited Children across the top.

Tommy looked at the poster and his mouth went
dry. "What'd he do?"

"He's wanted for kidnapping," Blanco said.

"Sergeant, that's the guy who took my car," Tommy
said, his eyes wide.

"You're sure?"

"I'm positive," he said, not taking his eyes from the
poster. "That's him."

"Come here, Tommy," Blanco said. He gathered the
law enforcement around him. "Looks like we have to
make a change in our APB. Seems the guy is now driving a burgundy Pontiac Bonneville with Rhode Island
plates." He placed his hand on Tommy's shoulder.
"Took it from this young man last night. What's the
plate, Tommy?"

"RCE 5398."

"Everyone got that? Rhode Island. Robert Charles Edward 5398. I'll put it over the system. Where'd that APB originate anyway?"

An older police officer spoke up, "Drifting, Connecticut."

"Drifting. How come that place sounds familiar to me?" Blanco asked.

The officer shrugged. "Dunno, Sarge."

"Who's chief over there?" Blanco asked. "That's what, about ninety miles from here?"

"Don't know, sir."

"Well, how about calling over there and letting me know."

The officer came back a few minutes later. "It's eighty-five miles from here. Sam Merrill is chief."

Blanco's face broke into a smile. "Sam Merrill. I worked with him twenty years ago back in Southport. That's why it sounded familiar. I heard he'd been promoted up there. Well, well, well. Get him on the line for me, would you?"

"Sam? John Blanco. Remember me? Yeah, long time. I'm over here in Hubbard, Rhode Island. We got your blue Taurus. Abandoned. Seems your buddy stole another car though. Here you go before the APB goes out. Burgundy Pontiac Bonneville. 1982. Plate Robert Charles Edward 5398. We'll keep you posted." He told Sam about Tommy Muldoon. "We're dusting the vehicle. Clean as a whistle except for a teddy bear in the backseat."

"We'll keep each other posted, John," Sam said. "Good to work with you again." He was about to hang up. "And, John, hang on to that bear, would you?"

"Will do, Sam," John said.

Sam called the Inn when he hung up the phone. Claire answered on the first ring.

"They found the Taurus," he said. "Looks like our friend got himself another vehicle."

Eli and Claire were drinking coffee on the veranda. Neither had slept the night before. They'd watched the sun rise over the ocean. "Where?" she asked, reaching for Eli's hand. "Where are they?"

"Hubbard, Rhode Island. Listen, Claire, does Kayla have a teddy bear?"

"Yes," she said, her voice trembling. "Oh God, why?"

"They found it in the backseat of the car."

"I don't understand," she said.

"He got another vehicle," Sam said again. "Bought it off some kid. Stole it really."

"How do you know?"

"Because he got a little sloppy and we got a little lucky. He paid some kid up there for a car and promised to come back this morning and transfer title but he never showed. The kid called the cops and the rest is history. I'll explain more later. We've got the make and plate on the car he's driving now, Claire. We're going to get this guy. I can feel it."

"But you don't know which direction he's headed."

"No, but no matter which direction he can't be too far. We'll broaden the APB and hopefully FBI will give us a callback this morning."

"You'll keep us posted, won't you, Sam?"

"You have my word."

"Tell me what's going on," Eli said when she hung up the phone.

She leaned her head against her husband's chest. "I didn't listen to Jack," she whispered.

"To Jack?"

"That first day, I saw the blister on her foot. I saw the expression on her face when she wanted to hide the cane from her father. Her jacket wouldn't close. The zipper was broken. I listened to her cry when her eyes hurt. Even Annie said she looked like a boy." She leaned her head back to look at her husband. "And you. Even you said there was something about him. . . ."

"I don't understand," Eli said. "What does any of this have to do with Jack?"

"Don't you remember what Jack used to say? He said to always watch the details of living. I didn't watch carefully enough." Her eyes filled with tears. "Maybe I just didn't *want* to see."

Chapter 17

Claire and Eli awakened before dawn on Wednesday morning after a restless night. They had stayed with Annie and Sam at headquarters until nearly midnight the night before, waiting by the phone that never rang. Claire awakened before Eli. She reached across his chest and in his sleep he took her hand in his.

"What time is it?" he murmured.

"Just before six," she said.

"Did you sleep at all?"

"A little. Not well," she said.

He pressed her hand to his mouth. "I'm not going in today."

"You're not?"

"I'm not leaving you alone."

"I'll be fine," she said.

"No, you won't be fine. And I won't be fine if you're by yourself." He reached for the phone. "Daisy? Listen, I'm sorry to call so early, but I figured you'd be up.

I'm not coming in today. Call the client list and cancel, would you? Give the emergencies to Brandon over in Meadville." He was silent for a moment. "No, everything's okay. I just have some things I need to tend to around here. I'll call you later." He rolled over and turned to Claire. "There. See? It's good to be king."

She rested her head on his chest. "Want to go down to the beach?"

"Sure," he said, stroking her hair as she lay across him. "Do you know that I love the way you look in the morning? Do you know I always want you beside me at the beginning and end of every day?"

"It scares me lately," she said.

"Scares you?" he asked, placing his hand on her bare back.

"Because I don't know what I'd do without you," she said, the words coming out in starts and stops.

"Why would you be without me?"

"It feels like too many people in my life are gone lately. Jack. The kids." She swallowed hard. "Sulie."

"Well, I tell you what," he whispered. "Wild horses couldn't take me away." He shifted her weight from his chest and placed her head against the pillow beside him, drawing his large body over hers. "I'll tell you something else, there are advantages to the kids being away at college."

"Like?"

"Like I can't remember the last time I made love to you before sunrise," he said.

The sun was still low on the horizon when they walked down the beach steps after Sam called, steaming mugs of coffee warming their hands in the cool au-

tumn air. The sky was still filled with shadows, sil-
houettes of seagulls swooped over the water like
phantoms. A small plane flew overhead as they sat
down on the seawall.

"I wonder where they're going," Claire said, gazing
upward.

"Who?"

"The people in the plane."

"When all this is over and done, I want to go to Key
West."

"Why Key West?"

"Because I read," he said, tightening his arm
around her shoulders, "that you can sit at the pier
and watch the sunset. And if you're with the one you
truly love, you'll see a flash of green as the sun sinks
in the sky."

"Is it legend or truth?"

He turned to her. "Legend probably. But I know
we'll see it, Claire. So I guess it would be truth."

"I love you, Eli. Too much," she said, sinking into him.

"Too much?" he said with a laugh.

"Too much," she said, wrapping her arms around
him and burying her face in his shoulder. She lifted her
face to his. "Was there ever a time when you wanted to
leave?"

"Leave?"

"Leave me. The kids."

"How can you even ask that?"

"Because we've been married so long I just want to
know."

"I never wanted to leave. Sometimes I wanted the
world to go away."

"What do you mean?"

"Oh, when the kids were babies and I'd come home at night and you and I were so exhausted from the day. I sometimes wished we could have each other back for just one night the way it was right in the beginning. There were times I wanted to leave but I never wanted to leave without you." He kissed the top of her head. "How about you?"

"I never wanted to leave, but sometimes I wished I could just freeze moments in time and go back and re-live them. Like the moment that you asked me to marry you and the way you asked Jack for my hand and the moment Jonah was born and you held him and just wept. I wished, I still wish, I could have those moments just once more."

He nodded and held her close to him. "That's what's so good about memories. But we're still making mem-ories, aren't we?"

"I keep thinking about Kayla's mother. All she has right now are her memories."

"You don't mistrust her anymore?" he asked tenderly.

She didn't answer right away. "I thought about it during the night. No one has the right to take a child. It's like Solomon. He knew who the mother was when he threatened to cut the baby in half. You don't kidnap your child out of love. That's just not love."

The phone was ringing in the lobby when they walked into the inn.

"Inn at Drifting," Eli answered. "Hey, Sam."

"What happened?" Claire asked, reaching for the phone.

Eli raised a splayed hand. "That's fine. Bring them over. We're here."

"What is it?" Claire asked as he hung up the phone. "Who?"

"Two FBI agents are driving up from New Haven. They're going to ask us some questions."

"Why us?"

"Routine," Eli said.

"What did Sam say? What did they tell him?"

"They broadened the scope of the APB from Maine to Florida. Entire East Coast."

"What if they drove west, though?"

Eli sighed. "I don't know. Come on, I'm going to make us some breakfast. Fuel up for the day."

"I want to call the kids."

"It's too early."

"I don't care. I need to hear their voices. I need to know they're there."

Chapter 18

In San Anselmo, Phoebe Parsons's dawn on Wednesday morning held no promise of a sunrise. She tiptoed down the hall to the kitchen in stocking feet, her shoulder-length thick auburn hair strewn about her face so that her features appeared even more delicate. Her eyes, deep-set jade fringed with dark lashes, were red-rimmed. Her narrow nose was flushed at the tip; her shapely thin lips were pale and chapped. She wore loose navy sweatpants and an oversize long-sleeved black shirt. Her face was strained and weary, making her appear far older than her thirty years. Her sister, Caroline, was visiting from Chicago. Their mother, Corinne, who came to stay with Phoebe the day after Kayla disappeared, was still sleeping. Caroline was already in the kitchen.

"I made coffee," Caroline said.

"How come you're up so early?"

"The time difference, I guess. I'm still on Chicago time. What's your excuse?"

"I don't sleep," Phoebe said, reaching for a coffee cup with a thin hand, the short nails encrusted with paint.

"Maybe we can go and get you a manicure today," Caroline urged gently.

"It's hardly worth it. They just get messed up again." She looked at her fingertips and then at her sister. "I painted a window in someone's home last week. First time since the accident. Not really a window, you know, a mock window on a wall. I still can't hold the brush very well."

"You're going to keep getting back more mobility."

Phoebe stretched out her fingers. "That's not what I need back." She looked at her sister, her eyes filling with tears. "I'm trying so hard not to give up hope. I had a bad night."

Caroline put her arm around her sister. "Listen, how about you and Mom and I take a little hike someplace? Mom loves that kind of thing."

"I don't want to. I just want to stay here by the phone."

"Phoebe, you have your beeper. Your cell phone. You can't just sit here all the time and wait."

"I did that job the other day."

"That was last week. You need some air."

"Next week will be seven months. Seven months."

"I know," Caroline said.

Phoebe's eyes glistened. "I will never give up, Caroline. Never. But I can't even go into her room anymore. I used to go in there and just sit on her bed and now I can't even stand to do that." She looked at her sister. "She took her bear that night, you know. The one you gave her for her first Christmas. He left everything of hers. Books. Clothing." She turned to Caroline, her grief turning to anger. "He left her eye drops. I keep them in that little red silk pouch on the bedpost. You know the one that Daddy kept his cuff links in? He left them. I keep thinking"—she covered her mouth with her hand, the words barely coming out—"that she's in pain. It's been seven months. Seven months."

Phoebe's recollection of the night was vague. He came to the door around ten, maybe eleven o'clock. Kayla had been sleeping for hours. He looked so forlorn, his blanched skin blending into a monochrome with his hair that had become grayer over the past several months. His sport coat was wrinkled and tattered. He hadn't looked like that when she first met him. He hadn't looked like that when she had taken care of him and been his wife.

"Just let me look at her," he pleaded as he stood in the doorway. "You can find it in your heart to do that, can't you?"

He'd never been interested in Kayla before the custody battle. She was a burden to him. The one time Phoebe insisted that he go with her and speak to the school psychologist had taken such coaxing. He never wanted that baby. He never wanted any baby. She should have left him years ago, but she always thought he might come around. She always had hope. Even that night, part of her trusted him. That night. The last time she saw her baby. Why did she let him in?

"So, you got what you wanted," he said, standing in the middle of the kitchen.

"This is not what I wanted," she whispered. "I wanted us to be a family."

He picked up a ceramic bottle of olive oil that sat on the counter. "Right," he said, setting the bottle down again hard.

"I'm sorry it ended this way."

"Sorry? You're sorry?" he asked. "You've got it all, sweet Phoebe. The house. The child support. The kid. Why the fuck are you sorry?"

"Maybe you should go, Nick," she said nervously. "I don't want to fight with you."

"Have you got a boyfriend?" he asked, slowly running his finger down the side of her face.

"No, I don't have a boyfriend," she said, turning her face. "I think you'd better leave."

"Well, I guess one day you'll have a boyfriend, won't you?"

She stepped backwards, looking at the wall phone from the corner of her eye. "Nick, please. I really think you should go."

"I told you. I want to see Kayla."

"I'll take you to her room but then you have to leave."

"You'll *take* me to her room? I still know my way around this place. I don't need you taking me anywhere. You and your fucking supervised visits like I'm some kind of criminal."

"I'm sorry, Nick. If you hadn't . . ."

"If I hadn't what?"

He grabbed her arm and twisted it behind her back, disabling her. That was the last of her memory from that night. She awakened on the cool kitchen tile, the mangled fingers of her right hand broken and bloodied. She ran to Kayla's room and saw the empty unmade bed. She ran through the house screaming

Kayla's name, flinging open closet doors, dripping blood down the carpeted hall, streaking it along the ivory walls as she steadied herself while she ran. She ran from room to room calling Kayla's name, her eyes clouding over as she tried to maintain consciousness and then, as she was passing out again from the pain and more from the disappearance of her child, she dialed 911. The next thing she remembered was the paramedic holding ammonium salts under her nose. She nearly vomited as she came to. "Not me!" she cried. "You don't understand. It's my baby," she heard herself cry. "He took my baby."

Corinne came into the kitchen. Her rich auburn hair, once the color of Phoebe's, was flecked with gray around the temples and tied back in a kerchief at the nape of her neck. "Look at you two girls. Drinking coffee and not a piece of toast or anything. Especially you, Phoebe. You're thin as a rail. You need your strength." She opened the refrigerator and took out the tray of eggs.

"No, Ma," Phoebe said. "No eggs."

"Oh, yes," her mother said, raising her eyebrows. "I should make you a nice big steak, that's what I should do. I've been here long enough without making a fuss. Now you heard what the doctor said. You're slightly anemic. You're going to eat if I have to force you."

Phoebe smiled wanly at her mother. "And how do you propose to do that? Going to make like an airplane, Ma?"

"Never you mind. And you, too, Caroline. I've had quite enough from you as well."

Caroline laughed. "What have I done? I've only been here for two days."

Corinne smiled. "You know I hate to single out."

"Oh, great. So Phoebe gains an appropriate amount of weight and I can just add to the slippery five."

"You'll do it for your sister," their mother said, cracking eggs over a frying pan. "That's what family's for. And after this we're doing something outdoorsy. We can go up to the Headlands. What's it called? The Point Bonita Trail? That's an easy hike. Not even four miles. You can't spend every waking hour surfing the Internet and sitting by the phone, Phoebe."

"But, Ma," Phoebe protested.

"No buts. I want you out in some fresh air. Gets the blood flowing," Corinne said. "Good for the soul." She looked at her daughter's crestfallen face. "And then when we get back we'll go back on that Internet. Get back to the phones." She took Phoebe's face in her palms. "Phoebe, if you're not strong you're no good to your daughter, never mind yourself. Listen to me."

Phoebe swallowed hard and nodded. "I dreamed last night that she was sick. That she was cold and sick and hungry. She was in this place and I kept calling to her and she heard me and she called to me but I couldn't get to her."

"We'll never stop looking. I promise you," Corinne said, taking her daughter in her arms. "I just want to get you outside for a few hours, sweetheart. You need to be strong for when Kayla comes home. Now, you go take a hot shower and fix yourself up a bit. Go ahead now."

By nine-thirty the three had finished breakfast, showered, and dressed in their hiking clothes. Phoebe placed her beeper on her hip and her cell phone in the small leather holster she wore on her belt. She checked the answering machine and listened to her voice.

"This is Phoebe Parsons. Please leave your message at the tone. If anyone has any information regarding my daughter, Kayla, please page me immediately at 415-555-4626 or call my cell phone at 415-555-3446. I thank you with hope."

Corinne and Caroline listened as the message broadcast from the desk in the living room.

"I swear to God on your dead father's soul," Corinne said. "If I ever see that son of a bitch again, I'll . . ."

"All we want is Kayla," Caroline said.

"I know that, Caroline. But I look at your sister and she's just wasting away."

"I see it, Ma," Caroline said in a whisper. "Tell me the truth, do you think we'll ever . . ."

"Some days I'm hopeful and other days I feel like we'll never see that baby again," Corinne said. "All I know is if I ever see that man, I'll kill him. I swear it."

Nick had pulled into Dennis, Massachusetts sometime after midnight Wednesday morning. He wondered how long the boy at the gas station would wait for him come dawn. Kayla had been sleeping for hours, sleep induced by pain that was a natural soporific. As he drove down the narrow street looking for a small motel he felt a sense of panic spread through his body from his head to his toes and back up again. He had to keep driving. This was a dead end. If he continued to drive northeast he would trap himself at the tip of the Cape. There was no interstate where he could get lost in the crowd. The town was dead. He'd stick out like a sore thumb. What had he been thinking? He had to turn around. He drove back through the town on Route 6, making sure to stay within the speed limit, holding the wheel at ten to two. He didn't dare turn on the radio for fear it might awaken Kayla. He didn't open the window. He turned west at Interstate 93 and got on the connector to Interstate 95. For sure, Cape Cod was far too claustrophobic. A trap, if nothing else. He would head to Manhattan. Talk about getting lost in the crowds. No one paid anyone any mind in that city. Besides, he'd given Manhattan as his home address. Who would ever think he'd head back to the scene of the crime as it were? That, of course, assuming that two-bit excuse for a cop Sam Merrill and his friends even thought there was a crime at this point. Dumb cop never even wrote down his plate. Not that any of that mattered. Pretty soon he would blend into the throngs on Madison Avenue. The only problem was there was only around twenty-five grand left in the briefcase. Kayla's college fund. It wouldn't take him that far in New York City. Hotels were expensive unless he stayed in some fleabag and he wasn't up for that. As if a kid like Kayla would ever go to college.

Nick was falling asleep at the wheel. He dug his fingers into his thighs. He needed coffee but didn't dare stop. His stomach was growling. Kayla was still curled up in a ball in the backseat, the seat belt slipped up around her neck. He would never make the next hour's drive into Manhattan. Besides, it wouldn't look right. It wasn't even five in the morning. He exited Interstate 95 at Playland Parkway in Rye. Playland. Must be a place filled with kids where Kayla could easily go unnoticed. The Parkway led to U.S. 1 where he made a left turn where the sign said TOWN OF HARRISON. Mario's Motel sat on the corner across from a McDonald's, a Dunkin' Donuts, and a Freight Liquidators. Perfect, he thought. Just busy enough.

He pulled into the lot and turned to awaken Kayla. "We're stopping," he said. "You have to wake up."

"Where are we?" she asked. Her eyes were red-rimmed and swollen.

"New York," he said. "Wait here. I'm going inside to check in. And no shenanigans, Kayla. I'll be right back."

He hit the small silver bell on the front desk and a pretty young girl with long dark hair came around from the back. She wasn't more than nineteen or twenty, Nick guessed. She looked like she'd been sleeping.

"Single room, please," he said.

"MasterCard or Visa?"

"Cash," Nick said, reaching for his wallet.

"I'll need your license, then."

Nick handed her the Texas driver's license. "Just hate getting saddled with those bills a month from now, you know?" Nick said.

"Well, you're far from home."

"Relocating. Looking at houses."

The girl nodded. "How many nights?"

"One. Maybe two. How much?"

"Eighty."

He handed her four twenty-dollar bills.

"Thanks," the girl said as she took a key attached to a large block of wood stenciled with ROOM 16.

"Around the back and to the right. There's parking in front of the door."

He had a feeling she was used to people like him passing through or just spending an afternoon there. She seemed to buy the relocation story. At least for now. All he needed was an overnight at the place, a few hours' sleep and he could move on. He slung the briefcase over his shoulder, took his suitcase from the trunk, and opened the door to the room. He went back to the car and looked around before carrying Kayla inside and placing her on the bed. Her face was swollen and red. Not just her eyes but her cheekbones as well.

"What is this place?" she asked.

"Motel," he said. "We're just going to stay the night."

"Why?"

He didn't answer her.

"Why?" she repeated.

"Look, I'm going across the street to get us some breakfast. I'll be twenty minutes," he said. "And quit rubbing your eyes."

"Can you get me drops?" she asked tentatively.

For a moment he felt her tug at his heartstrings. "I'll do the best I can," he said. He'd look in the yellow pages later and see if there was an eye doctor in the area. A woman, he thought to himself. Someone sympathetic. He'd come up with a story the way he always did. Right now, he couldn't think straight. She had to stop rubbing her eyes. She looked like someone had beaten her up.

Kayla heard the door to the room slam shut. Sadness overwhelmed her. She hated the new car. The motel room smelled like hard-boiled eggs and oranges and made her stomach feel queasy. She lost Bear. She never got to say good-bye to Claire, or Eli, or the lady at the candle shop. Just like she never got to say good-bye to Mommy. But Daddy's doing the best he can, she thought. Yet, for the first time in months, she was having trouble convincing herself that he really was.

Chapter 19

~

The Dunkin' Donuts was hopping at seven o'clock Wednesday morning when Patrolman Steve D'Angelo got his coffee and cheese Danish before his tour started at eight. He made certain to get there early so he could go across the street to Mario's where Gina worked the morning shift. He'd had a thing for her since he was a junior at Harrison High and she was a freshman. Now she took evening courses at a local college and he thanked his lucky stars every time he thought of the day she told him she would stay in town and not go off to school. Normally, he would have worked night shift on Wednesday but he'd flip-flopped the schedule with Patrolman Day since Day's youngest kid got an ear infection and his wife had to get to work on time.

"I missed you last night," he said, leaning over the desk to kiss her cheek.

"I had to study," she said. "And then Mario asked

me to come in early this morning because he had to get a wisdom tooth pulled."

"When did you get in?"

"Quarter to five," she said, yawning. "I'm so tired between this and school."

"I know, baby," he said, handing her a cup of coffee. "I got you a jelly doughnut, too. Pretty crowded there this morning."

"Lots of truckers. Especially on Wednesdays, for some reason," she said, sipping her coffee.

"One guy, I swear, he had a stench like you wouldn't believe. And the friggin' guy had to order an egg sandwich, which took forever," he said. "It's quiet in here. You should close your eyes for a while."

"Can't," she said, picking at the doughnut. "We already had a check-in anyway. Not ten minutes after I got here. Some guy from Texas who's relocating. Come to think of it, he had a stench, too. Maybe he was your egg-sandwich man."

Steve's radio crackled on his hip. *Attention all cars. All points bulletin for New England states and all East Coast. Be on the lookout for burgundy color Pontiac Bonneville license number Richard Charles Edward 5398. Rhode Island. Fugitive parental abduction with endangered female child. Originating agency is Drifting, Connecticut.* Steve silenced the radio. "Give me a kiss, Gina," he said. "How about tonight? You think you can forget the books for tonight?" The radio crackled again. *Car sixteen. Accident on Post and Mercer Lane. Please proceed.* "Shit, that's mine," Steve said. "You'd think people could slow down this early in the morning. So what do you say? No classes tonight, right?"

She smiled. "Pick me up around seven, okay? And be careful today."

"I'm always careful." He answered the radio call, "Car sixteen. Heading to Post and Mercer. Ten four."

He slid behind the wheel of his patrol car. He didn't see the Bonneville with the Rhode Island plates parked three spaces away or the man peering from behind the curtain, watching with relief and feeling victorious as the patrol car pulled away.

Nick said he was going to the doughnut shop across the street. As soon as he left the room, Kayla moved in the direction of the motel door. Counting. Fifteen steps. She passed her hand over the door and felt the familiar plastic card in its center that held what her father told her were instructions in case of fire. She counted the fifteen steps back to the bed and moved up to the pillow, reaching her hand to the nightstand, feeling what she guessed was a clock or radio, a phone, a lamp. She swung her legs over the left side of the bed and counted steps. Ten steps to a wall. She felt along the wall to her right and came to another door, not the same one she'd felt at first. She turned the knob and felt her way slowly as she stepped. Six steps. A door. She pulled it open and reached her hands up and felt a steel rod and thin metal hangers. She turned and counted again back to the bed and then from the starting point crossed the room. Another door. Counting. Still counting until she felt the cool tiles under her fingertips. The bathroom, she thought. It wasn't so bad. It smelled clean and fresh. Maybe this place wouldn't be so bad after all, although she missed the scent of the inn. She felt her way to the toilet, sat down and peed. Her eyes were sticky. She felt for a washcloth and then for the sink and bathed her eyes with water. She wished she had her toothbrush. Her mouth was taut and sore from sleeping. From crying. She wrung the washcloth in her hands and counted the steps back to the bed, sitting obediently in its center until her father returned. She reached behind her and took a pillow, hugging it to her. It wasn't her bear but it would have to do. She needed something to hold. But more, she needed someone to hold her. The way Claire held her that day in the car when her eyes began to ache. When was that day? Yesterday? The day before? She'd lost track of time. It was the first time since she and her father had been away that she was frightened. Truly frightened. Not just because she didn't know where they were and her eyes hurt so much, but because for the first time her father frightened her—to the point that she wondered if he would come back to that motel room at all. She heard a key turn in the door and then the door shut quietly.

"I'm back," Nick said. His voice sounded tired, she thought. "I brought you an egg sandwich and an orange juice. Here."

They must have been away from Drifting a very long time, she thought. Despite her pain, she was starving.

"I smell coffee, Daddy," she said. "What else?"

"A muffin," he answered with his mouth full.

"What's the name of this place?"

"Not sure," he muttered. "Listen, I need to rest for a while. We've been driving all night while you were sleeping. Watch TV or something, would you?"

He placed a remote control in her hand. She didn't tell him how sad he made her just then. She clicked on the television and knew from the sound of his breathing that he'd fallen fast asleep. She wished Mommy were reading her a story right now. The one about the bunny who keeps telling the mother bunny he's going to run away and the mother says she'd always find him. *The Runaway Bunny*, that was it.

"If you become a sailboat and sail away from me," said his mother, *"I will become the wind and blow you where I want you to go."*

For the first time in months, she wished Mommy could become the wind.

Chapter 20

It was nearly noon when the two FBI agents opened the glass door of the inn with Sam leading the way. Agents Susan Morse and Tim Hunt introduced themselves, flashing identification.

"Is there someplace we can talk?" Agent Morse asked.

"Out there," Claire said, pointing to the veranda. "Would you like some coffee or tea?"

Agent Morse looked at Agent Hunt, who shook his head. "Nothing, thanks," she said.

The five settled themselves around the large glass coffee table on two wicker sofas. Agent Morse pulled a flyer from her briefcase. "Are these the people who checked into the inn?"

Claire recognized the flyer from the National Center's Web site. "Yes," she said. "As Nick Pierce and Kayla."

Agent Morse scribbled on a pad. "When did they arrive here?"

"Monday morning," Claire said.

"What time?"

"I guess it must have been shortly after nine."

"How did the child appear to you?"

"He came in to register without her. She was asleep in the car. After Nick checked in, we went out to his car to collect her and the luggage and she was gone. Did Sam, I mean Chief Merrill, tell you?" she asked, glancing at Sam, who nodded.

"Yes, ma'am, he did," Agent Morse said.

"I called Sam from the beach phone."

"Did the father know you were calling the police?"

"No. I'd suggested it, but he appeared uneasy. I figured it was because calling the police meant she was really gone as opposed to the notion that she would turn up at any moment. Anyway, I called from the emergency phone. By the time I came back with her, Sam was standing with Nick."

"Did she appear to be running away?"

"Not at all. Just a child who had wandered."

"Did Mr. Parsons appear nervous?"

"You mean because he was with Sam?"

"Yes, did he appear nervous?" Agent Morse repeated.

"No. I mean he was nervous when he couldn't find Kayla but once he saw her he was relieved. He was very emotional as you can imagine." Claire hesitated. "Just as any parent would be who recovered a child."

Agent Morse tossed back her hair and smirked. "How long had the child been gone?"

"Fifteen, maybe twenty minutes."

"How did Mr. Parsons pay his bill?"

"Cash."

"And that didn't strike you as odd?"

"At first, but then he explained that he didn't like getting the credit card bill a month later."

"Did he sign the register?"

"Yes. He gave his address as Manhattan. I can show you the form. . . ."

"Could we see phone records from the room?"

"There are none," Eli said, speaking for the first time.

Agent Morse turned to him. "How do you know this, Dr. Bishop?"

"I checked them," he said. "You're welcome to look at the computer, to see for yourself."

"What made you check, Dr. Bishop?"

"I didn't like him," he said matter-of-factly.

"Did you suspect him?"

"I can't say that I suspected him. There was just something about him that bothered me. I checked the phone records out of curiosity, not suspicion."

"I see," she said. "Did he use a cell phone?"

"No," Claire and Eli said in unison.

"Was there anything unusual about Kayla?"

"Other than her blindness?" Claire asked.

"Yes."

"No."

"What about her demeanor? Her physical condition?"

"She was clingy with me. She mentioned almost immediately that her mother wanted to send her to a boarding school."

"When did she say that?"

"When we were on the beach. But when I pressed her, she didn't want to talk about it anymore. I didn't pursue it. I'm a psychologist and I know better than to force a child to talk about something they prefer not to discuss." Claire tilted her chin in the air. "I'm also a mother."

"And physically?"

"She had a blister on her foot. Her shoes, sneakers, were too tight. Her toenails were long."

"And how did you see this?"

"I saw her feet that day on the beach. I noticed the toenails when we went shoe shopping the next day."

"She went alone with you?"

"No, with Nick."

"I see," Agent Morse said. "Did the condition of her feet make you feel she was untended?"

"Not really. In retrospect, yes. But children often refuse to part with old shoes and they get blisters and such."

"Nothing else? Bruises? Skin tone?"

"She's small for her age and thin. She looked like a child who'd been premature. But yesterday her eyes began to bother her. She had some swelling and dryness," Claire said, stopping to swallow. She could feel her eyes fill with tears. "She was in quite a bit of pain. She has juvenile glaucoma and Nick forgot her eye drops. I told him to ask her doctor to call them in to the Drugmart and I could pick them up, but he said it would make him appear negligent and compromise his custody battle. In other words, the doctor would tell his wife that he hadn't thought to bring them. He'd explained that he and his wife were in the process of a divorce. He was afraid of losing Kayla."

Agent Morse shot up her eyebrows at Agent Hunt. "Go on, Dr. Cherney."

"Anyway, my husband called a friend of ours, Dr. Boyd, and he called the prescriptions in to the pharmacy. By the time we returned, maybe an hour or so later, he and Kayla were gone. That was Tuesday night."

"And that's when you called Chief Merrill," Agent Hunt said. "What made you call him?"

"She was sick when they left. She'd been in pain all day," Claire said. "I couldn't understand how he could leave with her in that condition unless he was running from something. He said that Phoebe was off with her boyfriend and he'd promised Kayla some time at the shore. It didn't make any sense. I mean, why would he just up and leave like that? He said they might even stay the week until her school started. Why would he leave like that with a sick child?"

"Was there a situation that might have precipitated his flight?"

"Nothing," Claire said. "Eli was right there when I told Nick we were going to the drugstore."

"Did you speak with him, Dr. Bishop?" Agent Morse asked.

"Only to tell him that I called the doctor for Kayla's prescription."

"He got spooked," Agent Hunt said, turning to Agent Morse.

"How was the child when you went to their room?" Agent Morse asked.

"We didn't see her," Eli said. "He only opened the door a crack."

"Anything else?" Agent Morse said, looking from Claire to Eli.

"He never let go of his briefcase. The whole time he was here, even when they went for a walk on the beach," Eli said.

"Did you ask him why?"

"He said it had original blueprints and he was worried about losing them. He said he was an architect."

"The only truthful thing he said," Agent Morse said with a huff.

"He really is an architect?" Claire asked.

Agent Morse nodded as she took notes.

"So why the attachment to the briefcase?"

"I'm sure it contained cash."

"He paid for everything in cash. The bill. Kayla's sneakers. As I said, he hated getting bills at the end of the month."

"Don't we all," Agent Morse said, continuing to write.

"Were the domestic charges against him bogus?" Claire asked tentatively.

"No, they were not," Agent Morse said, looking up at Claire. "At least not according to San Anselmo police."

"And I take it they're already divorced. The Web site for NCMEC said he's the noncustodial parent."

"That's correct," Agent Morse said. "The child has been missing since February. She was abducted the night after the custody hearing was finalized. The mother was awarded sole custody."

"Then how?" Claire asked, visibly shaken. "How did he take her?"

"He came to the wife's house around ten o'clock that night. Mrs. Parsons let him in. He said he just wanted to look at Kayla who was sleeping in her room in the back of the house. He followed his wife into the kitchen and grabbed her. Slammed her hand in the door of the steel wall oven and broke her fingers. She passed out. When she regained consciousness, her daughter was gone."

"Oh, no," Claire said, her mouth dry. "He also said that Phoebe had a skiing accident when she was pregnant with Kayla and she was born prematurely. That's why she's blind."

"According to Mrs. Parsons he pushed her down a flight of stairs when she was seven months pregnant. The baby was born prematurely the next day."

Claire felt the color drain from her face. "Did he ever hurt Kayla?"

"Not physically that we or the mother are aware of. Emotionally, of course, is another story entirely."

"Has the mother been contacted?" Eli asked. "Does she know that Kayla was here?"

"Not yet," Agent Hunt said. "We don't want to get her hopes up just yet. Months ago there was a sighting in New Mexico that led to a dead end. He took off before we got there. Needless to say, the mother was distraught. Someone in the department called her when they should have waited."

"We have APBs up and down the East Coast," Sam said. "We've got the make and license on the car he took out of Rhode Island. Now we just have to hope that he's paranoid and agitated enough that he screws up. And the FBI has a UFAP on him now that we placed him here out of state."

"A UFAP?" Claire asked.

"Unlawful flight to avoid prosecution," Agent Morse explained.

Claire recalled the phrase from the Web site. "And if all this doesn't work?"

No one answered.

"Where could they be?"

"Anywhere and nowhere," Agent Morse said, closing her notebook. "Needless to say, if by some remote chance he contacts you, you'll call us." She reached into her briefcase. "Here's my card. Thank you both for your time."

The two agents stood up.

"I'll show you out," Eli said.

"Go ahead," Agent Morse said. "I'd like to speak to Dr. Cherney for just one moment in private."

The three left the room and Agent Morse turned to her. "Was there anything between you and Nick Parsons?"

"Of course not," Claire said.

"Your husband didn't like him, Dr. Cherney."

"I know."

"There wasn't a hint of romance? The slightest flirtation? You realize if you withhold any information about his whereabouts . . ."

"This is ridiculous," Claire said hotly.

"Your husband had quite a strong reaction to him."

"He didn't like him from the moment he met him. It had nothing to do with anything else."

"You were sympathetic to him. As a psychologist and a mother, you saw nothing unusual about this man and his child?"

"I was raised by a single father," Claire said. "I was always alone with my father. As for your insinuation that there was anything untoward between Nick Pierce or Parsons or whatever his name is and myself . . ."

"I apologize, Dr. Cherney. He used you as a facilitator for his crime, you do understand that? I just wanted to be sure there was no further involvement or attachment where he might feel safe enough to contact you. . . ."

"There was no involvement," Claire said firmly.

"What kind of medicine does your husband practice?" Agent Morse asked.

"Veterinary," Claire said.

"Ah," Agent Morse said, softening. "I'm sorry if I upset you, Dr. Cherney. You understand, I had to ask."

Claire nodded. "I understand."

"If you think of anything else, please give me a call."

"Do you think you'll find them this time? Kayla needs medical attention."

Agent Morse slung her purse over her shoulder. "The fact that she needs medical attention may be the one thing that slows him down this time."

"What will happen to him in the end? If you find him, I mean."

Agent Morse set her lips tightly. "Not nearly enough," she said.

Chapter 21

Corinne pulled the car into the parking lot of Rodeo Beach.

"Quite a breeze today," she said, buttoning her jacket under her chin. "Ready, girls? Phoebe, button up that jacket."

"Ready," Phoebe said, feeling for the beeper and cell phone on her hip.

The three slung their knapsacks over their backs and headed out to the beach.

"Ma, remember when we took Kayla out to the beach? She always talked about that weekend. The drip castles."

"I remember," Corinne said. "She looked like a little mud pie by the end of the day."

Phoebe followed along the trail behind her mother and sister. Something about her dream the night before tugged at her consciousness. Her footsteps crunched along the trail and it was as though she heard Kayla coming to her. It was a feeling that Kayla was closer to her somehow than she'd been in the last several months. The doctors had let her hold her for only a moment the night she was born, the knuckle of Phoebe's finger larger than Kayla's fist. And yet that tiny baby flailed and screamed with the energy of a survivor and she knew, even when the doctors told her she was blind, that Kayla would surpass all the odds. She sat beside her Isolette for nearly three weeks, watching her little chest go up and down, the hideous tubes and electrodes dwarfing her tiny body. She didn't leave her side except to use the bathroom or shower or take a meal that wasn't allowed to be eaten within the unit. She pumped her breast milk into tiny bottles and fed it to her as she sat draped in a sterile robe. Nick came at the end of each day and stood at the glass window, telling the nurses he couldn't bear the pain. And each time Phoebe saw his face, she turned the other way. It's stressful, one of the nurses said sympathetically. In time, both of you will heal.

The day she brought Kayla home, the baby clamped hard to her breast, sucking firmly on her nipple, her strong little fist holding tight to Phoebe's finger. Soon she turned her head to the mobile that hung over her crib and played Brahms' lullaby. Weeks later she smiled at the sound of her mother's voice and looked around the moment Phoebe stepped into her room. Through Kayla's sightless eyes, Phoebe saw visions she never knew existed. A world of touch and scent and sound that might otherwise have gone unnoticed. The way grains of sand feel as they slip through the fingers, the scent of wind and rain, the soothing heat of the sun in winter, the sound of laughter before it bubbles into full force. How many times had she sat with Kayla and closed her eyes, entering Kayla's world of possibilities and beyond?

"You're a slowpoke," Corinne called as Phoebe trailed behind them. "Another mile and we're at the top."

"I'm coming," Phoebe said.

"We'll stop for lunch at the top. You'd better have a good appetite, Miss Phoebe. I'm going to get some meat on those bones or else. . . ."

And Phoebe thought of Kayla's smooth little body. The soft folds of baby flesh. How she loved to kiss the curve of her neck as she held her swathed in a thick towel after her bath. The way Kayla spoke in full sentences from the time she was only two years old. The way her smile grew when she spooned chocolate ice cream and fudge into her mouth. How her laugh came from her belly, deep and low, and ended in a song. The way she sat her bear beside her while she said her prayers at night and tucked him under the covers. Her long auburn hair that spread across her pillow when she slept so that when Phoebe lay next to Kayla it was nearly impossible to tell where one ended and the other began. How she cried when she banged her funny bone and said it was stupid to call it funny when it hurt so much and made her pinky feel like a porcupine. How they stood for hours bouncing the ball into the ceiling until Kayla learned to catch. The way Kayla melted into her body as she read to her at night. A gust of wind blew and Phoebe closed her eyes. The sea spray miles below the Point stung her cheeks. She smelled the salt air. She stood motionless for a moment, palms up, and felt the wind ripple every hair on her head.

She sat down in the middle of the trail and held her face in her hands, her body collapsing in a weary accordion fold, her shoulders heaving uncontrollably. Corinne and Caroline were beside her in a moment. She felt their arms around her. Heard their voices as they said now, now in unison. She felt the warm sun on her face. Miles below, she heard Pacific waves slapping the shore in a vista that Kayla would never see. She inhaled so deeply her breath caught in her chest. She was overcome with a sense that Kayla was trying to reach her. A worse sense that something had befallen her. She shut her eyes tightly, afraid if she opened them, the image of Kayla might disappear.

If you become a sailboat, I will become the wind.

I am the wind, she thought. I have to be.

Nick slept until three o'clock Wednesday afternoon in the artificially darkened room, the heavy vinyl shades pulled tightly over the windows. He was disoriented, uncertain whether the time was three in the morning or three in the afternoon. He parted the vinyl shades and saw the sunlight.

"Daddy?" the weak voice called from the other bed. "You're up?"

"I'm up," he said, his voice still thick with sleep.

He turned on the lamp on the nightstand and looked over at his daughter. Her face was flushed, her eyes shut.

"They hurt," she said.

He was unmoved. "You keep rubbing them. I told you to stop, didn't I?"

"You have to help me," she said haltingly, her lips barely moving.

He started to pull the phone book from the nightstand's drawer but placed it back again. If he took her to an emergency room, they'd ask too many questions. A doctor's office would do the same.

"Maybe you can call Claire and she can bring us the drops," Kayla said. "I bet she would."

"I'm going to get us some food," he said.

"I'm not hungry."

"I'll bring you something anyway," he said.

"Can I come with you? I don't want to stay here anymore."

"Not yet."

"Why? Please?"

"Not now," he said firmly, pulling his trousers over his boxer shorts, shoving his wallet into his back pocket. Not with your face looking like someone beat you, he thought. "Chain the door when I leave."

She followed behind him and counted the steps to the door. Her hands felt for the chain. She counted the steps back to the bed, making sure to remember the number so she could open the door when he returned. She reached for the phone. What would happen if she called Mommy, she wondered. Her fingers dialed the phone number. A woman's voice came on.

"Can we help you? You have to dial nine before making an outside call," Gina said. "Hello? Hello?"

But Kayla hung up the phone, dispelling her fantasy, reminding herself that Mommy was the one who wanted to send her away.

*　　　*　　　*

Gina's shift ended at four o'clock but Mario said it was all right if she wanted to leave at three-thirty given the fact that her day had begun so early. She was packing her books into her knapsack when she saw Nick walk across the Post Road and around the back of the motel. His hair was greasy and tousled. He carried two bags from the McDonald's, one leaking coffee as he walked. Strange guy, she thought. But then Mario's often had strange types. She hefted her backpack and walked to her little blue Neon parked in the front lot. If she hurried, she could paint her toenails before Steve picked her up that evening. She didn't realize she'd left the notebook for her morning Chem class on the front desk.

When the FBI left on Wednesday afternoon, Eli finished going through some bills and called his office. Claire went to the barn to check her messages. The answering machine was empty except for a message from Linda Taylor, the supervisor at child welfare in Meadville, acknowledging receipt of the papers. It had taken Claire a long time to know Linda. In her early thirties, Linda was always perfectly coiffed and did everything by the book, seemingly cold and unreachable but Claire asked her to have coffee one morning, determined to break through the iciness and get more than monosyllabic answers. As she guessed, Linda had a side to her that was vulnerable and human. She'd moved to Meadville with her fiancé three years before and the day after the wedding he decided that not only was small-town living not for him but marriage was probably a mistake as well. He left without explanation save a note on the kitchen table stating he simply didn't want to be married and felt there was life out there beyond Meadville. It said he was sorry for any pain he had caused her. The marriage was annulled with little fanfare and she never heard from him again. She'd filed a missing person's report but knew from the look on the reporting officer's face that he was not to be recovered. Her parents encouraged her to come home to their small town in Westchester County, New York but Linda decided to stay in even smaller Meadville where she was more anonymous. Claire had listened sympathetically and since then the two had become about as friendly as Linda could be with anyone. More important, Claire was one of the few people whom Linda trusted. What Claire didn't know was that an alert was handed to Linda shortly after she'd left the message for Claire. A missing child had been sighted in Drifting. In the three years that she'd held the supervisor's position, it was the first missing person's report Linda had seen besides a copy of the one she'd filed for her husband. She tossed the paper aside and shut her eyes. She didn't notice Claire's name on the report. She looked around the dingy gray windowless office and felt a sense of hopelessness seep through her skin. Recovery was a word no longer in her lexicon.

Chapter 22

Steve D'Angelo arrived at Gina's house Wednesday night at six o'clock. He'd gone for a few beers after his shift, headed for the gym although he was feeling a little on the high side, showered, and changed into black jeans and a black T-shirt. The day's tour had been typical. The fender bender first thing in the morning, two stolen bicycles at the middle school, a broken window at the unoccupied house on Wilding Lane, two false alarms and an elderly woman who fainted at the Stop & Shop. And now he got to see Gina who smelled like that strawberries-and-cream body wash she used in the shower. She'd leave him covered with the scent of her even though he returned her to her parents home each night. It wasn't enough anymore, he thought. He wanted her to spend the nights beside him. He wanted her there in the mornings.

He parked his black Honda Accord in Gina's driveway and rang the doorbell, looking around him out of habit as he waited on the stoop for her to open the door. She wore blue jeans and a black V-necked sweater, her long dark hair cascading down her back all shiny and silky.

She wrapped her arms around Steve's neck and kissed him on the lips.

"So I guess the policeman's your friend," he said with a grin. "You're in a good mood."

"Mario let me off early," she said, skipping down the stoop. "I'm starving."

"I thought we'd go over to McHenry's," he said. "Good burgers. I could use a burger."

"Perfect," she said as he opened the door to the Honda for her.

He placed his arm on hers before she stepped into the car. "You look beautiful," he said.

"Thanks," she said, smiling at him with her head cocked to the side.

He walked around to the driver's side and knew this evening was going to be one of the ones they'd remember for a long time.

McHenry's was one of the oldest taverns in Portchester, New York. Far enough from Harrison so Steve wouldn't run into any of his drinking buddies from the job who'd razz him the next day about being with Gina and close enough to his apartment so they might spend a few hours together before she had to get home to her father who waited up with a stopwatch in his hand.

"So, easy day?" she asked. "Sometimes I worry about you out there."

"You shouldn't," he said, taking a sip of his beer. "That's why I'm here and not in the city. That's a whole different ball game."

"I worry about you when you put on that siren and take off down the road," she said with a pout.

"Most girls would get turned on," he said, his eyes twinkling.

"Not funny," she said. "I'm not most girls."

"Don't I know it." He reached across the table and took her hand. "I love you," he said, looking into her eyes.

"I love you, too."

"So live with me. I don't like to be away from you."

"I can't live with you. My father doesn't even like it when you take me out at night," she said.

"Then marry me," he said spontaneously.

She stopped with her glass of wine in midair. "What did you say?"

"Marry me," he said.

"You're serious?"

"No, I'm kiddin' around. Of course I'm serious, Gina." He took his high school ring from his right hand and took her left hand in his. "This'll have to do for now. I promise I'll get you a real nice ring. I swear it. So will you?"

She gazed at her finger as he slipped on the ring and then turned her face to his. "I will," she said.

He pounded his fist on the table. "I swear to God, Gina. I knew before I left tonight that this night was going to be something special. I had this feeling something was going to happen."

He brought her hand to his lips. "I guess this was it."

They were leaving Steve's apartment at midnight that night when Gina remembered the chemistry notebook she'd left at the front desk.

"So we'll swing by and get it," Steve said.

"It's so out of the way," she groaned. "I can't believe I left it there. I was in such a hurry to leave. It was nuts later in the day."

"How come?"

"You know, the usual suspects. The guys who check in and sneak out like I don't see them leaving a few hours later. And then that creep who came in this morning."

"What creep?"

"I told you about him. The one who said he was relocating."

"Oh, right. Why? Did he bother you?"

"No, nothing like that. He stayed in the room all day except for when he got breakfast and then he went out later on and walked over to the McDonald's. I swear he looks like a homeless person. I don't know what his story is but I can bet he doesn't have any family back in Texas." She shuddered. "Who could be married to him?"

"Texas?"

"That's what his license said. He's just so grungy looking. Sometimes that place gives me the shivers and Mario keeps saying how it's the last respectable motel in the area. That's a laugh."

Steve pulled into the front lot of the motel.

"Drive around back, would you?" Gina asked. "I can go right in the back door with my key and grab the book. I'll just be a sec."

Steve pulled the Honda close to the back entrance. "Want me to come with you?"

"No! If Mario sees you he won't stop yapping," she said.

Steve turned on the car radio and opened the sun roof of the Honda. The midnight sky sparkled with stars. He hadn't planned on asking her to marry him that night. He'd planned it so differently—champagne and a diamond ring. Getting down on one knee. But all in all, it was just the ~~way~~ it should have been. The way it had been since they were kids, so nice and easy. She came walking out of the motel, the notebook in her hands.

"Was Mario there?" he asked.

"No, Loretta was on duty. She's Mario's cousin. He's taking painkillers for the tooth. She said he's really out of it."

Steve drove the car through the lot, looking around him as he drove. "That car has a low front tire," he said, pointing to the Bonneville.

"That's the creep's car," she said.

"I thought you said he's from Texas."

"He is."

"That car has Rhode Island plates." His heart began to race. "Hang on a second," he said. He turned the Honda around in a wide U and pulled behind the Bonneville. "You got a pen?"

She fumbled in her purse. "What for?"

"Write this down. RCE 5398."

"What for?" she asked, scribbling on the cover of her notebook.

He drove into the McDonald's across the street.

"What are you doing?" she asked.

He took his cell phone from his belt clip and the notebook from her lap. His buddy Sergeant Reid Wilkins answered the line. "Hey, Reid. Listen, I got it in the back of my mind you guys sent an APB this morning. Run that plate by me, would you? Sure, I'll hold."

He was silent for a few minutes. "That's it. Pontiac Bonneville. You're not going to believe this but I got the car. Back of the lot at Mario's Motel. Unoccupied. Hang on." He turned to Gina. "You remember the guy's name?"

"Nicholas something," she said. "What's going on, Steve? You're scaring me."

"Nicholas something. Gina checked him in early this morning." He listened for a few moments and then responded, "I'll wait until your guys get here." He snapped his cell phone shut.

"Now are you going to tell me?"

"We got an APB on that car this morning," Steve said. "The guy is wanted for kidnapping."

Gina put a hand to her mouth. "Oh my God."

"Gina, he came in alone? He didn't have a child with him?"

"No."

"You're sure?"

"Steve, for God's sake, I would have seen if he did."

"Okay, look, I'm sorry. As soon as the unmarked gets here, I'm taking you home."

"And then what?"

"And then we're going to make sure that our friend there doesn't go anywhere without us."

"Are you coming back here?"

"Oh yeah. I'm sticking around to see what happens."

Fifteen minutes later he pulled up to Gina's house. "I'll call you in the morning."

"No," she said adamantly. "I'll leave my cell phone on and you call me tonight."

"So this is what a wife acts like, is it?" he asked, pulling her close to him.

An unmarked black Ford Crown Victoria sat with the headlights out and the motor idling at the entrance to the back lot's driveway; another sat blocking the path to the front lot. Steve walked over to the window of the Ford in the front. Detective Todd Walker was in the driver's seat.

"Anything?"

"It's tough to see if there's light on in those rooms what with those blackout shades Mario has on the windows. I swear to God, this place is like a glorified whorehouse."

"Without the glory," Steve said. "So what's the guy's MO?"

"Noncustodial father. Left with his daughter last February from San Anselmo, California after he beat up his wife pretty good. History of spousal abuse. Apparently the guy's been crisscrossing the country. A real scumbag."

"Where's the APB origin?"

"Some beach town up in Connecticut." The detective punched a button on the built-in laptop computer in his car. "Drifting, Connecticut. Car was stolen out of Hubbard, Rhode Island." He looked up at Steve. "You get the APB this morning?"

Steve's face reddened. "I flicked it off. When I saw the car there tonight it was like it was stored somewhere in my brain space."

"You want to hop in? Could be a long night here."

Steve opened the passenger door. "How old is the kid?"

"Seven."

"Anything else?"

"Yeah, she's blind."

"Jesus. I take it there's a UFAP on the guy."

Todd handed the NCMEC poster to Steve. "The sad thing is even if we get the guy he'll get his wrist slapped and then he's home free," he said. "Pretty fucked up."

Corinne took her daughters to dinner Wednesday night after the hike. She was, as Phoebe recalled from her childhood, what neighbors described as indefatigable. If she wasn't gardening or volunteering at the local Women's Club, she mentored children at the high school or worked soup kitchen lines. And all the while Corinne had dinner on the table and an ear to lend her daughters or her husband, Henry. When Henry died, her world came crashing down but she threw herself into her good works, as she called it. And then Kayla disappeared and Corinne packed two suitcases, left the key to her house with a neighbor, and drove from Denver to San Anselmo. She'd been there since February, nursing Phoebe's broken hand but more, nursing her broken spirit.

"Now, then," Corinne said, opening the menu in front of her. "This place is known for its soups. What do you think, Phoebe? Lentil's good for you. Lots of protein."

"I don't feel very well," Phoebe said.

"Because you're hungry."

"No, Ma. You know how you always wake up at night before the baby cries? You lie there and listen and not a moment later you hear that little squeak and you get up and she's wide awake in her crib?" Her eyes filled with tears. "It's like I can hear her crying. And it's killing me."

"We'll get some food to take out," Corinne said, closing the menu. "I'm taking you home."

Corinne feared her daughter was starting to fall apart.

Chapter 23

If Sam Merrill could have kicked himself, he would have. He kept going over that Monday morning when Kayla took her walk on the beach as it came to be called. He'd pulled up to the inn and there was that man, twisting his hands and standing frozen in one position. Why wasn't he combing the road or looking under the gap in the porch? Why didn't he greet him in the way that most people greet the cops when they're in need of help and help arrives? The guy was stiff as a board. Answered his questions in short clipped sentences. And that damn white paint on the dented fender. He should have picked up on it right away when the guy said he had a run-in with a New York City cabbie. Cabs are yellow most everywhere. And besides, Sam had seen enough movies set in New York City, even though he'd never been there in his life, to know that New York City cabs are yellow. He felt like he got sucker punched.

The door opened and Claire and Eli came in.

"You can't just sit here without eating," Claire said. "We brought you dinner."

"Don't tell Annie. I've been refusing her all night."

"We just spoke to her. She's on her way over," Eli said. "She said she's run out of drawers to clean."

"So what we going to have here? A vigil?" Sam asked bitterly.

"If we're not going to sleep, we might as well be together, right?" Claire said.

"I should have run his plate on Monday morning," Sam said.

"You said there was no cause," Claire said gently. "I didn't see any of this coming either. I was with them for two days straight."

"I should have punched it in before you came back with the girl. That would have given me cause. A child was missing."

"Hindsight is always twenty-twenty," Eli said, thinking of Power. "We're only human, Sam."

"Except people like Nicholas Parsons who are sub-human," Sam said angrily. "I'll never forgive myself if we don't find that kid."

Annie had been listening at the door. "What am I going to do with all of you?" she asked, standing with her hands on her hips. "You've been off-duty since eight o'clock, Sam Merrill. I brought a bottle of wine and we're all having cocktails." She took out a bottle and four plastic cups. "And we're drinking to our children and Kayla."

It was nearly one A.M. when the four decided to leave headquarters. "Enough," Annie said. "Nelson's got the desk now until morning. We all need to get some sleep. We're useless otherwise."

They were on their way out the door when the phone rang.

"It's for you, Chief," Nelson called from the reception room. "Harrison New York PD."

"Merrill," Sam answered. He listened for a moment and his face lit up. "I'll be at this number all night." He hung up the phone and turned to the three faces staring at him. "They sighted the Bonneville at a motel on U.S. 1 in Harrison, New York. They have stakeout on the vehicle."

"Where is he? Is he at the motel?"

"One would assume."

"So why can't they just go in and get him?" Claire asked.

"Because they can't do it that way," Sam said, obviously frustrated. He wanted to be there worse than anything. He wanted to grab that stinking guy by the lapels and slam him against the wall and tell him what he thought of guys like him who beat up their wives and torture their children.

Kayla heard her father shake the pills from the bottle. She knew that sometimes he took something to help him sleep. He'd brought her a cheeseburger and French fries from McDonald's and a Coca-Cola. He had some kind of fried fish sandwich and the room reeked with the smell of stale oil and made her feel sick to her stomach. He turned on the fan and it rumbled and made a noise that hurt her ears but she knew better than to say a word. Now she heard him breathing, deep scratchy sounds, and knew he was sleeping again. Her hair felt oily and her eyes stuck together. She hadn't taken a bath in days. Mommy's baths were always the best, she thought. She had bubble bath that smelled like bubble gum and soap that smelled like flowers and Mommy would squeeze the washcloth so the water ran down her back and felt so warm like she was under a waterfall. And then she would bundle her in that great big towel and rock her on her lap while she shivered and Mommy made her feel all warm and toasty. And the powder. It went on so soft and silky and then she'd zip her into those soft pajamas and brush her teeth with the toothbrush that played a song while you brushed. She wondered how long it had been since she slept in pajamas. Thinking about the times that used to be made her as sad as they made her happy. It was what Grandma always said about Grandpa, she thought. At least she had her memories. But then Grandma would cry. Poor Grandma. Mommy once said people died of broken hearts. If she had Bear she might feel just a little better. When she pictured him sitting somewhere on the backseat of the old car she hoped he wasn't scared like she was. She hoped he knew that one day she'd find him and have him back safe and sound.

Kayla didn't know it was nearly one in the morning. She wished she could sleep.

She heard the opening and closing of car doors in the distance. A man's voice that sounded muffled and gravelly. She wished they could have simply stayed in Drifting. It was the closest thing to home.

Phoebe ran to the answering machine as soon as she opened the door to the house on Wednesday evening. There was a message from Caroline's husband, Frank, assuring her that the kids, Tara and Frank, Jr., were tucked in and fine. She pictured Kayla in the bed where she used to sleep in the room beside hers, the night-light shining on the wall so Phoebe could see her way in the dark if Kayla called to her. The covers would be up to Kayla's chin and the moon would shine through the bedroom window and light her baby's head as though it were a halo.

"You think I'm losing it, don't you?" Phoebe asked, staring at her mother and sister.

"Phoebe, don't . . . ," Caroline said, reaching for her.

"Stop," Phoebe said, stepping back from her sister. "Don't you understand? This is the first time since she's been gone that I can feel something. I'm telling you, she's coming home."

She walked down the corridor and slammed the door to her room.

"What do you think, Ma?" Caroline asked, turning to her mother.

Corinne wrapped her arms around herself. "I think I have to get her out of this place tomorrow before she makes herself crazy."

"But what if she's right?"

"What if she's wrong?" Corinne set the paper bag of take-out food on the kitchen counter. "She's like a rock, your sister. But even rocks get worn away after a while."

Phoebe awakened just after four on Thursday morning. A warm breeze blew through the open window. She swore she heard her daughter's voice on the whisper of the wind. *I'm coming home.* She rolled away from the window and curled up in a ball, certain she felt her daughter sleeping beside her.

At eight o'clock that morning, Corinne tiptoed into Phoebe's room and sat on the edge of her bed. As she had when Phoebe was a child, she brushed the hair from her face and smoothed her palm down her cheek. "Get up, sleepyhead," she said.

"I'm sorry, Ma," she said, her eyes still shut. "I didn't mean to take it out on you last night."

Corinne laughed. "You've been taking it out on me since you could speak."

Phoebe scooted up on her pillow. "Where's Caroline?"

"On the phone with Frank." Corinne drew in her breath. "I'm getting you out of here again today."

Phoebe groaned. "Another hike?"

"Just over to Faude Park. Not a big deal. We'll bring a picnic."

"Do we have to?"

"We have to," Corinne said firmly. "I won't have you sitting here." Corinne pulled up the window shade.

"It was so windy last night."

"Was it? I didn't hear a thing. Well, it's a beautiful day. Maybe the wind blew all the clouds away," Corinne said.

Chapter 24

❦

Nick slept only until six o'clock on Thursday morning and awakened believing his own lies. He looked at his child in the bed across the nightstand and around the room at the soiled beige walls. Kayla was coiled into the tightest of fetal positions, her fists clenched under her chin. His trousers were crumpled on the floor beside the bed, his wallet and keys on top of the ubiquitous briefcase. He inhaled the stench from his body. Once he was the slick, groomed senior partner at Parsons and Blanchard, the most well-respected architectural firm in Marin County. Now he was a fugitive. It was all Phoebe's fault. If only she had complied. If she hadn't taunted him all those times so that his fist flew against his will. If she hadn't called the police and had that woman from child welfare monitor each and every one of his visits with the child. The child Phoebe wanted to send away. But she doesn't want to send the child away, a voice inside his head taunted him. He saw Phoebe's face before him, her translucent skin that turned ashen as her hand caught in the oven door and she melted onto the white ceramic kitchen floor. He began to perspire and his heart began to pound. He wrapped his hand around his wrist and placed two fingers at his vein, but despite the thumping of his heart he couldn't find a pulse.

"Time to go!" he cried in a voice that came again from somewhere beyond himself.

"Daddy?" Kayla said. "Daddy?"

"I'm sorry," he said. "I must have been dreaming."

"What time is it?"

He looked at the clock. "Six."

"Night or morning?"

"Morning."

"What day?" she asked.

"Thursday," he said although part of him was uncertain. He was losing track of time.

"Can we go outside today?"

"Later."

"How much later?"

Too many questions, he thought. Why did she constantly have to ask him questions?

"Where are we?" she asked again.

"New York," he said, still searching for his pulse.

"Is that far?"

Far from what? he wondered.

"Is it?" she asked again.

"I don't know," he said breathlessly.

"My eyes won't open, Daddy," she said, her voice quivering. "They're stuck together."

"What do you mean they won't open? Open them,

for Christ sake. Open them." He might have a heart attack, he thought. He was dizzy and his skin was clammy. "Open them," he demanded.

"Maybe I can take a bath," she said softly, afraid to rile him. Her teeth were clenched so tightly her jaw ached. "If I splash water on them it helps."

He sat on the edge of the bed. "I have to shower." Maybe it was just the damn sleeping pills that were making him feel this way. "I'll help you after I finish."

She sat with her back against the bed pillows and listened as her father ran the shower. She could smell the steam from the bathroom. Maybe this would be the day they'd get the eye drops. Maybe things were going to get better. She heard the shower shut off and the bathroom door open.

"Much better," Nick said. His heart had stopped pounding. He wasn't as dizzy anymore.

She heard the latches open on his suitcase. Heard the zip of his trousers. Heard him take a shirt and shake it out the way he always did before he put it on. The bed creaked when he sat down and she guessed he was putting on his socks.

"Come," he said. "Your turn."

"Make sure you give me something soft to wear," she said. "Okay, Daddy?"

He stopped. "I left your suitcase in the trunk," he said. "Just sit back down and I'll bring it inside."

"Then I can take a bath?"

"Right."

"And then can we get some breakfast?" she asked.

"We'll get it on the road," he said.

"On the road? Where are we going now?" she asked.

"The Carolinas," he said almost dreamily. "It's getting cold up here. Look, sit tight. I'll be right back." He was calmer now. He'd get some coffee across the street. They'd probably catch the morning rush on the highway but it didn't matter. He would fill the car and check the tires and head down South. They hadn't been south yet. They'd been Midwest and north and by the Eastern Seaboard. The South was warm and people were friendly, he thought. Savannah, maybe. Or Charleston. Melt into the old architecture and Southern charm. He could start a new life there.

He jammed his wallet into his pocket and slid the briefcase under the bed. He looked around him as he opened the door to the motel room. The sun was just rising and the sky was painted with streaks of purple and orange. He looked around at the empty lot and spied the black Ford parked at the lip of the driveway. He hesitated for a moment but decided to think nothing of it. It was, after all, a motel. There were bound to be cars around even early in the morning. He didn't see the other black car partially hidden by a wide oak tree where the lot exited a side street lined with neat white cookie-cutter condominiums. He crossed U.S. 1 to the Dunkin' Donuts and ordered a large black coffee, a bag of doughnuts, and grabbed a glass bottle of some sort of red juice drink for Kayla. He returned not minutes later, placed the Dunkin' Donuts bag on the roof of the car, and placed the key to the Bonneville in the lock of the trunk. He heard footsteps grating on the cement behind him. Two men in dark pants and long-sleeved T-shirts, the new morning sun glinting from objects in their hands, walked toward him.

"Nicholas Parsons?" the larger man asked.

Nick didn't answer. He didn't turn around.

"Nicholas Parsons?"

Nick looked to either side of him and ran forward as the car near the side street lot pulled toward them, a red light flashing now on the dash of the car.

"Put your hands in the air," a voice boomed from the car.

Nick dropped the key to the Bonneville on the ground and placed his hands in the air. One of the men walked behind him, patted him down, and picked the key to room sixteen from his pocket. He twisted one arm and then the other behind Nick's back, the handcuffs going on with ease.

"You didn't read me my rights," Nick said. "I have rights."

"You have no rights, you asshole," the cop said. "You get rights when we have questions." He pulled the NCMEC poster from his back pocket and shook it in Nick's face. "We know who you are, you piece of shit."

The cop tossed the key to Steve D'Angelo who came from the car on the side street. "Room sixteen in front of the Pontiac," he said. He wrenched Nick's arm. "Is the girl in the room?"

Nick nodded. "Don't hurt her."

"Don't hurt her?" Steve asked incredulously.

Steve entered the room and saw Kayla propped up against the pillows on the bed.

"Daddy?" she asked breathlessly. She knew it wasn't Daddy. "Who's there?"

"I'm a police officer, Kayla. Your daddy's outside with us. He said it was okay if we came to get you."

She hopped off the bed and began counting the steps to the door. "I want to see my daddy," she said, beginning to cry.

"I'll take you to see him," Steve said. "Give me your hand."

"No," she said defiantly.

"I'm going to take you to your daddy right now. I promise you."

She froze in front of him. Her hair was matted down on her head, her eyes swollen and red. Her clothes were wrinkled and looked as though she'd slept in them for nights. "Where is he?" she asked, her lips quivering.

"He's outside with the policemen," Steve said gently, thinking they had to call an ambulance. The child's face was red and swollen around the eyes. She looked beaten. "I promise. No one's going to hurt you, Kayla."

"Are you going to hurt him?" she asked.

"No one's going to hurt him either. I promise you. How about giving me your hand?"

She extended her arm and placed her hand into Steve's. He felt afraid to hold too tight as though her little hand might break.

Steve sat Kayla in the other unmarked car. "She wants to talk to her father," Steve said to Todd Walker. "I'm going to call for an ambulance. Her face is all swollen."

"The guy can't be trusted. I don't know."

"Look, the kid is blind. Just let her talk to him."

"I don't like it," Todd said. "But go ahead."

Nick was sitting in the back of the unmarked car. Todd leaned his face into the backseat. "You pull anything funny and you'll be really sorry when we get you to headquarters. Now you tell her it's okay to come with us. You try any bullshit and believe me

you'll be sorrier than you ever thought you could be."
Todd pulled Nick from the car. "Here's Daddy, Kayla.
Now he's going to tell you that it's okay for you to
come with us."

"Daddy?" she called as Steve walked her over to Nick.

"Don't believe them, Kayla!" Nick cried. "They're
going to send you back home and she'll send you
away! Your mother's doing this to me, Kayla! I'm the
one who loves you, Kayla! I'm the one!"

Kayla began to scream. Steve D'Angelo picked her
up in his arms while Todd shoved Nick back in the car.
"You son of a bitch," he said. "You goddamn son of a
bitch."

Kayla heard the beep of a siren and then the rush of
tires pulling into the parking lot. A female paramedic
hopped out of the back of the ambulance. She walked
slowly over to Kayla and stroked her back as Steve
held her. "I'm Melissa," she said tenderly. "And I'm
going to take you to the hospital, okay, sweetheart?
There's an ambulance here. Everything's going to be
okay." Melissa took Kayla from Steve's arms.

Kayla trusted Melissa's touch. "My eyes hurt," she
said. She began to sob. "Claire was going to get me my
drops."

"Who is Claire? Is she here with you?"

Kayla shook her head. "No."

"How long have they been hurting, sweetheart?"
Melissa asked.

"I don't know," Kayla said. "I don't know. Where's
my daddy?"

"Your daddy is going with the policemen," Melissa
said. "But we're going to take real good care of you,
okay? Come, we'll ride in the back of the ambulance

together. You know I have a little girl just like you at home. What are you, about six?"

"Seven," Kayla said. She was holding her breath and trying not to cry. "Why's my daddy going with the policemen?"

"They're going to help him sort out a few things. They have to ask him some questions. He's fine, sweetheart."

Kayla leaned her head against the woman who had a little girl just like her at home. Chief Sam back in Drifting was a policeman, she thought. He was nice to Daddy. Daddy said not to be afraid of Chief Sam.

"Are we almost there?" Kayla asked.

"About another three minutes," Melissa said. "The doctors are going to make you all better."

"Will you come inside with me?" Kayla asked.

Melissa's eyes misted over. She swallowed hard before she could get out the words. "I'll ask them if I can. At least for a little while," she said, folding Kayla into her arms.

On Thursday afternoon at twelve-thirty, John Blanco called Sam at headquarters.

"I wanted to be the one to tell you," he said. "They got them down in Harrison, New York. Father's in custody. The kid's at St. Agnes Hospital."

"She okay?" Sam asked.

"Seems to be unharmed," Blanco said.

"What time did they pick them up?"

"Around seven this morning."

"How?"

"One of their patrolman spotted the car behind the motel down there."

"Why the hell didn't they call me with the hit confirmation? We were the ones who put out the original APB."

"Yeah, but the car was stolen here in Hubbard. Besides, it's been total chaos all morning."

"What about the mother?"

"They left several messages on her answering machine. Her cell phone doesn't respond. They're still trying to locate her."

No sooner did Sam hang up with Blanco when he called the inn. Claire answered the phone.

"They got him," Sam said. "Down in Harrison, New York. About four hours from here. Father's in custody and Kayla's being treated at St. Agnes Hospital."

"Treated for what?"

"It's routine. They check her. You know, for signs of abuse. That sort of thing," Sam said grimly.

"You don't think . . ."

"It's routine, Claire. I told you."

"They should know about those eye drops," Claire said.

"The doctors will examine her."

"Did they reach the mother?"

"They're still trying," Sam said.

"Where's St. Agnes?" Claire asked.

"White Plains, New York."

Claire hung up the phone and walked out to the veranda where Eli was reading the paper.

"They found them," she said.

"Where?"

"Harrison, New York. They just took her over to St. Agnes Hospital in White Plains. They're trying to reach the mother."

Eli tossed the paper on the floor beside the chair. "White Plains. That's about three hours from here." He stood up. "I take it you're up for a drive."

The calls to Phoebe's answering machine started coming in around ten AM Pacific time on Thursday morning, just as Corinne and Phoebe and Caroline trudged through Faude Park. There was no wireless service in the park area and Phoebe's phone was painfully silent for the next seven hours until they walked in the door of the house around four o'clock. Phoebe saw the red light blinking on the machine and pressed it down with trembling fingers. The first message was from Detective Tom Warren from the San Anselmo Police Department. The lead detective on Kayla's case.

"Phoebe, it's Tom Warren, San Anselmo Police. 415-555-1200, extension 201." The next six messages said the same.

Phoebe dialed the number while Corinne and Caroline stood on either side of her.

"Detective Warren, please," she said. "This is Phoebe Parsons."

"I'm sorry, ma'am. He's gone for the day."

"I'm returning his call," she said.

"One moment please," the voice said.

"Detective Brennan," a different voice said.

"I'm trying to reach Detective Warren," she said. "My name is Phoebe Parsons."

"Your daughter's been recovered, Mrs. Parsons. She's fine, Mrs. Parsons."

Phoebe stood frozen in place. The voice came to her again from someplace far away. *"Mrs. Parsons, your daughter's been recovered. Do you hear me, Mrs. Parsons? Are you all right? Is anyone there with you?"*

"I hear you," she said. Her heart pounded. "Am I dreaming?"

"You're not dreaming," Detective Brennan said tenderly. "Your daughter's been found. And she's just fine."

Phoebe leaned against the wall, sank slowly and deliberately to the floor, and began to sob, the receiver on her lap, her shoulders heaving spasmodically.

Corinne took the receiver. "This is Phoebe's mother, Corinne Albert. My daughter's overcome at the moment," Corinne said, reaching her hand down to Phoebe's back. Tears smarted in her eyes. "You found Kayla?"

"She's been recovered, Mrs. Albert. She's under observation at St. Agnes Hospital in White Plains, New York. Only routine. She appears to be in good condition," the detective said. "Detective Warren was trying to reach your daughter all day."

"We were hiking," Corinne said breathlessly. "The cell was out of range. Where did you find her?"

"At a motel in Harrison, New York, ma'am. We tried the cell but prefer not to leave messages on mobile numbers."

The phone beeped for call waiting. "Hold on, would you?" Corinne said, trying to remain calm as she flashed the signal.

"Detective Warren, San Anselmo Police," the voice said. "Phoebe Parsons, please."

"Tom, it's Corinne," she said, shaking. "I have Detective Brennan on the other line. We just heard. Phoebe's, well, she's overwhelmed."

"I understand," the detective said. "There's a ten P.M. out of San Francisco. They're holding three seats for us. I assume you're coming along, Mrs. Albert. I'll pick you up around six. I'll be escorting you to New York."

Corinne flashed back to Detective Brennan. "That was Tom Warren," she said. "He's on his way."

Caroline sat on the floor beside Phoebe, her arm around her shoulders. "Take a deep breath, sweetheart. Breathe."

Phoebe looked at her sister and tried to inhale. "I can't," she said with what nearly sounded like laughter.

"The detective booked us on a ten o'clock out of San Francisco," Corinne said, kneeling in front of Phoebe now. She turned to Caroline. "He only booked three seats, honey."

"You go, Ma," Caroline said. "I'll go food shopping and clean this place up."

"I'm going to throw some things in a suitcase," Corinne said, tugging Phoebe's hands. "Okay? Come, get up now."

"See? I was right, Ma, wasn't I?" Phoebe rose like a colt standing for the first time. She smiled through her tears. "I'm telling you, I heard her calling to me." She took a deep breath and shut her eyes. "Kayla's coming home."

Chapter 25

Claire wished she'd called Linda Taylor for a lunch date before she made the call to her on Thursday afternoon. She knew that more often than not in cases like Kayla's, the child would be placed in either a group home situation or foster care before the custodial parent arrived to recover her. She remembered in the back of her mind that Linda had transferred from Westchester County, New York. She knew that Harrison was in Westchester. Maybe Linda still had contacts in the area.

Linda listened in silence while Claire unfolded the saga of Nick and Kayla. "The report came in yesterday," Linda said softly when Claire finished.

"Then you knew?"

"No. Only that there had been a child sighted. Why didn't you call me?"

"It was too late by the time I realized what was happening," Claire explained.

"It's out of our jurisdiction now."

"I'm hoping you know someone in child welfare down in Westchester County."

"Which police department is it?" Linda asked.

"Harrison. We're driving down there now. I'll give you our cell number."

"I may not be able to do anything," Linda warned. "These things get very involved. It's not so easy. I can't make any promises."

"I just want to see her. I just want them to let me into the hospital so I can see her," Claire said. "Wait with her until the mother arrives."

"I'm going to try my best, Claire." Linda's voice dropped. "How long was she missing?"

"Seven months. Can you imagine what that mother's been through?"

"Yes, I can," Linda said with a sigh.

"We need to have a heart-to-heart lunch one of these days, don't we?"

"Absolutely," she said, brightening. "I'm going to make some calls. Keep your fingers crossed."

Eli came in with two small overnight bags. "Don't even ask me what I packed for you," he said. "Pajamas. Jeans. A couple of shirts. Two sweaters."

"Underwear? Socks?"

"Check," he said. "Toothbrush."

"You are amazing," she said. "Truly amazing. We'd better call the kids from the car and tell them what's going on." She turned to get her coat. "What about Stella?"

"We can drop her at Annie and Sam's. I already called them."

"That was some day when you walked into Cherney's Drugs," she said. "My hero with the egg cream."

Officer Joan Matthews was sitting in a chair outside when Claire and Eli stopped at the door to Kayla's room.

"My name is Claire Cherney," Claire said. "This is my husband, Eli Bishop. Kayla and her father were staying at our inn in Drifting, Connecticut, and—"

Officer Matthews interrupted her. "We have the whole story," she said. "We got a call from Child Welfare about an hour ago. You're cleared, but I need ID. The doctors want to keep her overnight for observation. She's been through quite an ordeal. She's dehydrated. They have her on an intravenous drip."

"Did they reach the mother?" Claire asked. Linda came through, she thought.

"She's taking a ten o'clock flight out of San Francisco. We expect her around eight in the morning."

"How was she?"

"I don't know. But I imagine this is the longest flight that woman's ever going to take in her life."

Claire nodded. "Can I see Kayla?"

"She's sleeping, but go ahead."

Claire pushed open the door slowly. Kayla was lying on her back, her head turned to one side, swollen eyes closed. The intravenous plugged into her tiny arm. Claire stood at the foot of her bed. She was about to leave the room when Kayla stirred.

"Kayla?" Claire whispered. "It's me, Claire."

"Claire! How did you find me?"

Claire walked over and sat on the edge of Kayla's bed. She kissed her forehead and took her hand in hers. "Same way I found you on the beach that morning." She squeezed her hand gently. "You okay?"

"My eyes feel better," she said. "The doctors gave me drops. The police are helping Daddy."

"Well, those are all good things," Claire said.

"The police said that Mommy is coming," Kayla said, tightening her grip on Claire's hand. "I'm afraid. I'm afraid she's going to send me away."

"Listen to me, Kayla," Claire said. "Your mommy doesn't want to send you away."

"But Daddy said she did. He said that was why we had to run far away from her so she wouldn't do that."

"Well, he wasn't telling the truth, Kayla," she said with trepidation. "He made a mistake."

"Did he lie?"

"Mommy is going to come get you and no one is sending you anywhere but back home with her to San Anselmo."

"Will Daddy go to jail?"

Claire drew in her breath. "I don't really know, Kayla."

"One time I faked being sick at school and Mommy told me that I couldn't listen to my tapes that night because I didn't tell the truth. I got punished when I lied. If he lied, then he'll get punished, too, right?"

"Sometimes people have to learn lessons the hard way, Kayla. But I bet you never faked being sick again after that, did you?"

"Never. I never lied again except when Daddy said I had to. Like I was never supposed to tell anyone that we'd been away for so long."

"Not telling something isn't a lie, though."

"But how come he said stuff that wasn't true?"

Claire shook her head. "I don't know. But you know what? I think the best one to answer that is your mommy. You ask her and I'll bet she'll explain everything to you. Right now, you have to know two things. You have to know that Daddy will be fine and that your mommy would never send you away. She loves you very much, Kayla."

"Will you stay with me?"

"Until Mommy gets here," she said. "Then she's going to take you home where you belong."

Kayla was sleeping in the crook of Claire's arm when the door to her room opened at eight-thirty on Friday morning. A woman with auburn hair flecked with gray at the temples walked in behind a young woman who barely looked much more than a girl to Claire. The girl's eyes were a startling shade of deep green with thick fringed lashes, though red-rimmed and liquid. A shock of thick auburn hair framed her delicate features set in an alabaster complexion. She was rail thin, her clothes hanging from her body in loose folds as though they were bought several sizes too large. Hardly a showgirl, as Nick had described her. In fact, she was the image of Kayla. The girl walked cautiously over to the bed. Claire let go of Kayla gently, slipping her arm out from beneath her, and stood to the side without saying a word. The girl stood for a moment and looked at the child, then gave a gasp as her eyes filled with tears. It was her child despite the short-cropped mousy brown hair and the roses that were gone from her cheeks. Despite the swelling that remained around her eyes and the hideous tube that stretched from the metal pole beside her bed. Despite the veins that tracked her arms once covered by dimpled little-girl flesh. She placed her fingertips on Kayla's forehead as though a firmer touch might break her in half.

"Mommy?" Kayla asked, opening her eyes. "Mommy?"

"It's me," Phoebe whispered, trying not to cry. She sat carefully on the edge of the child's bed and took Kayla into her arms like a rag doll, kissing Kayla's face, the soft curve of her neck, her bare shoulder where the hospital gown had slipped down. She rocked her slowly back and forth. "My baby," she said over and over. "My baby."

Corinne came behind Phoebe. "Kayla?" she said softly.

"Grandma?" Kayla sat bolt upright. "Grandma! Daddy said you died."

Corinne inhaled a breath filled with anger and grief. She shook her head from side to side, her lips pressed so tightly together they were nearly white. She walked around the other side of the bed and moved the pole so she could find a spot where she could get to Kayla. Phoebe pulled back for a moment, still holding her daughter's hand in hers as Corinne took the child's face in her palms and kissed both cheeks. "Daddy was wrong," she said, the statement laced with fury. She tempered her tone. "We have far too many drip castles to build now, don't we?"

"Why did he say that?" Kayla asked. "Mommy, I knew it was you when you came in the room, but I thought I was dreaming. I smelled the perfume. Angel, right?"

"I put it on just for you," Phoebe said, her face breaking into a smile.

Although Phoebe walked past Claire as though she were a ghost when she came into Kayla's room, she knew from Detective Warren that Claire and Eli were the two responsible for Kayla's recovery. It wasn't until Kayla asked Phoebe if she had met her friend that Phoebe rose from Kayla's side and went to Claire who stood beside Eli in the doorway of the room.

"I don't know how I can ever thank you."

Claire took her hand from Eli's and folded Phoebe into her arms. Both women wept. And at that precise moment two truths occurred. Kayla knew her mother was indeed the wind and Claire witnessed a reunion she could no longer deny was a longing deep in her soul.

Chapter 26

The nurse unhooked Kayla's intravenous, vehemently stating the child was hydrated enough and the best therapy was the sanctuary of her mother's arms. Eli showed Corinne how the armchair in the room could tip backwards and she might get some rest herself, but Corinne explained she was too keyed up.

"Tell me what you know," she whispered to Claire. "I know you must be tired, but please." She looked at her daughter and granddaughter in their embrace. "I swear in the last couple of weeks I was certain I'd lose my daughter, too."

"There's a lounge down the hall where we can sit and talk," Claire said. "I don't even know your name."

"Corinne," she said. "I know you're Claire and Eli. Detective Warren debriefed us on the plane." She covered her mouth with her hand. "He dyed her hair, the bastard. And he cut it. It was auburn like Phoebe's and flowed down her back. She's thin as a rail."

"Shhhh," Claire shushed her. "Let's talk down the hall."

They settled into the worn purple couches in the waiting room.

"She was such a robust child. She looks like an urchin," Corinne said, pulling a clump of loose blue tissues from her purse and blowing her nose.

"She was always so hungry when she was with us," Claire reassured her. "She'll gain weight in no time."

"We never wanted Phoebe to marry him. My husband was alive at the time. To this day I can't understand why she was so taken with him. They met on the job. She does faux painting and he was the architect on a project out in San Francisco. He was handsome and well-to-do and she had just come off a relationship with a young man who couldn't seem to commit, as they say. Nicholas was her rebound, I suppose. Her rebellion," Corinne said bitterly. "She'd never rebelled as an adolescent. I guess it was time."

"How long were they together before Kayla was born?" Claire asked.

"Not even a year. Oh, he was mad as a hatter when Phoebe got pregnant. He pushed her down a flight of stairs when she was seven months pregnant. Can you imagine what a monster? Of course, I should have seen the signs before then. It was summer and she was wearing long-sleeved shirts to cover the bruises. She told me she was always cold because the pregnancy made her feel that way. I barely saw her when she was pregnant. She called me the night he pushed her down the stairs, but she said she'd fallen. I had my doubts, mind you, but I was afraid I'd alienate her more if I said I didn't believe her. She said he was away on business, but he ran off that night. I came to the hospital after Kayla was born the next morning. He slinked in later in the day and I couldn't look at him. I suppose a part of me felt like I could lose my daughter if I intervened. If I didn't say I believed her. There were incidents after that. Of course, she didn't tell me until she decided to divorce him. Times when he struck her." Corinne began to cry again. "I blame myself."

"You can't blame yourself," Claire said, gently touching Corinne's arm.

"They had the custody hearing after the divorce and naturally she got custody of Kayla. He came to her house the night after the hearing and she let him inside. He broke her fingers. She passed out and when she awakened he had taken her." She took a deep breath. "That was in February. February twenty-sixth. Two months after my husband, Henry, passed away. Sometimes I think if he hadn't died this nightmare would have killed him anyway. He loved that child." She looked at Claire. "What did Nicholas tell you?"

"He said that Phoebe wanted to send Kayla away to a school for the blind. That she would live there and he couldn't bear to be away from his child." She dropped her voice. "That you had died."

"And I suppose he told the same to Kayla and she believed him," Corinne said, her face pained.

Claire nodded. "It's going to take a long time for her to understand why he did what he did. She has a tough road ahead of her. A lot to be undone. All of you do. But at this point I think Kayla understands that he was lying to her. I just don't know when she'll be able to process the reasons. Even adults can barely process the reasons."

"Punishment," Corinne said.

"What?"

"He did it to punish my daughter."

"Punishment, control, anger," Claire said. "Using the child as a weapon in his personal war against his wife. It's all in the books but all the reasons are still unacceptable. And even when we know them, it's hard to fathom."

"He was married before, you know," Corinne said. "It wasn't until we lost Kayla that we found out from Nancy, his first wife, that he had abused her as well. She stayed with him for over twenty years. The abuse began after their first child was born."

"What finally made her leave?"

"She joined a support group. Of course, he had no idea she'd done that. God knows, he might have killed her. She ended up in a women's shelter. His sons from that marriage won't speak to him. And Nancy wouldn't even tell us where she lived."

"And Phoebe had no inkling of this before she married him?"

Corinne shook her head. "None whatsoever."

"It's over now," Claire said.

"What will they do with him, do you suppose?"

Claire took a deep breath. "Not enough, I'm afraid. Not enough."

"I watched my daughter waste away these past seven months. I watched her wait by the phone and sit up all night long working that computer hoping she might find someone somewhere who saw something or heard something. Her sister came a few days ago and the three of us were on one of the trails in Marin County when the calls came through, but the beeper and cell were out of range. You can't imagine how tough it was for us to even get her to go out. She said she had this instinct that they were going to find Kayla. At that point I thought she was delusional." She sighed. "And I must tell you, I had nearly given up. And then when we got home and that message was on the machine." She looked from Claire to Eli and back to Claire. "There is something so powerful about motherhood. It's the fiercest bond on the face of the earth."

The morning sun shone through the slatted window shades in Kayla's hospital room and although the sunlight normally would have made Kayla close her eyes and look away, she coveted the warmth of the sun on her face as she lay in the crook of her mother's arm.

"We're going home soon," Phoebe whispered, bringing Kayla even closer. "The doctor said you're good to go."

"With Grandma?"

"With Grandma."

"Why did Daddy say she died?"

"I don't know," Phoebe said, stroking Kayla's cheek. "Claire said sometimes people tell lies and they don't really mean to tell them."

"That's probably true."

"I lost Bear, Mommy," she said tearfully. "He was in our car and then Daddy got this new car and he got lost."

"We'll ask the police, sweetheart. Maybe they found him."

"Like they found me, right?" Kayla asked hopefully.

"We need to get you some breakfast and get you dressed. Come, let's get you showered."

"Daddy used an icky shampoo. We don't use that, right? It smelled like the cleaning stuff at school."

Phoebe ran her fingers through Kayla's hair. It was the only time she was grateful the child couldn't see.

"Mommy?" Kayla took a deep breath. "Daddy said you wanted to send me away. He said there was this school for blind kids and you wanted to send me there. He said I would live there." She started to cry. "That was another lie, right, Mommy?"

Phoebe kept herself from crying. "Kayla, I would never send you anywhere."

"So why did Daddy say that?"

"Daddy was very angry at me, Kayla. People say things they don't mean when they're angry. All I want you to know right now and forever is that it's simply not true. Grandma's here and I'm here and Aunt Caroline is waiting for you back at home."

"I don't want to talk about it anymore."

Just at that moment the nurse came into the room. "Detective D'Angelo just sent this over," she said, handing a small pink shopping bag tied with a white bow to Phoebe. "He thought Kayla might want this."

Phoebe handed the bag to Kayla and guided her fingers to pull the ribbon. Kayla reached inside the bag. "It's Bear, Mommy!" she cried, hugging the worn stuffed animal to her. "Everyone's home now."

Detective Warren picked up Phoebe, Kayla, and Corinne on Friday at noon for their flight to San Francisco. Kayla wore pink pants and a pink-and-white-striped shirt that Phoebe had brought with her from home. The swelling in Kayla's eyes had abated and the slightest tinge of rose had come back into her cheeks. She would not let go of her mother's hand even as Claire knelt before her and touched her chin.

"I'm going to write to you," Claire said.

"It's better if we can talk on the phone," Kayla said. "But Mommy can read me the letters."

"I'm going to have Annie send you some of those lavender sachets, too."

Kayla smiled and turned to Phoebe. "Claire has a friend who owns a candle shop. She makes these hearts you can put in your drawers and everything smells really nice from them," she explained.

There was no need for words. Corinne and Phoebe and Claire hugged one another with Kayla in their center, Bear held tightly in her arms.

Chapter 27

No one waved from the window of the car as it pulled away from the hospital. Phoebe climbed in first, Kayla cuddled beside her, then Corinne. Detective Warren shut the door behind him and took his place next to the driver. Claire raised her hand in an instinctive wave even though she knew that Kayla wouldn't see. She also knew that Kayla had everything she needed on either side of her.

"I'm tired," she said, turning to Eli.

He nodded. "Me, too. Too tired to make the drive back home."

"You said you wanted to go to Manhattan. How about that? It's what, about forty minutes from here?"

They checked into a small hotel on lower Madison Avenue, purposely avoiding the tourist mecca of midtown, preferring a part of town they'd never known. It was a neutral part of town, one that lay dormant at night when shops and offices were closed. Restaurants and bars were sparse in the quiet neighborhood. They showered and peeled back the covers on either side of the queen-size bed, falling asleep on their backs, their hands clasped together at their sides, awakening around six o'-clock that evening to the sound of sirens from the street.

"I remember when we first moved to Drifting," Claire said in the darkness. "The birds would wake me at five in the morning, yet I slept through the sirens in Manhattan all my life." She looked at the digital clock beside her. "They're halfway home now."

"We should go out," Eli said sleepily. "Get some dinner. Walk around."

"This is so crazy, isn't it?" she asked, propping herself up on her elbow. "Did you ever have a feeling about something and you just couldn't quite put your finger on it? Like you know how something feels but you can't exactly remember the feeling?"

"Déjà vu?"

"Not quite," she said. "It's more like anticipation, I guess." She thought for a moment. "It's like this jack-in-the-box I had when I was a kid. It played 'Pop Goes the Weasel' and I'd wind it and wind it and I'd always jump when the clown popped up."

"It didn't pop up on the same note every time?"

Claire laughed. "I'm not sure. Maybe it did, but it always surprised me. That's kind of how I feel." She sighed. "I don't know. I can't explain."

"You've been through quite an ordeal," he said.

She fiddled with the satin trim on the blanket. "Which one?"

"Which one?" he asked, puzzled.

"I want to find her," she said. "But it's been so safe without her. I'm afraid."

"Sulie?"

"Sulie."

"What are you afraid of?" he asked, turning on his side to face her.

"Of what I'll find."

"Did you ever try to look before? Tell me the truth, Claire." He took her in his arms. "This is the one place you never took me along, you know," he said tenderly.

"Only because I wasn't going there until now," she said. "I wasn't shutting you out, Eli. I would never do that."

"So, have you ever looked?"

"Just this past Monday," she said, drawing in her breath. "That was the first time. I went on one of those people search sites on the Internet. There was nothing. It's probably for the best."

"There are other sites. Or private investigators."

"I thought of that. But you know, she could find me, too. I even kept my name. I'm listed professionally. It's easy to find people nowadays if you want to."

"Maybe she's as scared as you are."

"That gives me too much hope," she said. "I'm wise enough to know I shouldn't romanticize her at this point. She left me."

"But until you know why, you'll never rest, will you?"

"But what if I don't rest even after I have the answer?" She ran her finger along his chest and down to his stomach. "We should get dressed. Let's go someplace fun."

They had dinner that night at a small pub on East Twenty-ninth Street. Burgers, fries, a bottle of red wine.

"When the kids were little I took them on 'explores,' " Claire said, smiling. "We'd go shelling and feed the ducks by the bay." She laughed. "I always had Cheerios in my coat pockets back then. And some nights I'd give them backwards dinners. Of course, they didn't know it was because I didn't have dinner ready on time and they were hungry. Those were the easy days. I was the dream weaver. Their only truth."

"I remember those dinners. Start with ice cream, end with spaghetti."

"Sometimes I wonder if she realizes how much she missed with me." She sipped her wine. "I tell you what, let's start backwards. Let's go downtown to the Village. Start at the apartment where we lived with Jonah."

"Why backwards?"

"Compartmentalize," she said with a smile. "I've always been good at that. Start from where I began with you. Then tomorrow go back to the Upper West Side where I began with Jack."

"And then?"

"Then we'll see."

The building on West Fourth Street had been renovated. The lobby, painted a dark gray when they lived there, was now papered in a gold brocade. A heavy steel door had been placed between the corridor and the stairs, a buzzer system installed with small white pearl buttons above brass mailboxes. Claire took her finger and scanned the names. "No more Eileen Latimer," she said.

"She was elderly back then," Eli said. "She'd be well into her nineties now. Most people don't live alone in their nineties."

"Look, here's Murphy. You think it's the same Murphy?"

"Could be. He wasn't much older than we were."

"Strange guy, remember him? He used to walk down the stairs with that rag in his hand and wipe the bannister as he walked."

"Germ phobic."

"Phobic altogether, I think," Claire said with a laugh. "You know, Sulie once sent a postcard from this place called Cakebread."

"That's a non sequitur."

"My mind is going a thousand miles a minute. Cakebread. In Missouri or Arkansas or someplace. I can't remember. I just remember it sounded like such a sweet place. Jack used to show me the postcards and pretend it was a happy thing. I hated her." She dropped her chin. "One day I told him to stop pretending that I had a mother and he got so upset. I remember thinking he looked so helpless. It was my birthday and he was trying to make everything so nice. I never told him I hated her though because I always had the feeling he still loved her."

"How could he still love her after what she did?"

"For the same reasons that Phoebe stayed with Nick even though he beat her. We turn things on ourselves and excuse those around us."

"Jack once told me Sulie was like a wild mare who couldn't be tamed. He almost exalted her. He said she was simply too young."

Claire got tears in her eyes. "He said that? When?"

"One night when he and I were drinking together. You were in the living room nursing Jonah."

"Why didn't you tell me?"

"For what reason? You had a new baby. We were

happy. Besides, Jack was drinking that night. It was also the vodka talking."

"You see what I mean? He loved her in spite of everything. I think he blamed himself."

"You have to remember one thing," Eli said, reaching for her hand. "You can look for her, but you can't look for your mother. You can look for the woman who would have been your mother if she'd stayed. She gave birth to you. She never mothered you."

"I know," she said.

"Nature and nurture, you know?" he said gently.

"You think I'm setting myself up for a fall."

"I told you I would catch you."

She smiled up at him.

He straightened his shoulders. "Claire, I have to ask you something. Did you ever think she might be . . ."

"Dead?"

"Yes."

"She's not dead, Eli."

"How do you know?"

"Something tells me I would have heard. I just know, that's all." She gathered her hair and twisted it on top of her head and let it fall. "I need to hear the sound of her voice. I need to look at her hands and her fingernails and the way she walks. I want to know if her skin is supple or wrinkled or if she has gray in her hair. If she cooks, if she draws, if she sings. I used to sing myself to sleep at night." She paused. "If she has other children. If she fell in love and maybe that's why she took off. Maybe she fell in love with someone else and the only way to be with him was to leave."

"What would be the best reason she could give for leaving?"

"Passion."

"The worst?"

"Passion."

"I don't understand."

"There's no passion in the world like the one we have for our children. For me, the greatest sin in the world is forsaking a child."

They walked down the street and a fortune-teller beckoned them inside her storefront.

"Aunt Helen told me that Sulie fancied herself a gypsy. She was Italian. Her father was a tailor. Her mother cleaned houses. Helen said that Sulie thought they weren't good enough for her. Just like us. I guess we weren't good enough either." Claire's eyes looked faraway. "I remember her from the pictures. She was very dark. Very beautiful. She *looked* like a gypsy." Claire stopped and wrapped her arms around Eli's waist. "You know what one of the worst things is? What if I find her and I actually like her?"

"What would be so bad about that?"

"I don't want to like her. She should have been *my* dream weaver and instead she unraveled all the threads."

Chapter 28

Jack and Claire's old apartment on the Upper West Side had new windows. Black steel-framed panes of smoked opaque glass that appeared to block the sunlight. There were no more boxy air conditioners hanging precipitously over the street but rather vents in the sides of the building indicating central air and heat. The lobby had a crystal chandelier and a new marbled floor replaced the old black-and-white tiles Claire often skipped as a child, using them as a hopscotch, deciding whether she would step on only the black ones or only the white ones before leaping into the elevator bay.

"I used to live here," she said to the doorman, looking around her.

"Oh? I've only been here for two years. When was it?"

"When I was a little girl. Do you think I could see the basement? My father and I used to do our laundry down there."

"The tenants have their own machines now."

"So what's in the basement?"

"Pipes. Storage rooms. Cable wires. You can't go down there."

"The super's name was Walter."

"It's Eddie now," he said, disinterested.

"Oh," she said, turning to walk out of the building. She stopped. "Who lives in apartment Ten A now?"

"I really can't tell you that," he said, clearly annoyed.

"That was our apartment," she said. "It looked out over the Hudson."

The doorman nodded. "Well, it still does, I guess. River's still there."

"I thought it would be the same," she said to Eli as they walked across Riverside Drive to the park.

"Sometimes it's a bad thing to stir up those memories," he said, holding her hand.

"Well, at least the cannons are still here," she said. "Jack and I came here every Sunday morning." She looked over the stone wall into the playground. It was a labyrinth of wooden climbing structures, tunnels, and forts. "It used to be metal swings and slides. There was a wading pool with a sprinkler." She threw her hands palms up to either side of her. "Progress, huh?"

They walked over to Broadway. Stanley Drugs. The neon display hung over the empty storefront. A FOR RENT sign with a phone number scrawled in black magic marker was taped in the window. They walked into the pizza parlor next door.

"When did Stanley's go out of business?" she asked.

"About a year ago. CVS came in and ran them out."

"My father used to own it."

"Your father's Stanley?"

"No, Cherney. My father was Jack Cherney. He owned it before Stanley took over. About nineteen years ago, I guess."

The man shrugged as he put a pie in the oven on a long wooden spatula. "I been here for fifteen years. I must have just missed him."

They left the pizza parlor and Claire linked her arm through Eli's. "It's time to go home," she said. "No Farabutto. I don't want to know."

The chimes on the door to Annie's store tinkled when Claire and Eli walked in. Stella, who had been sleeping at Annie's feet, struggled to get up, walked over to them, and wagged her tail.

"So there is life in the old girl," Annie said. "I was just getting ready to close." She hugged them both. "I hear all's well that ends well."

"It was really something," Claire said.

"What a story. You know Sam was the one who made sure the bear got to her," Annie said proudly. "He called John Blanco up in Hubbard. So how was the city?"

"So-so," Claire said, sniffing a scented sachet. "What's in this one?"

"Rosemary. So how come just so-so?"

"It's so different now." She sighed. "Everything's changed."

Annie looked at Eli. "Think you'll ever work again?"

"I may not," Eli said with a grin. "I'm enjoying these days with my wife." He looked at Claire and read her thoughts. Go away just for a moment, her eyes told him. Not for long. Just for a moment. "I'm going to go next door and get some coffee. Want anything?"

"Hazelnut?" Claire asked Annie.

"Absolutely," Annie said.

"You are like an open book, my friend," Annie said as the door closed behind Eli. "What gives?"

"Nothing, really." Claire sighed. "We went back to the old apartments. The one where we lived in the Village. The one I lived in with Jack. The pharmacy. Did the whole nostalgia tour."

"And?"

"The pharmacy's for rent. It's all shuttered. The apartments are renovated. Nothing looks the same."

"Did you speak to the kids?"

"Before we left for Harrison. I'll call them tonight. Obviously you got my message. You knew we went to Manhattan."

Annie nodded. "I almost called Eli's cell, but I didn't want to bother you. I figured you needed a break."

"I have something to tell you."

"Uh-oh."

"What 'uh-oh'?"

"Tell me you're not pregnant."

"Oh for God's sake, Annie. Have you lost your mind?"

"Well, you know. All these days off he's taken. A night alone in Manhattan."

Claire laughed. "So what am I—a minute pregnant?"

"I got you to laugh, didn't I?"

Claire's face became serious. "Strange thing is what I'm about to ask you is sort of about birth." She straightened her shoulders in the same way she had at thirteen when she had something to say to Jack. Something perhaps painful that required courage or an undue amount of strength. "I need you to help me find my mother."

"Me?" Annie asked, her mouth agape. "How can I . . . ?"

"Sam has that computer. That NCIC."

"Oh, Claire, it didn't even help us with Kayla. You found her on that Web site."

"That's because we didn't have her real name. Why can't we can try?" Claire said.

"It only works if someone has a criminal record or if they're a missing person or something."

"She is a missing person," Claire said softly.

"Yes, but from forty years ago . . ."

"Forty-two. It's my last resort unless I hire an investigator and that's so expensive."

"Claire, I can't."

"Why not?"

"Because only Sam is authorized to use that thing. He could get in a lot of trouble."

"No one has to know."

"I just can't. You know I would do anything for you. . . ."

"You know his code, don't you?"

Annie reddened. "I'm not supposed to, though."

"Oh, come on. Husbands and wives always know those things. Pillow talk. That's what Eli and I call it. You think I don't tell him some of the cases I deal with?"

"Sam would kill me."

"Even if he knew it was for me?"

"He's pretty rigid when it comes to regulations."

"Well, maybe he wouldn't mind looking the other way. Just this once."

"If I ask him and he says no, then I can't sneak behind his back. I can't deceive him, Claire."

"But I'm not asking you to deceive him. Please,

Annie. Ask him. We may not find a thing. But please, help me try."

"What about those people-search things on the Internet?"

"I tried that. It came up empty. She's probably not listed. For all I know she was running from something and she's still running."

"Maybe she's . . ." Annie tipped her head sympathetically.

"She's not dead," Claire said adamantly.

"How do you know?"

"Because I just know," she said.

"And if you're wrong? What if we find out otherwise? Then what?"

"Then I'll have to bury her all over again, won't I?"

Annie studied her friend's face. "Just let me figure out how to ask Sam. I'll help you. I promise. Why did you want Eli to leave?"

"So he wouldn't try to stop me from setting myself up for a fall."

"Are you going to tell him?"

"Only if we find her."

"You're not going to tell him that you're looking?"

"He worries about me."

The door opened and Eli walked in with a box of coffees. As they left he turned to Annie and kissed her good-bye. "Careful with her," he whispered in her ear. "Very careful."

Deputy Nelson was watching the cable crew and Deputy Kent was at the school crossing when Sam showed up at the inn to help Eli with the storm windows on Monday afternoon at two-thirty.

"Storm windows?" Claire asked innocently. "He's going to do the storms today? He's at the office."

"You're a lousy crook, Claire," Sam said. "Your accomplice is waiting for you at the shop."

"Annie? You mean . . ."

He raised his hand. "Why don't you run down to the shop. Kent is going to be back at headquarters at three-thirty. You've got an hour."

"Sam, thank you," Claire said, reaching for her purse. "Oh my God. I have a patient coming at four."

"Well, you better hurry then. Now get going."

Annie was waiting in her car when Claire pulled down Main Street. She rolled down her window. "Follow me to headquarters," she said.

Claire pulled a chair over to Annie as she booted up the NCIC computer. She punched in Sam's code.

"Spell her last name for me," Annie said.

"T-E-R-E-N-Z-I."

"You think she uses that name? Not Cherney?"

"I don't know. Yes, I think so. That was the name on her stage photographs."

"First name?"

"Ursula."

"Last known address?"

"One-oh-two Riverside Drive." Claire swallowed hard. "That's the last one known to me."

"New York City," Annie said aloud as she filled in the empty field.

"Date of birth?"

"What?"

"Her birthday?"

Claire's mouth opened. "I have no idea. Isn't that amazing? I have no idea."

"The year she was born?"

"She was fifteen years younger than Jack. I guess it would be around nineteen thirty-eight."

"We'll make up a month and date."

"Why?"

"It's quirky. It would rather have something than nothing," Annie explained as she typed. "Place of birth?"

"Italy, I think."

"Italy?"

"Yes, why?"

Annie looked at Claire over her glasses. "You are the least Italian-looking half Italian I ever met, that's why. Okay, now here goes," Annie said, hitting the enter key.

Rows of white type popped up against the black screen. The computer came to a stop.

Ursula Terenzi Cherney. Missing person. Originating agency NYPD Missing Persons Unit. Original date of report January 22, 1959. Five foot seven inches. One hundred twenty pounds. Black hair. Brown eyes. Mole on inside of left thigh. May use Terenzi as surname. Contact information: Detective Charles Wagner 212-555-2246. Miscellaneous: Last sighted August 11, 1991, at Morley's Bar and Grill in Bar Harbor, Maine. Wearing black trousers and red sleeveless shirt. Reported by customer Vincent DiFalco.

"Vincent," Claire said, shaking.

"Who is he?"

"My father's friend. He died about five years ago."

"He never told you that he saw her?"

"Maybe he wasn't sure. Maybe he didn't want to get my hopes up."

Annie printed out the form and exited the computer. "We have to go," she said, handing the form to Claire. "Everyone will be back soon."

Claire took the form in her hand. She pulled her coat over her shoulders.

"What are you going to do?" Annie asked.

Claire didn't answer.

"Claire?"

"Try not to dream."

Claire was sitting on the veranda when Eli came home that night.

"So?" he said.

"So what?" she asked.

"Sam told me."

"What did he tell you?" she asked.

"That you and Annie used the computer to look for her."

"Are you angry that I didn't tell you?"

"You needed to be on your own with this one." He poured himself a glass of wine. "I wanted to give you time."

"How long were you going to give me?" she asked with a smile.

"Until now," he said, sitting beside her.

"She exists," Claire said.

"You always knew that."

"They still have the missing person report. It's there."

"After all these years?"

"I didn't know her birthday." Her eyes glistened. "Or the town where she was born. Vincent's name was on the report. He thought he saw her ten years ago in Bar Harbor, Maine."

"Vincent?"

"I guess it was like with the police and Kayla. They didn't want to tell Phoebe until they had Kayla for sure." She looked out the window. "Vincent saw her in a place called Morley's Bar and Grill."

"Did you call? Is it still there?"

"Yes."

"Who did you speak with?"

"No one. I only got the phone number. I haven't called yet."

"It could be a dead end," he cautioned. "You have to brace yourself for this."

"I know," she said, turning to him. "That's why I waited for you."

"What should I do?"

"Stay beside me while I make the call." She smiled at him. "Stand behind me."

"Behind you?"

"In case I fall backwards."

"Morley's Bar and Grill," a man answered. "Brad Morley speaking."

"I'm looking for Ursula Terenzi," Claire said, her voice trembling.

"And you are?" he asked guardedly.

"I'm her daughter," Claire said. The words tumbled from her lips as visions haunted her. A ghost framed in silver sitting on the mantel. Postcards with frilled edges and three-cent stamps. Her father's face forcing joy as he took her into his arms, sat her on his knee, and showed her pictures of the woman he called her mother. The few phone calls where she said merely Happy Birthday, Claire—the change running out on the pay phone in the midst of the call.

"Her daughter?" he asked, unable to mask surprise.

"I'm trying to locate her," Claire stammered.

"She used to work here," he said. "Long time ago." He paused. "I don't quite understand. You're her daughter. Is this one of those adoption things?"

"No," Claire said, collecting herself. "I lived with my father. Do you know where she is now, Mr. Morley?"

She'd worked summers there for half a dozen years. In the winter, she was in Nevada or California or Florida. In the beginning, she waited tables, but then he discovered she could sing and she put on a show every weekend. One night, after the show, she took her tip money, slipped out the back door, and never returned. It was the night a man at the bar had asked about her. Brad couldn't remember his name, just that the man thought he knew her. He had put money in the glass on the piano and he swore there was some recognition from Sulie as well. He told Brad he thought she was the wife of a friend of his. The last Brad heard, she was working at a café in Quebec. A little town called Sainte Agathe. That was where he'd mailed her last paycheck—but that was about ten years ago. She was, he said, like so many of the summer people who got lost in the glare of the summer sun and didn't want to be found.

Claire hung up the phone and covered her mouth with her hands. She walked over to the window where a full moon trailed silver over the ocean. Eli stood behind her. She pictured her mother's dark hair cascading down her back. She recalled Aunt Helen's revelations. The secrets she told Claire about the day Sulie left. Secrets Claire never let on to Jack that she knew. She envisioned a young woman not much older than Natalie standing at the door with a suitcase by her side. A man coming home and rocking a baby to sleep in his arms. She wondered what compelled Sulie to run. Anger surged within her. How do I ask my mother forty-two years later why she left? My mother, she thought, shivering involuntarily.

Chapter 29

Neither Ursula Terenzi nor Ursula Cherney were listed in Sainte Agathe or any of the other small villages and towns that dotted the Laurentian Mountains. Claire scrolled through Web sites, searching towns and directories for her mother's name. One night, after Claire was sleeping, Eli went downstairs to the office, booted up the computer and pulled up names of the local newspapers and went into their obituary archives, holding his breath, his heart pounding, as he put in Ursula's names. Had he found Ursula, he wasn't certain how he would tell Claire who was so convinced that Sulie was alive. Although he found no matches under either Cherney or Terenzi he remained more than convinced that Sulie died under a different name. Claire, on the other hand, preferred to think that perhaps Sulie lived under a different name.

On Friday afternoon, Claire's last patient canceled her five o'clock appointment. She gathered her papers, her briefcase, her jacket and gloves since the autumn had become more like winter overnight. She called Natalie and Jonah and listened to each nuance of their voices. The way Jonah said Mom more as a statement than a question when he answered the phone. How Natalie's greeting was more questioning, or perhaps it was exclamatory. Mom? Mom! She hadn't seen either of them for nearly two months now. She wouldn't see them until Thanksgiving. And she wondered how a mother could go for years not wondering, not watching from some secret place to see how her child fared and grew. She leaned back in her chair and closed her eyes. Was there anything Sulie left behind that Jack hadn't shown her? The closet in Jack's bedroom that once was Sulie's was filled with coats in summer and summer suits in winter. It reeked of mothballs and cedar. There were dishes and vases and china figurines and the lace antimacassars, but it never occurred to her they might have been Sulie's. Where was the rest of her? Surely she couldn't have taken it all in that small suitcase or had Jack made a decision one day to remove all traces of her? She closed her eyes tighter and tried to remember. Somewhere in the recesses of her mind she thought Aunt Helen said she had been the one to remove the remains as it were. Sulie's clothing went to the church and the personal effects were tossed except for some that were placed in a cardboard box and Jack said he would tend to them. There were no rings, no bracelets, no bottles of perfume. Only the photographs—and those became ashes.

What if she found her and saw traces of Sulie in herself? What if Sulie's reason for leaving was one that was best left buried? Did Jack know Sulie the way a husband should know a wife? The way that Eli knew her, she thought. He could read a gesture of her hand, a look on her face, a tone in her voice that said something was not right with the simplest hello.

The door to the barn opened with a soft knock.

"I didn't see anyone's car so I figured you were alone," Eli said.

"My last patient canceled," Claire said. "Flu season's starting, I guess."

"How come you're still here?"

"I called the kids. Did some paperwork."

"How are the kids?"

"They're good," she said with a smile. "Sometimes I talk to them and they're so grown up but I still picture them as little ones."

He settled himself into the sofa. "Claire, I looked up her name in the local obits in Quebec. She wasn't there."

"You what? When?"

"I did it last night while you were sleeping."

"Why?"

"I was afraid you might do it yourself when you were alone." He leaned forward. "I didn't want you to find . . ."

"You tried both names?"

"Yes."

"I know what you're thinking—she could have married. Taken someone's name." She rose from her chair and sat beside him on the sofa. "But I'm telling you, she's not dead, Eli."

"You're not going to rest until you find her, are you?"

Claire shook her head. "I've finally succeeded in torturing myself."

"Sainte Agathe is about eight hours from here by car. If we leave now we can get to Montreal by midnight. It's about seven hours from here. We can stay there and drive up to Sainte Agathe in the morning. It's about an hour out of Montreal."

"But she's not listed there."

"First of all, you just said it yourself—she's unlisted. That doesn't mean she isn't there. It also doesn't mean that someone there doesn't remember her." He hugged her to him. "It's going to be cold up there."

"I want to drive straight through to Sainte Agathe. I don't want to stop," she said, wondering how cold it might really be.

Sainte Agathe was sleeping when they drove in shortly after one in the morning. There was a bed and breakfast at the edge of town, a miniature of the Inn at Drifting. Red-and-white awnings and the Canadian maple leaf flying. Pots of plastic red and white geraniums hanging from the porch. The proprietor opened the door in his robe and slippers. Despite the lateness of the hour, he was welcoming, walking ahead of them to the small room at the end of the hall on the inn's third floor. Claire parted the curtains on the windows half expecting to see the ocean, but instead there was an old stone church, its golden cross illuminated by the same moonlight that played on the stained-glass windows. She turned to Eli who had opened their suitcases and was hanging their jackets in the closet.

"Come look," she said.

He stood behind her for a moment as they looked out the window.

"Let's go to bed," he said, kissing her neck. "Make love with me."

They were under the white down comforter, their bodies intertwined, when the door of the church opened and a woman descended the steps. She lifted the hood of her coat over her head, dropped her chin against the wind, and walked down the street, silhouetted by the street lamp.

Chapter 30

Sainte Agathe was in between seasons. The leaves had already fallen from the trees and the air smelled like snow. It began to drizzle in the morning, sharp daggers of icy rain that bounced off their cheeks as Eli and Claire walked the narrow streets. There was a candle shop like Annie's, a store that sold rough leather coats and winter boots, a bookshop, a bakery. The town, except for the French spoken, was not unlike Drifting. They sat at a corner table in the bakery, drinking coffee and eating ham sandwiches stuffed into croissants.

"What else I can have for you?" the young waitress asked.

Claire looked to Eli and back to her. "Do you live here?"

"Upstairs," the young woman said. "With my husband. This is our bakery."

"Everything is delicious," Claire said. "It's very beautiful here."

"I am grown up here," she said, beaming. "You are Americans?"

"From Connecticut," Claire said.

The woman nodded. "Vacation?"

"Yes," Claire said. "But I am looking for someone. Do you know a woman named Ursula Terenzi?"

"No."

"She sings."

"Comment?" she asked in French.

"Chanteuse," Eli said.

"Ah, une chanteuse. You want to hear the songs. They sing at La Nuit Magique."

"La Nuit Magique?" Claire asked.

"Magic Night," Eli said, turning to Claire. "Where is it?"

"The club? In Saint Jovite. Twenty-nine kilometers from here," she said. "I can get you nothing else?"

"Just the check," Eli said.

"Since when do you speak French?" Claire asked.

"I don't." He laughed. "It's that long-term memory invoking high school French."

"How far is twenty-nine kilometers?"

"About eighteen miles."

The waitress came back with their check. "I speak to my husband. The woman she sings at La Nuit Magique? She is not Ursula. She is Sulie Bernard. But my husband he says she does not sing now anymore."

Chapter 31

⟟⟡

La Nuit Magique was strung with small red lanterns and tiny carnival lights, its name painted in iridescent blue on a sign surrounded by silver half-moons and shimmering stars. It was an oasis of sorts along the desolate highway that led into Saint Jovite, situated between an Esso with a small dairy mart and a fast-food shack advertising hot dogs and pommes frites. The tables were covered in blue-and-white-checkered oilcloth, glimmering candles in cobalt votives, a single rose in a cut-glass bud vase. A menu written in faded chalk hung on the far wall. An easel with a photograph of a young man named Jean-Louis sat in the corner. It said he would sing that night at eleven o'clock.

Claire and Eli stood at the small podium at the front of the café. A man with white hair was seating the couple who had arrived before them. A woman in a flowing black skirt painted with small red rosebuds that touched the middle of her calves, a black lace top, décolleté with three-quarter sleeves, a wide black belt accentuating her small waist, walked from table to table. Her jet-black hair was swept up in a chignon, gold earrings with red stones dangling from their centers hung from her ears. Her high cheekbones were blushed with a touch too much rouge and her perfectly heart-shaped lips were painted red. She was nothing like Claire. Nothing like Claire's slender up-and-down boyish build, pale skin, and fine golden hair. The woman cocked her head, her ear pressed into the lips of a young man who took her arm by the elbow, pulling her down to the table. If there had been the slightest doubt in Claire's mind, it was then she knew: the woman's head tipped back in laughter, the tilted angle from the photographs. The line of her angular jaw. The sparkle in her dark gypsy eyes.

The white-haired man gestured to a table near the piano but Eli said they preferred a table in the rear. Ah, lovers, the man teased with a wink. He looked to be in his late sixties, the white hair combed straight back from his forehead, a blue-and-white pinstriped shirt, navy blazer with a silky red pocket square, dark gray trousers. The man pulled out the chair for Claire and bowed from the waist. Enjoy the evening, he said. She murmured thank you under her breath but couldn't take her eyes off the woman, following her from table to table that lined the front row by the small platform where Jean-Louis would sing at the ebony piano. Don't come here, Claire thought as the woman walked toward them. Not now. Not yet. Don't come here.

"You are here for the show?" the woman asked.

"We are," Eli said.

"You will like Jean-Louis. He's come for the week as a favor to my husband. My husband used to own a club in Montreal. I am Sulie Bernard. That's my husband, Edward, over there," she said, pronouncing his name with a French accent, pointing to the white-haired man. "Welcome."

Claire knew she was pale. She heard herself breathing.

"Are you feeling well, madame? Would you care to see our menu?"

"Please," Eli said. "We're quite hungry."

Sulie snapped her fingers and a young man brought two menus. "Enjoy your dinner," she said. "The wine list is on the back."

Claire watched her walk away, the skirt sashaying with each step.

"Claire?" Eli asked, reaching for her hand. "Claire?"

"She's still beautiful," Claire said.

"Do you want to stay? We can leave. Tell me what you want."

Claire nodded as her eyes grew wide. "She's Natalie," she whispered, unable to complete the breath she longed to take. "Her features. Her figure. She's Natalie."

Jean-Louis's set was interminable. Sulie sat at a corner table by the piano with Edward, joining Jean-Louis for one song, a rendition of Sinatra's "Something Stupid," much to the delight of the patrons who had coaxed her onto the stage, one of them saying she could sing like an angel.

"Enough," Sulie said in French, clearly enjoying the applause while she curtsyed deeply.

"Diva," Claire said, lost in thought. She blinked and turned her head like a mechanical doll. "I want to go now, Eli."

He motioned for the check.

"I'll meet you at the truck," she said.

Sulie and Edward were at the podium as she walked past.

"Did you enjoy the show?" Sulie asked.

"He was very good," Claire said.

"The night is young," Sulie said, waving her hand to the ceiling painted on with stars. "The night is magic. There's more. Another show. You're leaving too soon."

The words caught in Claire's throat. So did you, she thought. "Good night," she said softly. She was halfway through the door when she stopped and turned around. "By the way," she said just before the door shut behind her, "my name is Claire."

Chapter 32

It had become a ritual for Sulie and Edward. The bar closed at two A.M. and they spent the next hour alone. The chairs were stacked upside down on the tables save two the staff left down, knowing their routine. The votive candles were snuffed. Two brass sconces with fringed blue shades dimly lit the room. The stars on the ceiling no longer sparkled; the lanterns and carnival lights were dark. Edward poured brandies into oversized crystal snifters they kept for themselves in a small wooden cabinet behind the bar. Sulie unclipped the clasp that held the chignon in place, letting her hair fall past her shoulders, placed her hand on the small of her back and leaned backwards. Edward hung his blazer on the back of the chair and placed the gray metal cash box between them.

"So it goes," Edward said. "Quite a good night."

She took a sip of brandy. "All the regulars this time of year."

"Until ski season."

"Did you see the couple in the back?"

"The blond woman with the tall man?" He placed a stack of bills into a rubber band. "I offered them a table up front."

"Her name is Claire. When she left, she said her name was Claire."

He closed the metal box, turned the key, and walked over to the safe.

"Did you hear what I said?" she asked. "I said her name was Claire."

"I heard you. So?"

"That was my daughter's name, Edward." She looked up at the painted stars on the ceiling. "She was blond like her father."

"What are you saying?" he asked.

She placed her face in her hands and spread her palms on her rouged cheeks. "That woman is my daughter. She found me."

Sulie was silent throughout the ride back to their small house in Sainte Agathe. She stared out the window as Edward navigated the winding back roads. In many ways, Edward was much like Jack. Routinized. Decent. Stable. Qualities she longed for, needed, when she married Edward five years ago as she approached her sixtieth birthday. Qualities she couldn't bear in Jack when she was twenty-one. She wanted to fly to the moon back then. His feet stayed on the ground.

That day forty-two years ago remained vivid. Its memory never faded. Jack was dressed as usual in white trousers and white smock, the square white pin with his name in black letters pinned to his collar: JACK

CHERNEY. PHARMACIST. He was so predictable. Each morning, he had his black coffee, nearly burnt toast, a wedge of cheddar cheese, a scoop of blueberry jam. The newspaper was folded beside him into thirds. She wore a yellow quilted robe that morning and sat across from him at the gold-flecked dinette.

"Will you take Claire to the park today?" he asked. "Today is a beautiful day." That daily proclamation of his.

Claire sat in her high chair, a Zwieback broken into bits, mashed and wet between her fingers. She wore a crookedly fastened undershirt, a cloth diaper beneath voluminous rubber pants.

"She won't sit in her stroller anymore," Sulie said. "She runs and runs."

"She's supposed to run and run," he said. "This is what children do."

"She chases the pigeons."

He laughed. "So long as the pigeons don't chase her." He looked at the clock. "I'll keep an eye on her while you dress. Go ahead, Sulie."

She drew her bath and sank into the hot water. He had brought her a bottle of Sardo Bath Oil the day before. He forever brought her things, but never gave her what she needed. He brought home bouquets of spring flowers and trinkets from the store. Bath oils and chocolates. Fake gold brooches embedded with rhinestones in large floral sprays. Barrettes and pearled combs. He poured his vodka from the frozen bottle at six o'clock each night and read the evening paper in the overstuffed chair, the white outfit changed to belted beige trousers and an Oxford shirt, the sleeves rolled to the elbows, the collar open at the neck. On Saturday nights he made love to her, although before they were married he made love to her all the time.

She wrapped herself in a towel and sat at her dressing table, brushing her long dark hair that fell nearly to her waist and twisting it into a single braid down her back. He came into the bedroom with the baby in his arms.

"Ready?" he asked. "She's wet. You need to change her."

"Almost," she said, as she lined her eyes with a thin line of black and avoided his. "I'll be right there."

His hands felt cold on her bare shoulder as he kissed the back of her neck. "I'll put Claire in the playpen. I have to run."

"Good-bye, Jack," she said to his reflection in the mirror.

Her body wracked with sobs after he left, blending with the cries of the baby in the playpen who had her father's eyes and the pallid tone of his skin. She picked up Claire to calm her, bouncing her on her hip while she dialed Helen's number. She sat on the floor, the baby on her lap, after she'd hung up the phone.

"I can't do this," she whispered to Claire. "I'm not cut out for this." She placed her gingerly back into the playpen, afraid if she held her and kissed her the way she saw mothers do in the playground she might not be able to leave. She packed the worn leather suitcase that sat on the closet shelf, took her hairbrushes, her combs, and her Castile soap. She dressed in her best outfit and took the one hundred dollars she had saved from her allowance and stashed under the mattress. The doorbell rang and her heart pounded. The baby looked up at her with liquid blue eyes, her thin little thighs damp now from the leaking diaper she'd never changed. "It's not you," she said before opening the door to Helen. "It's me. He'll take care of you. I can't."

And as the Greyhound bus entered the white-tiled tunnel she disappeared. She was wise enough to know there would be nights filled with demons and days filled with regrets. She took her gloved hand and wiped a circle of frost on the window. The bus cleared the tunnel and she saw the Manhattan skyline become distant. She didn't know where she was going, but she knew there was no going back. She was, she thought, a detail Jack failed to notice, despite the way she had said good-bye that morning with such finality.

Edward pulled the car into the driveway. "Long night," he said, breaking into her thoughts.

"I'll be up shortly," she said.

"What are you going to do?"

"I'm just not ready to sleep."

Edward wore his plaid flannel robe and brown leather slippers when he came into the living room. Sulie was sitting where he'd left her hours before. "It's four-thirty," he said. "Come to bed."

"I will," she said. "Soon."

"Just because she's blond and her name is Claire, this doesn't mean she is your daughter."

"No. It's her," she said. "Last night I went to church. You were sound asleep. It was after midnight. Lately I've been thinking about her. Trying to picture her."

"Why church?"

"No distractions. I used to do that sometimes when I was on the road. When I was younger. I never made confession. My mother ruined that for me." She shook her head. "She dragged me to confession if I wore lipstick. When I liked Elvis Presley. My parents moved back to Italy after I left. They wouldn't speak to me again." She was silent for a moment. "The man with her. That was probably her husband. I wonder if they have children."

"She'll be back again," he said, sitting beside her, placing his hand on her knee. "I daresay that was not the end of it. Not if you're her mother."

She lifted her chin and turned her head to the side. "You're a sweet man, Edward," she said, placing her hand on his cheek. "But at this point in my life I realize any cat can have kittens."

"What does that mean?"

"I'm not a mother," she said ruefully. "Mothers don't leave their children."

Chapter 33

The next afternoon, Claire and Eli walked to the playground in the middle of town.

"I watched you sleep most of the night," she said.

"Was I peaceful?"

"Very." She smiled.

"But not you."

"Not last night."

"You have to speak to her, Claire."

"I don't know what to say."

A young mother wheeled a double stroller into the playground. She unstrapped her children one by one, kissing their cheeks as she placed them on the ground, double-knotting their shoelaces. Smiling, she stood and watched them climb the wooden fortress. "I miss Jonah and Natalie," Claire said softly. She looked at her watch. "Too early to call on a Sunday morning."

Eli nodded. "Way too early. Are you going to tell them that you found her?"

"When I see them. Face to face. It's not a phone call."

It began to drizzle. "We should get going," Eli said, looking at the sky. "It's supposed to pour."

Claire watched as the mother gathered up the children and placed them in the stroller, protecting them with a sheet of plastic. On the other side of the playground, on the path that wove around the park, a woman trudged up the hill. A baguette jutted from the brown bag of groceries in her arms. She wore dark glasses despite the dismal weather. Claire watched as she walked up a cobblestone path to a small, white frame house that sat on the corner.

"It's her," Claire said, quickening her pace.

"Where are you going?" Eli asked as she ran ahead of him.

The woman fumbled for her key, opened the door with her knee and shut it behind her.

"I'm going to ring the bell." She turned to Eli. "I have to do this alone. You understand?"

"I understand," he said.

Eli stood in place as Claire crossed the street and walked up the path to the house. He watched as she pressed the bell and waited until the woman opened the door. The rain was coming down harder. He pulled the hood of his jacket over his head and sat on a bench in the small wooden shelter at the bus stop.

Sulie opened the door, her coat slung over her arm. Gloves in her hand.

"I wondered if you'd come back."

Claire simply stared at her. I wondered if you would, too, she thought. "I wasn't sure if I would," she said.

"How did you find me?" Sulie asked as though she'd been expecting her. The way someone might tell a door-to-door salesman that they don't want any.

"You can find anyone these days. Computers."

"Come in," she said. "Come out of the rain."

The house was small but well appointed. A round mahogany table with four soft upholstered chairs sat in the el bend of the living room, a basket of fruit in the center. There was a red velvet love seat and two matching chairs. A tall brass lamp. Claire walked over to the fireplace. On top of the mantel, there were photographs in silver frames. The same ones of Sulie from long ago and one with the white-haired man from last night.

"Maine," Sulie said. "Our honeymoon. We were on our friends' sailboat."

"How long are you married?" Claire asked, taking the photograph in her hands for a moment and then replacing it.

"Five years." Sulie hung her coat in the closet and placed her gloves on a small table in the hall. "I was about to make breakfast. Are you hungry?"

Claire shook her head. "How long have you lived here?"

"Ten years. Give or take. Why don't you give me your coat?"

"Why here?" Claire asked, slipping her arm from her sleeve.

"Edward was born here. This is the house where he grew up." Sulie placed Claire's coat on the chair.

"Why did you leave us?" Claire asked suddenly.

Sulie stood straight in front of Claire and looked her in the eyes without blinking. "Because I couldn't stay. I had no choice."

"No," Claire said with more anger than she imagined was held inside. "You *chose* to go. You *made* a choice."

"Why did you come here? To punish me?"

"No."

"What then?"

"To understand. To ask you why you left." Her voice became nearly inaudible. "How do you leave a baby?"

Sulie walked over to the bookshelf and pulled a small leather picture frame from between two books. "This is you."

Claire studied the picture without touching it. "So?"

"I kept it all these years."

"Perhaps you'd like a round of applause. Perhaps you should take another bow."

Sulie placed the picture facedown on the shelf. "Go ahead. Keep it up if it makes you feel better. Or you can sit down with me and I will tell you why I left. I didn't leave you. I left him."

"You left us," Claire said, pronouncing each word alone. The words haunted her. *She left me*, Jack said. *No, she left us.*

"That's not exactly true."

"Not exactly? How reassuring."

"Do you want to hear or not?"

"I suppose."

"Then come into the kitchen while I cook."

Sulie took two eggs from a glass bowl in the refrigerator and set them on the counter. She pulled the baguette from the bag and sliced it into two diagonal pieces.

"Will you have something?" She motioned with her hand. "Sit down."

"I'm not hungry," Claire said, pulling a chair from the table.

"You might change your mind."

She sliced up peppers and poured olive oil into a pan, tossed in the peppers, pulled the centers from the pieces of bread, cracked the eggs into gaping holes.

"I take it the man with you last night is your husband. Where is he?"

"Waiting for me." Claire watched as Sulie deftly seasoned the concoction in the pan. "Where is your husband?"

"Sleeping." She turned down the flame on the stove. "How is your father?"

"How is my father?" Claire echoed, horrified. "My father is dead."

Sulie grabbed the edge of the counter. "When?"

"Nearly twenty years ago. He had a stroke."

"And Helen?"

"Gone. Five years ago. She would have been close to ninety now."

"Max?"

"Alzheimer's. In a nursing home in Raleigh. It was Vince who saw you at Morley's in Bar Harbor. He was the one who called the police so they reopened your case. If not for Vince you might not have been listed."

"Listed?"

"As a missing person."

"I recognized Vince that night." A faraway look came across her eyes.

"Why did you run?"

"I wasn't ready to be found."

"Vince is gone now, too."

"Everyone is gone," Sulie said more to herself.

"Jack was the only one who died too young," Claire said, unable to resist reassuring her.

Sulie took the eggs from the pan and set a dish in front of Claire and one in front of herself, pushing hers away at the same time she set it down. "Do you cook?"

"Jack taught me. He taught me everything. To do laundry. Grocery shop. Even sew," she said defiantly.

"I suppose the best I could have done was teach you to sing."

"I used to sing myself to sleep at night."

"So you sing?"

"Not really."

"What's your husband's name?" Sulie asked, changing the subject.

"Eli."

"What does he do?"

"He's a veterinarian."

"And you?"

"I'm a psychologist. And a mother." Claire reached for her wallet. "A mother first. I have pictures. Jonah is twenty-two. Natalie is eighteen."

"She looks like me," Sulie said, gazing at the pictures through the cellophane.

"She has Eli's coloring. Jonah has mine. Jack's."

"You called him Jack?" Sulie asked, handing back the photographs. "Why?"

"It felt right."

"I sent you pictures over the years."

"No. Only the first few years," Claire said. "I burned them."

"You what? You burned them?"

Claire's eyes filled with tears, but she refused to cry. "I was thirteen. It was my birthday. I threw them into the incinerator." She drew in her breath. She was thirteen again. "I'd just gotten my period a few weeks be-

fore. You weren't there. You weren't there for anything. I walked over to the five and dime with a washcloth stuffed between my legs and stood in the section
where the Modess was. A woman who worked there
came over to me. She showed me the belt and the pads
and took me to the bathroom in the back." I hated you
then, she thought but didn't say. "I thought you were
an actress. You're a singer."

Sulie shrugged. "I needed to make money. You can't
get up in a club and act on the stage."

"Do you have children?"

"Other children?"

Claire ignored the remark.

"I had an abortion when I was twenty-five. I became
infected. I couldn't have children after that."

"Did you want to?"

"No," she said quickly. "Are you going to eat your
eggs?"

"Not right now."

"Did your father marry again? Was there anyone
else?"

"He never married. I don't know if there was anyone else."

"How can you not know?"

"Jack was discreet. I never asked."

"Why not?"

"He was my father. Why should I have asked?" she
asked hotly. "Do you know how much he loved you?
Do you know it was I who had to convince him to let
you go? You were like a ghost that hovered over us for
years. Why did you marry him?"

"Because he loved me," Sulie said simply.

"But you didn't love him."

"Why are you asking me this now?" Sulie asked.

"When should I have asked you?"

"Why do you think I didn't love him?"

"Can you really ask me that without guilt? Am I supposed to feel sorry for you?" Claire said, nearly seething.

"I ran away, Claire. You have to accept that. You were a casualty, not the reason."

"And Jack? Was he the reason?"

"I thought he was my prison."

"What do you mean you thought? Was he or wasn't he?" Claire hit the table with her fist. The plates of eggs shook. "What are you saying?"

"I look back now. I'm sixty-four. Now I realize I was my own prison then," she said. Her eyes looked away. "I read the magazines nowadays about women who have this depression. This postpartum. Sometimes I wonder if that wasn't what I suffered. . . ."

"Oh no. Don't tell me that. I had that after Natalie was born. I think I was afraid to have a girl child. I loved her too much. I wanted to give her everything I never had. I was afraid I'd smother her. Every time I put her to my breast a wave of sadness came over me but I never would have left my children. That didn't figure into the equation."

"You think I'm grasping at straws. Making excuses."

"I don't know you well enough to think anything."

A door opened down the hall. "Edward's just getting up," Sulie said.

"Do you love him?"

"I suppose. Sometimes I wonder if I can truly love anyone."

"Why?"

She shrugged and let go a small laugh. "At sixty-four we look foolish if we say it's because we feel no one ever loved us. We should be beyond that."

"Is that what you feel?"

"Are you the therapist or the daughter now?" Sulie asked, her lips pursed.

"Neither," Claire said and closed her eyes for a moment.

"I suppose I was simply too young. For marriage. For children."

"No younger than I was. I was twenty-two when Jonah was born. So what were you? A year younger?"

"It was different times. Women were not as connected. Our grief, our dissatisfaction was unacceptable. We had no one to talk to. You didn't tell your friends how you suffered in your marriage." She looked away. "And I had no friends. The people Jack knew were much older than I."

"Jack died when Jonah was three. We left the city nine months later and Natalie was born nine months after that. I didn't have any friends at first."

"I can't sit here and defend myself, Claire." She ran her fingers through her hair. "I'm sorry you didn't find what you were looking for. You didn't find the blue-haired lady who would take you into her fleshy arms and give you a reason to forgive."

"You have the nerve to ask for absolution?" Claire asked.

"It's the very least I can ask for at this point."

Without the rouge and lipstick, Sulie was no longer glamorous as she had been the night before. Claire saw faint streaks of gray in the hair that hung over her shoulders. The once-smooth caramel skin was mottled now. Feathered lines sprung from her lips.

"I have to forgive you," Claire said, her breath coming in spurts.

"Why is that?"

"So I can live with myself."

"So this is about you then."

"Are you so heartless even now that you can't let it be about me?"

Sulie walked to the window and saw Eli standing on the sidewalk, his hands jammed into the pockets of his leather jacket.

"Your husband is standing outside. He could have come in."

"I wanted to do this alone."

"Do you love him?"

"Very much."

"He loves you?"

Claire nodded. "Yes."

"You're very lucky."

"I know."

"How long are you staying here?"

"Here? Right here?"

"In Sainte Agathe."

Claire felt embarrassed. "We have to leave today. We have work tomorrow." She looked at her incredulously. "Do you know where I live? You haven't asked where I live."

"I suppose other things were more important."

"That's fairly fundamental."

"Are you going to tell me?"

"Drifting, Connecticut. By the way, when is your birthday?"

"September twenty-seventh."

"Do you know mine?"

"Of course. December fourteenth."

"How long was your labor?"

"They put me out. They did that in those days. How long were yours?"

"They were both fast and furious. Not three hours each."

"Your husband was with you?"

She nodded. "And Jack. Jack was there when Jonah was born. Outside the delivery room. Jonah was fifteen minutes old when he held him."

"He loved babies. You nursed your babies?"

"For ten months." She hesitated. "Did you nurse me?"

"It wasn't done so much in those days. They bound me."

"Bound you?"

"To stop the milk. They strapped your breasts back then."

"I wished you were with me when I had my babies," Claire said softly. "Well, not you exactly. A mother."

Sulie let go a deep sigh. "Will I see you again?"

"I don't know. I have to go now." Claire took her coat from the chair. "Maybe," she said. "We'll see."

Sulie's eyes were liquid coals. "I'm sorry," she said. "You may not believe this but I've thought about you lately. More than before. I went to church last night."

"To pray?"

"Right. For my soul," she said sarcastically.

"I wasn't implying that."

"Not to pray. I don't pray. I went to think."

Sulie helped Claire with her coat.

"I'm sorry, Claire." She reached out her hand. Long slender fingers. Painted nails.

"So am I," she said, taking Sulie's hand, resisting the urge to get closer, to cover her mother's hand with both of hers.

Eli looked up as the door opened. Claire buttoned her coat to the collar as she walked down the steps. He never told her that he saw Sulie holding back the curtain, watching her go. Claire stopped before him. Tears rolled down her cheeks. She pressed her face into his coat as he held her.

"She's still missing," Claire sobbed. "I want to go home."

Epilogue

Claire placed yet another letter to Jack in the back of her dressing table drawer.

Dear Jack,

Today is a beautiful day.

It is one year to the day since Kayla was recovered. It doesn't feel like a year has gone by. It is roughly a year since I have seen Sulie. A year since Natalie went off to college. A year that Eli and I have been alone. Six months ago we went to Key West for a long weekend because Eli wanted to watch the sunset. I swear we saw the flash of green.

Lately, I see mothers and daughters everywhere I turn. The mothers wear boxy pantsuits and eyeglasses dangle from beaded chains over their ample bosoms. I watch them as they hold the helm of the shopping cart, a grandchild in the baby seat, while their daughters pack the groceries and pay the cashier. I see them in the nail salon, shaking their keys at the toddler in the stroller while their daughters get pedicures. The daughters ask their mothers if they like the color they've chosen. And the mothers nod their approval while they coo at the grandbaby. None of the women look like Sulie. She is exotic and glamorous. Although when I saw her that afternoon, I thought she had the potential to be simpler. More like the grandmothers at the supermarket. Perhaps it was just me dreaming again. But I am beginning to think there might be more to Sulie than she let me see. After all, you loved her, Jack.

I watch even older women with daughters around my age. They have lunch together at the coffee shop in town or at the food court in the mall, their shopping bags touching, their pocketbooks nearly matching. The mother places extra chicken salad on her daughter's plate because she knows she's always liked chicken salad, she says, even though the daughter protests. I hear them bickering sometimes and listen to their banter. I hear the somewhat impatient resignation of the daughter and then the mother trying to calm her, telling her she's been like this or like that since she was just a little girl, angering her daughter even more. I stare at them. I am an emotional voyeur.

It remains a daily struggle as I make my peace with Sulie though it's getting better. I still may never have the answer I would like to have. An answer where she says I looked everywhere for you and couldn't find you. Or I had amnesia. Or I was a spy and the government changed my identity. I think crazy things like that. They would all be better than the answer she gave me which was simply that she was a prisoner *and had to escape. I guess when you told Eli she was like a wild mare that couldn't be tamed, you were right. You knew.*

I miss my children but in a different way now. It's funny what we grow accustomed to, how we adjust to change. I awaken each morning in Eli's arms. We have become what we were twenty-four years ago with a better knowledge of one another. Our love is more patient. Wiser. Even more tender if that's possible. We know each other's strengths and weaknesses. We have fewer expectations. Can you read my smile now? We light candles in the bedroom and hooked up a stereo on the windowsill. Sometimes it frightens me—he is so much my world.

Natalie is in love (at least this week) with a boy named Ryan and Jonah is engaged to a girl named Angela. He bought her a gold band embossed with stars and moons that she'd admired in an antique shop.

This morning, a basket of flowers, Kayla's picture, and a letter came from Phoebe. It was good to hear from her. She said that Kayla has grown two inches and put on five pounds. Her hair has grown past her shoulders and is back to auburn. She goes to the neighborhood school. She remains fearful, however. When she hears a siren or someone knocks at their door, Phoebe says Kayla's face becomes pale. But Corinne lives with them now, so Kayla is never alone. Kayla won't talk about Nick. She won't talk about the seven months when they were running. Nick spent eight months in jail and is serving three years probation. Not enough. But the judge issued a no contact order so, for now, he can't come near Phoebe or Kayla. Of course, that didn't stop him be-

fore. I've enclosed the part of Phoebe's letter I want you to read.

Despite the lingering fear, it amazes me how the pain of losing her has left me. I suppose in some ways it's like childbirth. If we remembered, we would never have another child. She was reborn for me the day she was recovered. But I can't go back to the pain. The pain of losing her, finding her gone that night, was the most intensely physical pain I have ever encountered. I focus instead on the day I saw her at St. Agnes.

Sometimes I think the healing process will not be complete for Kayla until she sees her father once again. As much as I hate to think that, I have a feeling it's true. I know as she grows older there will be so many unanswered questions. She doesn't ask questions now, but one day she will. She must. Right now she's not ready. Of course, I wonder if she will ever be ready for the answers he will have for her—the answers any of us will have for her. On one hand I pray he will never want to contact her; on the other hand I know there will have to be an understanding and resolution when she's older so she can get on with her life.

My days are spent painting (just did a "yellow brick road" on the side of a nursery school in town) and volunteering for a support network for families with missing children. We're a great team. Unfortunately,

we've all been there. We've all suffered lost
children. Some of us are still there. Some of us
have not been as fortunate as I. The bottom
line is we are there for each other.

Kayla sends you a kiss (from Bear, too) and
Mom and I send our eternal gratitude.

With hope,

Phoebe

*I've read that part three times this morning, Jack.
One day, Kayla will also need answers.*

*Next week is Sulie's birthday. She will be sixty-five
years old. I've wandered into so many shops over the
years looking at gifts I might buy if I had a mother.
Though I've never stopped at the sections that say "For
Mother." Yesterday I drove into town and went to the
stationer. I bought a card. I looked in that section
marked "For Mother." The cards had shiny hearts and
embossed flowers. Happy Birthday Mother written in
large curly script and then on the inside there was poetry of sorts thanking the mother for all she had done,
telling her how meaningful she is. Jonah and Natalie
have often sent me those cards. I've saved them all—
along with their lacquered plaster handprints, paper
flowers, potholders, clay bowls, and key chains etched
with I love you. When they got older they bought me
talcs and bath salts, lotions, sachets, and candles. My
treasures . . . Anyway, I took a blank card painted with
lilacs and walked next door to Annie's shop. I wanted
to send her something. There was a basket filled with
heart-shaped sachets scented with lavender. I don't
know if Sulie likes lavender. And I felt odd sending her
a heart. I sent her one of those pillar candles instead. A*

red one. Her living room has a lot of red in it. It smells like cinnamon.

I suppose Phoebe is right when she says it's a process. It took me ages to decide what to write in that card. It was the best I could do, Jack. I wrote,

> To Sulie.
> Happy Birthday.
> With hope, Claire

Look for Stephanie Gertler's next hardcover coming from Dutton in November 2004. . . .

The Windmill

Known for her gift for reaching straight to the heart, Stephanie Gertler now tells the story of a couple whose seemingly perfect life is toppled in an instant and saved through their bold leap of faith. Olivia and Carl appear to have the perfect life: a son and daughter, weekends on Cape Cod, and satisfying work as professors at Belvedere College in the picturesque town of Willow, Massachusetts. Until, one day, the seemingly stable, dependable Carl disappears without a trace—leaving behind only a cryptic note. Alone and terrified, Olivia cannot help but relive the long-buried pain she felt when she lost her first husband. While Carl travels back to his childhood hometown to confront the demons he has hidden from his wife, Olivia takes a journey of her own as she tries to make peace with the memories that have always haunted her. Told with graceful skill and unflinching honesty, *The Windmill* is a story of the secrets we are entitled to keep in a marriage and those we must share—marking a splendid new level of achievement in this much-admired author.

Stephanie Gertler

The Puzzle Bark Tree
0-451-20884-6

When Grace Hammond Barnett's parents die suddenly, she is bequeathed a lakeside house she never knew existed. Leaving her city life behind, she travels to the house for refuge and meets a man who helps her unravel a devastating secret buried in her past.

"ENGAGING...INSIGHTFUL CONTEMPORARY FICTION."
—*MIDWEST BOOK REVIEW*

Jimmy's Girl
0-451-20516-2

Do you ever think back on your first love? This acclaimed debut novel explores the "what if" questions that live in every woman's heart.

"A PERFECT REMINDER OF HOW STRONG FIRST LOVE CAN BE...DEFINITELY A PAGE-TURNER."
—*REDBOOK*

Available wherever books are sold or
to order call 1-800-788-6262

Discover NAL Accent

Fiction for the way we live.